MY NAME IS ALISON

MY NAME IS ALISON

ALISON BROWNSTONE™ BOOK THREE

JUDITH BERENS   MARTHA CARR   MICHAEL ANDERLE

LMBPN

DISRUPTIVE IMAGINATION

LMBPN Publishing
PMB 196, 2540 South Maryland Pkwy
Las Vegas, NV 89109

First US edition, January 2019
Version 1.02, November 2020

MY NAME IS ALISON TEAM

A special thanks to Debi Sateren, Kathleen Fettig and Mike Robbins for being amazing early readers for this book.

Thanks to the JIT Readers

Angel LaVey
Nicole Emens
Daniel Weigert
Keith Verret
Misty Roa
Peter Manis
Diane L. Smith
Larry Omans
John Ashmore
Jeff Eaton
Paul Westman

If we've missed anyone, please let us know!

Editor
SkyHunter Editing Team

From Martha

To everyone who still believes in magic
and all the possibilities that holds.
To all the readers who make this
entire ride so much fun.
And to my son, Louie and so many wonderful friends who
remind me all the time of what
really matters and how wonderful
life can be in any given moment.

From Michael

To Family, Friends and
Those Who Love
To Read.
May We All Enjoy Grace
To Live The Life We Are
Called.

CHAPTER ONE

Hana knelt and smiled at the unconscious security guard on the floor. She examined the man and looked up to shrug at Alison. "It's so much harder when you can't kill everyone."

"Yeah." Alison groaned and scrubbed a hand down her face. "We can't be sure who knows about the illegal crap going down here, though. How did this job go so sideways? It was supposed to be a simple job for a damned pet food company CEO. I only took it because I thought it'd be good training for you. It's barely worth the money." She threw her hands up. "And now we're in the middle of some warehouse dealing with assholes smuggling Triffles, and the client knew the entire time. This is annoying."

Hana grinned and the glow from her pendant made her teeth and eyes brighter.

I wonder what having red, glowing skin from my ring does for my teeth and eyes, Alison thought. *I don't have any weird street names like Demon Alison or anything that I've heard. It might be kind of cool if I did.*

"Maybe we should grab one as a little bonus," Hana added. "A mascot or a pet. Every good company needs a mascot."

"Wait. Are you talking about the Triffles?"

Her friend nodded. "They're cute. Didn't you think so?"

Alison shook her head. "Just because they look kind of like cats doesn't mean they are. Those things are untamable fabric-eating, pee monsters. I've not heard anything good about them, and there's no way I'll bring one of them into the condo."

"Oh. That sucks." Hana sighed. "We should still consider a pet slash mascot."

"Sure." Alison grabbed the guard's own cuffs to secure him. "I'll take that under advisement, or you can be the mascot. You're the one who turns into a fox. We can get T-shirts printed up with you in fox form. You're cute as a human, fox, or..." She gestured to her nine glowing tails. "Half-fox?"

Hana grinned at her friend, her current yellow vulpine eyes wide with mischief. "I am cute. Can't argue that. It's like a law of nature or something."

Alison nodded. "First, though, we have to get out of here and deal with this situation, as annoying as it is."

"Shit happens, girlfriend. Don't sweat it." Hana shrugged, stood, and shook out her clawed hands. Her glowing tails swayed behind her and highlighted a new wardrobe choice that had shown up in the last couple of weeks—a long red leather overcoat.

Maybe Hana thought it'd show less blood, or she was trying to coordinate a little with Alison and her red denim jacket. February wasn't exactly warm in Seattle, but the last of the snow and ice had fled with January.

"Yeah, shit happens," Alison replied. She finished cuffing the guard. "That's the story of my life."

"I thought the client was a little too nervous." Hana frowned. "But I couldn't tell if it was because he was conning us, or if he was merely scared. Sorry. I think I let myself get too excited about the job. I should have thought more about a con."

"Don't worry. It's on both of us. That's what I get for not having Ava and Tahir crosscheck, but I figured it'd be an easy job so I didn't look too hard." Alison pulled her phone out and frowned. "They're still jamming us in here, so we need to get out of the warehouse and contact the cops. I'm not sorting through this mess, but we better continue to simply knock people's asses out. I don't want the cops to arrive to a bunch of dead bodies with, 'Sorry, I was confused about who the bad guys were' as an excuse. There's no reason to make any unnecessary enemies." She sighed. "I wish I had brought a few more sonic grenades. They always make it easier." She nodded toward the door out of the security office they currently occupied. "Let's get the hell out of here."

Alison threw the door open and stepped out. Her sword scabbard brushed against the door on the way out. She wouldn't need the weapon on the job after all, although with her crystal ring and Hana's pendant, she didn't even have to put in much effort. That was the only thing keeping her merely annoyed rather than outraged.

The women jogged down the hallway leading to the parking lot. The police could handle the smuggled exotic animals, so they had no reason to go back to the main storage room. The authorities could also deal with arresting their client. Killing a guy over an inconvenient job would be a tad excessive, even by Brownstone standards.

Over the last couple of months, Alison learned that going full Brownstone had a time and a place when it came to Seattle. Taking down criminals, thugs, and assassins was one thing, but the police and the PDA shook their fingers a little more when she brushed up against the white-collar types of scum.

The white-collar bastards often destroyed more people's lives than the average gangster, but a few expensive lawyers made most of their sins go away. Alison tried to thread the needle between protecting the city and her clients while also minding her own business when possible. She was already in the sights of one asshole billionaire and didn't need to add more to the list. More than ever, she started to understand what her Dad had gone through.

Alison and Hana turned the corner and stopped. Grimfaced men in gray uniforms and flat-billed hats filled the hall, all holding stun rifles. More security.

Good, you're giving me a reason not to have to kill you. That's always convenient.

One of the men stepped forward. Alison couldn't help but snicker at his ridiculous handlebar mustache. It looked more like drooping horns than facial hair.

"Something funny?" Mr. Handlebar narrowed his eyes. "For someone who broke into our building, you're not taking this shit seriously."

Alison waved a hand. "I'm sorry. But you do own a

mirror, right?" She nodded to Hana. "I'm not wrong, am I? You're seeing what I'm seeing?"

Hana shook her head. "Nope, not attractive, and I've dated—well, kind of dated—a lot of guys who could rock nice handlebar mustaches. This guy does not pull it off."

Several of the other guards chuckled. Mr. Handlebar shut them up with a glare.

"Put your hands on your head," he growled. "And get down on the ground. If you do that, we'll simply tie your asses up, and you can sit around until the client moves the merchandise. No one has to get hurt over some stupid animals."

"Good. You know what's going down here. It makes me feel better about what I have to do." Alison rolled her shoulders and channeled magic to her feet and legs. The shadows deepened around them. She wanted to end this quickly. "Don't be a hero. Or, I guess in this case, don't be a villain. You don't stand a chance."

"Don't get cocky, bitch."

"Look, asshole," Alison replied. "I don't know who knew what about what and when, so I won't kill every last one of you, but don't tempt me. I'm already annoyed, so stay out of my way if *you* don't want to get hurt."

His face twitched, and his gaze cut from her to Hana. He licked his lips. "Just because you're some witch with a… what the hell is she, anyway?"

"I'm a nine-tailed fox, you ignorant asshole," Hana responded. She pointed to her tails. "Even if you've never seen one before, I literally have nine tails!"

"Whatever. You're outnumbered, and if you try anything serious, we might have to shoot you with something a little more deadly than stun bolts. Don't make us hurt you." Mr. Handlebar smirked, confident in his victory over the two magical women. "My quote of the day calendar this morning said, 'Quantity is a quality all its own.'"

Alison sighed. "It seems like negotiations have broken down. Okay, I'll give you *one last chance* to get the hell out of our way. You don't seem to understand that you're such a non-concern that I don't even have to use much in the way of magic to take you down. If I was serious, you wouldn't last two seconds."

Hana nodded her head. "You should really consider it." She tapped her claws together. "I mean, I could have probably done this entire job by myself."

"You won't get me to surrender with only a little speech. I don't care who you are. I've got pride in my job." The man smirked and nodded at her feet. "Did you think I didn't notice you were prepping some magic? What's the deal with all those shadows, then?" He held his stun rifle up. "I think you're trying to bluff your way through. If you're so tough, you would have already bowled through us."

Alison shook her head. "You're really wrong about this."

He snorted. "I'm tired of this shit. Stun 'em, boys."

Blue bolts spat from the rifles and struck Alison and Hana. They arced across their bodies but didn't penetrate their magical defenses. The men continued to fire although the bolts accomplished nothing.

She yawned and patted her mouth with her hand. "Our turn."

Before they could react, she released the magical energy

she'd pooled and launched herself down the hallway. Hana sprang after her. Alison's fist collided with Mr. Handlebar's face and he careened into several men behind him.

Half the men dropped their stun rifles and reached for a handgun inside their jacket. The other half maintained their non-lethal assault.

Alison delivered quick punches and kicks. Men fell to the ground one after another or slammed against the wall and groaned. She chuckled.

Several thuds, shouts, and groans sounded behind her, preceded and then followed by the harsh buzz of a stun rifle going off. Hana's loud cackling completed the sonic tapestry.

Alison turned.

Hana had snatched up two of the bulky weapons and now fired both at the remaining guards.

Oh, yeah. That works too.

As the last man collapsed, drooling, Alison chuckled. "I think it took us longer to threaten them than it did to take them down." She knelt and patted the unconscious Mr. Handlebar on the cheek. "You should have simply let us through, asshole."

Alison hopped up. She headed toward the parking lot door behind the piles of stunned and unconscious men.

"And you're sure about the pet?" Hana whined.

"No pee machines!" Alison opened the door and stepped into the parking lot. "And no more backstabbing clients. Time to call the cops for clean up."

Hana tossed a fry into her mouth, chewed, and swallowed. Hitting Wendy's wasn't exactly Alison's normal post-job plan, but she wasn't in the mood for victory sushi. Instead, they'd gone to a drive-through and were now back on their way home in her Fiat. She still missed her original Spider, but she'd come to appreciate the charms of her newer vehicle, including how quiet it was.

"The police were really nice, don't you think?" Hana asked.

Alison shrugged. "We didn't kill anyone, and we helped them bust a major illegal smuggling operation, plus take down a major corporate asshole who helped finance the operation. Half of them are convinced I have some sort of Brownstone Effect for all types of crime, not only violent street crime."

"I think that one cop was really into me. And hot. Maybe I should have asked him out. Can you see me dating a cop?" Hana grinned. "I kind of like the idea of a man in uniform."

Alison snickered and shook her head. "I think you should keep away from men in uniform." She blew out a breath. "Anyway, I'm glad the cops didn't add to my trouble."

"I know you're kind of mad, but I liked the job." Hana shrugged. "Sometimes, it's nice to have something easy and not have to worry about anti-magic bullets, wizards, or evil billionaires. I think you're richer than that pet food guy anyway."

"Probably. Sometimes, I worry about getting too soft if things stay calm. As annoying as that was, it wasn't exactly a huge challenge to our abilities. Should we always push to the limit?" Alison shrugged. "I don't know. My dad would go sometimes after low-level guys, but usually because the police asked him to. But otherwise, he didn't bother much with them. Mom doesn't care about the challenge as much as the money and if she can learn something interesting."

Hana shrugged. "I don't mind easy jobs and easy money."

Alison stopped at a light and watched a pizza delivery drone zoom over her car. She had trouble eating delivery pizza anymore. The influence of Shay and Peyton remained etched in her soul and only high-quality pizza was palatable. She hadn't tried hard, and there had to be at least a few good delivery pizza places in a large, diverse city.

Her companion sighed and rested her head against the window. "And there's nothing wrong with things being a little calmer lately. We'll end up with white hair from the stress." She laughed. "Or maybe you'll end up with dark hair."

"Very funny." The light changed, and Alison pulled forward. "It's only calm because the Chesterton stuff is going slowly. You shouldn't get too used to easy jobs and paychecks. If Latherby ever gets off his ass, things might move forward quickly with Chesterton, or maybe Scott will come up with some sort of angle for us to work. For now, the best thing we can do is build up our rep and continue to train."

Hana laughed. "Don't miss out on the chance to hang out with your boyfriend. You should take advantage of all this calm time to do that."

Alison shrugged. "If anything, Mason's busier than I am

because I get to pick and choose jobs a lot more than him, but, yeah, I'm taking advantage of that. And him." She smirked. "But if you want to go there, I'm taking more advantage of this time than you are. It's hard not to notice that you've pointedly not asked Tahir out but you still are obviously into him, even as you've gone out with other guys."

"A girl's got to have some fun." Hana lifted her head and straightened against the back of her seat. "I'm trying different strategies—studying the target, that kind of thing. If something's going to happen, I don't want to screw it up. You have to understand, Alison, I'm not used to anything real, friends or boyfriends."

"What are you talking about?" Alison glanced her way with a frown. "You've told me all about old friends you had and guys you've dated."

"It's all a matter of definition. What's a friend? Someone who actually has your back, and not only because they think it'll help them later." Hana shook her head. "I didn't really have anyone like that until I met you. I merely had people I knew, and let's face it, given my old way of making money, most of them weren't the best people. I had guys I dated, but none I actually cared about. It's always been a game to me. When life's nothing but a game, it doesn't really matter if you win or lose on any one day. It's simply about the fun of playing. Now, I'm worried a lot more about other stuff than the fun of playing."

Alison performed a quick mirror check, but other than a surprising squadron of pizza drones, there was nothing suspicious. "I'm young, and you're younger than me. Don't beat yourself up so much."

The fox laughed and her broad smile returned. "You're right. Although I'd better get a move on it before some hackette comes along and steals the guy I like. Who would have thought my life would have got easier and harder at the same time?" She rubbed her hands together. "And I'll finally get to meet one of your old friends. She's still coming, right?"

"Lily? Yeah. A couple of days, from what she told me. I think you'll like her." Alison shrugged. "She's gotten more intense over the years working as a tomb raider, but she's practically my sister, especially since she was my mom's protégé or apprentice or whatever you want to call it. I'd love for you to meet Izzie someday, but it's not exactly like she can hop on a plane and stop in wherever she wants to."

Alison had received a self-destructing letter from Izzie a couple of weeks prior, not informing her of much other than that she was doing okay and had a little trouble in Tucson, but it'd been taken care of. When Alison checked the news, she found an article about a mysterious gas explosion in Tucson and wondered if that had anything to do with her friend.

"A Drow princess with a billionaire after her," Hana intoned, "and yet you still manage to have friends who have it worse than you and are on the run. Talk about drama. Anyway, I look forward to meeting Lily, assuming no one manages to kill us between now and then."

She snorted. "Yeah, assuming."

CHAPTER TWO

The next morning, Alison emerged from her bedroom in her favorite blue robe, her hair still wet from her shower, when her skin tingled at a huge surge of magic. She summoned a shield and a shadow blade and stepped back.

Hana was out already, having mentioned something about a sale. Whether that was code for her conning someone, Alison didn't know, but her friend not being there meant she could go all out against whoever was about to mess with her.

Damn. If I bust up my condo, will the condo board come down on me? Even if it's in self-defense?

Alison sighed as a dark, swirling portal appeared in her living room and expanded. She released her magic. This wasn't an assassination attempt.

A shadowy form stepped through the portal and solidified into Myna. The portal vanished behind her.

She hadn't seen Myna for a month, but in that time, the older woman had traded her robe in for a dark high-necked dress with a voluminous skirt. She wore her stark white hair up. There was something very Victorian about the entire look.

Alison pulled two chairs out at her dining room table and took a seat. "It's been a while."

Myna headed to the table and sat in the offered chair. "I'm unsure how long I have to live on Earth, so I thought it best if I spent some more time exploring it." She lifted her chin slightly. "And I also understood you might need time to fully accept my presence. Admittedly, my sense of time might be off. When enough centuries have passed, a month here and there doesn't seem as important, even when death is coming."

A quiet chuckle escaped Alison. "I wanted to thank you for some of the things you told me about my mom. The other Drow weren't as forthcoming. It's still weird to think she had this whole life before on Oriceran. She gave up all her status for love. It's sad that my dad couldn't be satisfied with it. No, screw Walt. He's not my dad. He never was."

"Avarice is the way of many species, but your new parents have trained you well. Made you strong and honorable." A hint of a smile appeared on Myna's face. "And they are wary, very wary."

Alison blinked. "What does that mean?"

"I wanted to see who had helped guide you. I watched them from afar, but they could sense me—your new parents, that is. I went to talk to some of your teachers at your school of magic. What an odd place. That is the true strength of Earth, a school where so many races work together." Myna's smile disappeared. "You should know, Alison, that I apologize for any inconvenience. It seems my wanderings caught the wrong sort of attention. The Fixer confronted me. I think he believed I was a new Drow assassin probing your weaknesses."

"Correk?" Alison chuckled. "Don't worry about him. He's sort of a…family friend in a way. Not like I talk with him all that much, but if I do run into him, I can explain the situation."

"Interesting. Though your offer is unnecessary. I've made my intentions clear, and the Fixer accepted my explanation." Myna stared at her. "He also gave no indication that he knew you. Be wary. Even if as Fixer, he's sworn to provide aid and protect all magical beings on Earth, he's still a Light Elf, and they have their own agendas. He has access to spell books and artifacts that would allow him to challenge a Drow queen with ease if he were so inclined."

"Like I said, I don't exactly see him a lot, but I'll keep it in mind." Alison cleared her throat. "That said, we need to discuss you simply portaling in here. You've been on Earth since December now, and you've spent a lot of time exploring Earth. You should understand how phones work."

Myna sneered. "I've seen these phones. People should control artifacts. Artifacts shouldn't control people. Humanity is brilliant in many ways but foolish in so many others."

Alison sighed. It wasn't merely a generation gap. It was a generation chasm. A Grand Canyon. Myna might have been born before England was a country for all Alison knew, let alone the United States. A lot of Oricerans might have kept tabs on Earth, but the ancient Drow had barely traveled to a planet she'd considered inferior for most of her long life.

"Phones have their uses," Alison countered. "Such as calling me ahead of time so I know you're showing up, rather than you suddenly appearing when I'm fresh out of the shower." She shrugged. "It wouldn't hurt. I could pay for one if you don't have money."

"I don't need your money nor your slaving artifacts." Myna sniffed disdainfully. "But I do apologize. You're right. I've been presumptuous about simply appearing when and where I want, and this is disrespectful toward you." She took a deep breath. "I am sorry…Alison."

Alison stared at her. It was obvious the woman wanted to call her princess. Myna might have claimed she was willing to accept Alison's desire to stay out of Drow politics, but that didn't mean the woman believed she couldn't eventually convince her.

"It's okay." She forced a smile. "Maybe you could contact me with some sort of spell, at least?"

Myna nodded. "I'll try to remember."

"Good. Thanks." Alison shrugged. "So why are you here, Myna?"

The ancient Drow leaned forward and an even more serious look settled over her wrinkled face than normal. "To teach you. It's time that I do more to instruct you in your magic. Yes, the Drow have trained you, but that was for a short time. I want to make sure that you can begin to walk in your true potential as Princess of the Shadow Forged, even if you don't care about the implications for the Drow."

Alison took a deep breath and released it slowly. A

dedicated and ancient Drow wise woman could be helpful in ways that even decades at the School of Necessary Magic might not be and given that there was still the possibility of some sort of power struggle among the Drow, it'd help if Alison could avoid having to go to them for aid.

"I'm very interested." She raised a finger. "On one condition."

Myna nodded. "Of course."

"You understand and accept that I don't want to become Queen of the Drow. If you help me, you help Alison Brownstone, security consultant, sometimes bounty hunter, and daughter of James Brownstone and Shay Carson-Brownstone. Yes, I'm Princess of the Shadow Forged, but I will stay on Earth and make my life here, even if there's a Drow civil war."

"As you wish, Alison. I'm a woman who wasted her life, so I'm not one to tell you how to live yours." Myna shrugged.

That still feels too easy, but at least I've made it one hundred percent official.

"Thank you for understanding," she responded.

"You're welcome." The old woman lifted her palm and a dark orb appeared. "From what I've seen, you already have much of your power. We shall work on refining things and expanding the types of non-pure magic you can use. Is there anything in particular you want to ask about?"

Alison furrowed her brow in thought. "I'm curious about shapeshifting. I can use illusion magic, but I was told before that Drow can change shape easily—almost like an inherent ability rather than true magic—but I've never been able to do it. My dad even had to deal with a Drow shapeshifting assassin years ago."

Myna gave a slight nod. "All you've said about the ability is true. I've had little use for it for centuries as I've never cared to hide my identity, but it's as you said, it's an almost inherent part of being a Drow. Some claim our race is so deeply part of the shadows that it only makes sense that we can obfuscate our appearance. It goes deeper than that—an actual change. I can only surmise that your mixed heritage is responsible. Although it has given you some advantages, including your ability to access different types of pure magical energy, in this case, it is a disadvantage."

"Oh, no big deal." Alison waved a hand. "It would have been useful, potentially, for some of my jobs, as changing shape without using a lot of magic would have—" She struggled not to grimace.

They'd not discussed her AMDS yet, but she knew it'd eventually come up.

This is silly. I intended to go to Oriceran anyway. I might as well take advantage of my old personal ancient Drow wise woman.

"I have a problem," she admitted. "A disease that saps at my magical ability. Human doctors don't know what to make of it, and they claim that Light Elves have had trouble healing it in others, but I came across some information that suggests it's not natural. That someone targeted me and certain others as part of a test."

Myna leaned forward and reached her hand toward Alison's chest. "May I?"

"Go ahead."

The ancient Drow placed her hand over Alison's heart.

A dark purple glow surrounded it. Myna narrowed her eyes.

A warm tingle spread through Alison's body, and she held her breath.

If this is all some sort of big trick, I'm about to die.

The warmth continued to spread through her body, and the purple glow moved from the withered hand and coated her chest. The examination stretched on for so long, Alison was forced to take another breath.

Myna pulled her hand away, frowning, and the warmth vanished. "It's like nothing I've ever encountered."

Alison winced. Considering how old the woman was, that wasn't a very encouraging sign.

Her nostrils flared, and a deep scowl covered her face. "I've healed many diseases over the centuries, and I've encountered many curses. This feels like some strange mix of them—not a curse causing a disease, but a curse as a disease. Who did this to you?" Her expression darkened. "I will destroy them."

"I'm not sure." She shrugged. "I have some suspects, but we can't go around taking revenge if we're not sure. I'm less interested in that, anyway, than curing it. I refuse to believe there's nothing I can do. I could have used the wish, but I saved it for...well, you know about that already."

Myna sat back, her breathing shallow. "I think I have an idea on how to take care of your problem, but I'll have to look into some things and go back to Oriceran to get some materials."

"Wait. Are you saying you can cure this?" Alison's heart kicked into overdrive, and she resisted the urge to jump up and shout for joy. She didn't want to look like a little kid in front of the ancient Drow, even if most beings on the planet were effectively children compared to Myna.

"I'm not sure," Myna admitted with a frown. "As complex as the magic is, the curse aspects do remind me of some things I saw long ago—a mix of various dark magic techniques. There's a ritual—an ancient Drow ritual—that hasn't been used in almost a thousand years. It might be able to help." She stood and lifted an arm. A swirling dark portal appeared behind her. "I'll go now and begin gathering the materials."

"Woah." Alison put up her hands. "Shouldn't we talk about this some more?"

"You've been attacked and your potential denied." Myna shook her head. "No. We must do this sooner rather than later. Then, you must track down your enemies and destroy them. You are an honorable warrior, Alison, but that doesn't mean those who attack you without honor deserve anything but utter destruction."

"Trust me, once I figure out for sure who did this to me, they'll pay."

"Good." With that, Myna's body turned into shadow and flowed into the portal.

Alison exhaled a long sigh as the portal vanished. She held out hope in the back of her mind for a cure, but she'd also wondered during dark times at night before falling asleep whether she'd ever get her full potential back. Now, this strange Drow woman who used to serve her mother might be the solution.

She snorted. "Myna's right. Whoever did this to me better start running while they still have a chance, even if they are a billionaire."

Alison tried to not let the possibility of her AMDS being cured distract her as Ava lead her through the first floor of the Brownstone Security building. Tarps, ladders, and workbenches stood everywhere, with construction workers spread throughout the rooms. They all offered her polite nods as they continued their remodeling efforts.

Alison, Ava, and Hana moved from the lobby and down a hallway. The scent of fresh paint drifted from farther down.

"They've made a lot of progress in six weeks," Alison commented. "I was worried about not having them start until after the new year, but these guys are cruising right along. Impressive."

Ava adjusted her glasses and swept some dust off her suit jacket. "You're paying premium money, Miss Brownstone, for a premium construction firm. If they were working any slower, I'd suggest switching companies."

Hana poked her head into an empty and freshly painted office. "I still get my own office, right?"

Alison laughed. "Yes. For now." She grinned and turned back to Ava. "And we're on schedule to finish by the original estimate?"

Ava nodded. "Yes, still looking at early May. They'll start work on your training room next week."

"Great. I know it's still a few months off, but I can't wait to settle into this place." Alison smiled at the woman. "You were right. It's good that we're starting off big. It's a lot of space, but we'll be able to grow quickly."

Ava stopped at the end of the hallway, looked both

ways, and nodded as if satisfied by the progress. "They are prioritizing the lobby and our first-floor offices, along with the obstacle course, gym, firing range, and the tactical training room, Miss Brownstone, at my request. The total remodel won't be finished until May, but you should be able to at least begin work, provided you don't mind the noise, by mid-March, and with at least partial use of those rooms."

"That fast?" Alison watched a man painting at the end of the hallway. Despite all the magic and fancy technology available, at the end of the day, the bulk of most construction was still handled by regular people using proven techniques.

"Money gets results." Ava shrugged and her expression suggested she didn't understand why Alison was so surprised.

I've never really splashed this kind of cash around before. The condo's nice, but it's not huge or anything, but this really does show what I can do when I push my resources.

It helped that the jobs they did brought in a significant monthly income, added to the odd bits here and there she managed to squeeze from the government when they needed her help. It felt better knowing that she wasn't simply spending everything without making enough to recoup the major expenses, even if it did take time.

Hana clapped Alison on the shoulder. "This will be badass. Even better than Two Worlds Security. Wait. Can we get some holographic globes, too?"

Ava pulled out her phone and tapped some notes into it. "It's definitely within the realm of possibility. I know of a supplier whom I could squeeze some discounts out of with little effort."

Alison rolled her eyes. "We don't need holographic globes. Figure out something else tasteful for the lobby."

Hana kicked at the ground, her face stuck in a pout. "Being rich is wasted on you. Tasteful is boring."

"Probably. Blame my parents." She nodded at Ava. "What about potential new hires?"

She tapped her phone for a couple more seconds before responding. "I've filtered potential employees in a variety of roles and scoured the net for people who might be useful in specialty direct offensive or defensive roles."

"Ass-kickers," Hana clarified, a gleeful smile on her face.

"Yes, that's one way to look at it." Ava shrugged. "But note that I'm not neglecting basic clerical staff and research staff as well. Did you want to bring them in earlier than April for interviews, Miss Brownstone?"

Alison shook her head. "No, Hana and I should be able to handle everything until then. I figure I bring on a few more specialists for our top-tier team, let them gel, and then we'll look into hiring people for a second team and some general-purpose teams for less dangerous jobs. Also, make sure you look for in-house repair and maintenance staff. The less we have to farm out, the less risk someone slips a bomb into the building when we're not looking."

Hana chuckled. "I can't figure out if it's terrible or awesome to be in your head."

Ava nodded, her expression unchanged. "Of course, Miss Brownstone. Wise precaution."

"It pays to be careful." Alison shrugged. "And—"

Her phone rang. The dedicated ringtone, an excerpt of

the finale of the "1812 Overture," let her know exactly who was calling.

Ava raised an eyebrow.

Alison cleared her throat. "I've got to take this." She hurried away from the smirking Hana and icy Ava before answering the phone. "Hey, Mason."

"Hey, A," he replied. "In the middle of kicking ass?"

"Nope, touring the remodel of the building." She smiled and almost leaned up against a wall before she realized at the last second it was freshly painted and jumped away with a wince. "It's coming along nicely."

"Great to hear. I don't even have an office. Maybe I should get one." Mason laughed. His laughter died quickly. "I know it's short notice, but are you interested in going to a concert tonight? A client gave me some tickets. Front row. A Light Elf choir, supposed to be really impressive."

Alison sighed. "It sounds nice, Mason, but I've got work stuff I need to take care of tonight and a few things I need to handle tomorrow, too. I'll probably be busy the next few days, to be honest."

The work statement was true, thanks to an unfortunately timed text sent an hour earlier. And her second statement was also true, even if her important task involved Lily visiting. Dating Mason was fun, but they weren't exactly close enough yet that Alison felt comfortable sharing the details of her tomb raiding friend's arrival. Lily operated a lot like Alison's mom as an elite tomb raider shrouded in mystery and false identities.

Alison was still learning to trust Mason, and she could see telling him more of her secrets in the future, but not yet.

"Don't sweat it, A," he replied cheerfully. "It's not like I didn't know that dating you wouldn't come with some complications. How about we have dinner on the weekend? Saturday night? Presuming the standard of no one trying to kill either of us."

"We don't need to be that strict." Alison grinned. "As long as no one's planning to kill me in the next few hours, I should be fine for dinner."

Mason chuckled. "Glad to hear it. I'll text you. Talk to you later."

"Talk to you later."

Alison glanced down the hallway at Hana who chattered excitedly with Ava and gestured toward the various offices.

Business is coming along. I've got friends. I've got an actual social life.

Sure, some billionaire has it out for me, but he's the one hiding, not me.

She smirked. After all, a man who couldn't even stop her from going out on a date couldn't be that much of a threat.

CHAPTER THREE

Alison maneuvered her way through the densely packed nightclub and the loud thump of the music shook her bones. It might be cool outside, but inside, the heat of hundreds of bodies mingled together to draw out the sweat from the dancers—at least the species that could sweat.

Still no breakdancing gnomes. Too bad.

She didn't mind a little dancing and Hana could make any situation fun, but every time she entered a club, she couldn't help but worry about the dangerous possibilities of someone targeting the place. Being the adopted daughter of Shay Carson-Brownstone meant always considering the worst-case scenario whenever she entered a building.

It didn't help that she wasn't there to have fun. That night, Hana wasn't with her, nor her boyfriend, and she was in jeans, a T-shirt, and her denim jacket—not exactly sexy clubwear. She wasn't at simply any club, either. She was at the True Portal.

A luminous nova of light exploded near the roof and small, glowing wisps of color flitted around in the air around the display. The crowd cheered and lifted their hands high as pulsating particles rained down from above. enough residual magic filled the area that Alison couldn't tell if spells or technology fueled the display.

Chesterton and Scott are both mixing things together. How long before the distinction between magic and technology no longer makes any sense?

Her attention focused on the colorful bounty from the sky, Alison bumped right into someone's wing.

She stepped back and held her hands up as a muscular Arpak woman turned with a raised eyebrow and a frown. Her wings weren't fully spread, but her irritation was obvious enough from her face.

"Sorry," Alison shouted over the music and pointed up. "I was distracted by the light show."

The Arpak's dance partner, a lithe human man, leaned in to whisper something into her ear. He put his hands on her hips and grinned. Her frown vanished, and she spun back to continue dancing.

Glad you're so smooth. Saved me some trouble.

Proceeding more carefully, Alison maneuvered past more dancers until she arrived at the stairs leading to a second-floor landing covered with tables. She bounded up and caught sight of tonight's not-so-fun date. Vincent.

She'd give the wizard small credit for changing things up. Instead of a purple suit, he wore a black suit with silver chains. The last couple of times she'd met with him, he'd stuck to variations on purple. Now, he looked more try-hard club douchebag than pimp.

Vincent's cool blue eyes focused on her from his table. He lifted a martini glass to his lips, green liquid inside. He might be experimenting with clothes but not his appletinis.

Alison walked past several other tables. The noise of the club died, a victim of Vincent's silence spell. She pulled a chair out across from the smirking blond-haired informant and sat.

"Good evening, Alison." He smiled and held up his drink. Delicious and could detect lies. A nice combination.

"It's all right." She shrugged. "I had to turn down something much more fun to meet you, though."

Vincent brought his drink to his lips to take a small sip. "What's more fun than talking to me? I give you useful information. You give me useful information or money. Both are fun."

Alison looked at the people enjoying their night on the dance floor. It'd been a long time since she'd been that carefree. At least when she was around Mason or Hana, she could approach that feeling. After all she'd gone through, she might never be able to truly let go again.

She returned her gaze to Vincent. "I paid a lot of money upfront for your help, despite that I don't like to work that way, and now, I want to know what you have for me."

The informant gave her a slow nod and rubbed behind his ear. "I value your patronage, Alison, and I also value being on the good side of a Brownstone. It's already opened up more doors for me than you can imagine."

Alison snorted. "Don't think I'll save your ass if you screw over someone you're not supposed to, Vincent. We have a business relationship. We're not friends."

"Friends like you and Mason Lind?" He smirked.

She narrowed her eyes and leaned forward. "Is that supposed to be a threat? I thought you just got done saying how you liked to be on the good side of a Brownstone. If you're trying to get leverage over me, you'll regret it."

Vincent sighed and shook his head. "You should take up yoga. You get pissed too easily. Nah, I was simply thinking he's a lucky bastard. Besides, you think I haven't checked him out? He might not be you, but he's no pushover either. Anyone going after him better not take him lightly."

"I'm glad to hear it." Alison took a deep breath and straightened. She kept her expression hard although she couldn't help the pride that welled up in her when she heard that even someone like Vincent who was in touch with the underworld understood her man wasn't a pushover. "Let's talk less about my love life and more about what I paid you for."

"Of course, of course. Just to make sure we're still on the same page, I spent my time, and some of that money you threw at me, to look into any magicals who might have done any work on a short-term basis, contract or otherwise, with Derek Chesterton or anyone associated with him, in less-than-public projects. Things they might be trying to hide."

Alison nodded. "Nothing's changed."

She also had some of the ex-Death Knights asking around, but while they had pull in her building's neighborhood concerning street matters, their influence and knowledge of the deeper bowels of the magical underworld had proven limited.

"It's been hard. The nature of this work means he hires

a lot of magicals. I've had to spend a lot of time going through dead ends to find what I think you want." Vincent tilted his head and a lopsided grin slid over his face. "You know, I'm impressed, Alison. I figured when you moved to Seattle, you'd make some noise and do the kinds of things you did to those gangs and the Eastern Union, but you're going straight to the top, swimming with the biggest sharks. People even you have to be careful of."

"A shark that doesn't want to get punched in the nose shouldn't come at someone." She frowned. "Chesterton's people have targeted me, and I have every reason to believe he's behind that, so it's too bad for him. He should have stayed the hell out of my way if he didn't want me to come at him."

"I saw it, you know." Vincent pulled his phone out and tossed it on the table. "You going all Drow on Johann and his little monster horde. It made an impression. Not only on me but on a lot of people locally. Lots of groups, big or small, are making changes—subtle, some not so subtle, but it all amounts to the same thing. They don't want the Eye of Brownstone to focus on them. You know what they call you now?"

"The Scourge of Jacobsen?" Alison shrugged. "The Union Killer?"

The informant shook his head. "Nah, nothing like that. The Dark Princess."

What the hell? Is it a coincidence? Or is whoever behind the AMDS spreading the name on purpose?

Alison's face twitched. "The Dark Princess?"

Vincent stared at her for a moment before laughing.

"What? You think it's insulting or something? It's a good thing, Alison. It means they're afraid of you. Fear is a currency all its own. I would have thought a Brownstone would already understand that."

"I'm fine. It simply wasn't as...cool as I hoped." She furrowed her brow, not bothering to kill her scowl.

"Just keep in mind, like the wise man said, for every action, there is an equal and opposite reaction." Vincent picked up his glass and took another drink. "Don't be surprised if some of the bigger players get scared and up their game. A cornered animal bites more readily."

Alison scoffed. "A lot of people have tried to kill me or mess with me since I came to Seattle. They all have regretted it. But enough with the stalling. Do you have the information I asked for or not?"

Vincent clucked his tongue and shook his head. "Calm down there, Dark Princess. I've got the information for you, and you don't know how hard this was to get, even before all that filtering I had to do. I've had to be very quiet about this to avoid alerting Chesterton or his people to me, but a little favor here and a lot of money there got me a name, a witch who worked on a hush-hush project associated with Chesterton. Madison Vance." He picked up his phone and tapped in a message. "I'm sending you her address. This took a hell of a lot of digging. Let's say you got your money's worth."

She chuckled. "I'm glad I'm making you work a little. I wouldn't want you to get lazy."

"I don't know how close your ear is to the ground, but from what I've seen and heard, no one attached to

Chesterton has messed with you since December." He shrugged. "It's only one man's opinion, but I think you've already made your point to him. Maybe you should simply let this one die down. Have you ever considered that? If Chesterton leaves you alone, maybe you should leave him alone, too. Everyone knows about your dad and what he did to organizations that crossed him, but he pounded people into the ground to make a point, not merely because of revenge."

"If you believe that, you don't know my dad at all." Alison stared at Vincent and watched his face for any sign that he knew more than he let on. She assumed the spell on his drink only reacted to her own lies despite some protestations to the contrary. "Let's say I have my own reasons to keep pushing that go beyond petty revenge."

There was no way she'd ever let a scumbag like Vincent know about her AMDS. She didn't know for sure how Johann knew about the condition but assumed Chesterton had told him directly. Myna offered some hope for curing the disease, but until that happened, Alison needed to be careful.

The man nodded. "It was simply a little advice. As always, feel free to do what you want with the information I've given you. All I guarantee is the information's accuracy."

"I'll keep that in mind." Alison stared at the green alcohol in Vincent's glass. "And what about the other thing I asked you about?"

He sighed and shook his head. "Yes, I know people who can get you magical items without unnecessary attention, but you should remember what I said about actions and reactions. That comes into play. Here's the thing. I'm worried that if I send you to some people I know, that on any given day, maybe you go all Drow on them, and that looks bad on me. If you want black-market hidden sourced magical artifacts, Alison, you'll have to deal with some unsavory people."

She shrugged. "Who says I'm not prepared to do that?"

"Me, for one. You have your thing you're doing, and that's fine. You go clean up whatever neighborhoods you want." Vincent leaned back with a smile. "But I intend to squeeze every last dollar out of Seattle until some Brown-stone Army runs me out, and that means I can't be seen helping you take out people who haven't done anything to you. Even if you promise not to, you can't know what'll happen in the future."

Alison rolled her eyes. "Fine. I'm only looking for a little something here and there that I might want to get without a huge government paper trail. How about you act as the middleman, then? If I need something, I'll come to you, and you can get it for me for a nice finder's fee. I get what I need, you get some money, and your contacts don't need to be in the same room with me. Does that sound fair?"

Vincent scratched his cheek. "I can't say it's a bad deal. You're shrewder than I expected. Fine. I'll do it. All the players and centers of power are changing now in this city. It's a good time to make a profit if a man can seize the opportunity." He smiled, but it didn't reach his eyes. "Or a good time to get killed if you don't pay attention."

Alison stood. "I don't need anything at the moment, so

I'll let you know. Thanks for the information on the witch." She turned to leave.

"Will I hear about her death tomorrow in the news? Not that I care. I'm simply curious."

"It depends on what she says and does," she explained over her shoulder. "I always give people one last chance."

CHAPTER FOUR

Alison almost leapt out of her seat in excitement when a knock sounded on her door the next morning. She'd sat at her dining room table and waited for Lily to arrive at her condo after her friend's text saying she'd arrived in Seattle. Alison hadn't given Lily the lobby code or called ahead, curious to see if her friend could easily get through the security at the condo. A little game, along with a little test.

Something I need to think more about for the future. They've got security and drones, but not enough to hold off a major attack. Most people don't have to worry about that, but I do. Maybe I should consider a more isolated place, or should I secure this place myself somehow?

Whatever. Lily's here now. I can't be up my ass about something that hasn't happened yet.

Hana hopped up from the couch. "Another little slice of your past. I can't wait." She clapped and grinned. "Your mom is a total badass, and I loved meeting her. I've got as much of a girl crush as I can have on her without turning into a straight-up lesbian."

"Lily's impressive, but she's not my mom." Alison returned the grin and hurried to the door. She opened it.

Lily stood on the other side, smiling in her black, asymmetrical, belted wool coat with a gray leather handbag slung over her shoulder. She looked the same as ever—an attractive young woman around Alison's age with gray hair and gray eyes, an artifact of her half-Gray Elf heritage. Like Alison, her elven half expressed itself through minor appearance quirks and magic rather than pointed ears.

The women exchanged tight hugs.

Alison was the first to pull away. "It's been a long time since we've actually been in the same room together."

Her friend shrugged as she stepped inside and smiled brightly. "We're both so busy, but you seem like you're busier. You've moved twice since we last saw each other, and you started a business and blew up half of Seattle, not to mention D.C. I still don't know why you didn't want the news announcing loudly about how you stopped a bunch of terrorists."

Alison laughed. "I didn't blow up half of Seattle, and I have enough people looking to start something with me without adding a major terrorist organization to the list. At least with criminals, I can count on them to care a little about their own survival." She pointed at Lily. "And you should talk. Just because you blow up stuff in caves where people can't see it doesn't mean you're any less destructive. I've never caused an earthquake."

"That area was tectonically unstable anyway." Lily walked over and extended her hand to Hana for a quick shake. "You must be Hana, right? Nice to meet you. Alison has told me a lot about you. I'm glad to know there's someone here watching her back. She gets a little headstrong, and her martyr complex is bad."

Alison snorted. "I don't have a martyr complex."

"Sure, sure. Like you're not constantly thinking, 'Got to save the city; got to protect my friends.'"

Hana laughed. "She totally has your number, girlfriend."

Alison chuckled. "I don't *constantly* think that."

Hana smiled. "Yeah, she's down to probably a good eighty percent of the time." She waved a hand. "But enough about Alison. I live with her. I want to know more about you. Is it really true you can see the future?"

Lily shrugged. "Yes, but it's not as cool as you think. It's taken me a long time to actually get some control of it, even with an artifact of my dad's that helps. It used to come and go." She patted her handbag. "But even though I can control it more often than not, it's only a few minutes in the future at present, and I still have to be careful. If I go overboard with it, I can get stuck looking at the future instead of the present—not a good thing if you're in a room filled with guys or monsters trying to kill you."

"That's still pretty damned cool." Hana sauntered over to the couch.

"Says the woman who can turn into a fox." Lily winked. "That's just as cool."

Hana grinned. "It's neat, sure."

Alison smiled and happiness threatened to spill out in an embarrassing way. She hadn't realized how much she missed some of her old friends, and it was nice to see her new friend getting along with the old.

"How's Harry?" she asked.

"Oh, he's fine. Busy running his little info empire." Lily removed her coat and handbag and hung them on a rack by the door. She wore a black A-line sheath dress underneath. Alison hadn't noticed her heels earlier.

She almost laughed at a sudden thought. In some ways, Lily had ended up more like Shay, the ass-kicker who could turn elegant and feminine on a dime, whereas Alison ended up more like her dad, even if she'd never fully embraced the glories of barbecue.

The two women made their way to the couch.

Lily turned toward Hana. "I can see snatches of the future, and it's saved my ass a few times, sure. And I hope it'll save my ass tomorrow if there's any trouble, but it's simply part of the overall toolkit."

Alison nodded. "I wasn't sure if you would end up doing a job or not. You were kind of unclear about it in your last message."

Hana's eyes widened. "An actual tomb raid? Is there like some ancient dragon buried in Elliot Bay lying on top of a treasure horde? Or is there a hidden tomb underneath the Space Needle? A secret passage under the statue of Chief Seattle leading to the Lost Treasures of Rhazdon?"

Lily laughed. "Nothing like that. It's in the Seattle Underground. Sort of. Even before it was…the Underground and they built over it, there were a lot of hidden passages and rooms that magically inclined people liked to use, with a few even leading to the kemana and the town around it. They called it the Secret Underground. Many of these passages and rooms had enchantments that required magic to open them. Before the full return of magic, that helped to guarantee only magicals could get through them. But when the portals opened fully and magic flooded back in a big way, a lot of the passages opened as well." Her smile faded. "But the destruction of the kemana meant a lot of the spells were disrupted, and people were so focused on the kemana's loss they didn't care much about exploring the other hidden parts of the Underground, especially with the new dangers. The Secret Underground is a dangerous maze, but some people manage to live in parts of it." She chuckled. "Just like I used to live in the tunnels underneath L.A. Even with those people, most of it is long abandoned."

Hana shook her head, her eyes filled with awe. "That is so cool, girlfriend. I didn't even know about this place, and I was born and raised here."

Lily shrugged. "You'd be surprised how many tomb raiders don't even know about it. There have been a few tomb raids down there, but not as many as you'd expect." Her voice and face grew more somber. "It remains danger-ous, and a lot of gear doesn't work down there. There was lots of electromagnetic interference from the very begin-ning, and it's only gotten worse since the kemana was destroyed. Most fancy electronics don't work down there. That's kept a lot of non-magical tomb raiders out of the place, and even with magic, things can get confusing."

Alison crossed her arms. "I know you're good at the job, but unless you learned a bunch of magic I don't know about, this sounds like a death trap even for you, Lily."

The other woman shook her head. "You know how I like to be prepared. A contact of mine gave me something very nice. Not only did she give me a line on a healing bowl, but she even gave me a copy of a good, old-fashioned paper map, and I've already lined up a buyer."

Hana bounced a little on the couch. "This is everything I thought tomb raiding would be. Secret places lost to time and filled with ancient treasure, a brave woman descending into the deadly tomb using her skills and wits, and the occasional spell to earn the treasure."

Lily furrowed her brow. "Are you two busy tomorrow?"

Alison shrugged. "No. I cleared out my schedule because I knew you would be here. I'll tell you what I always tell my boyfriend. 'I should be open as long as no one is trying to kill me at the time.'"

"So, maybe fifty-fifty?" Lily smirked. She looked at Hana. "What about you?"

"They haven't even finished building my office yet," replied Hana with a sigh. "And we're not working a job, so I don't have any plans. Why?"

Lily looked from one to the other. "I do almost everything solo in the field these days. Shay's more concerned with the old homestead than doing jobs, but it's not like I can blame her. She has more money than she knows what to do with and plenty of reasons to stay close to home. Every time I try to get a new partner, they turn out to be an idiot or try to betray me." She sighed. "I've got a good tech as backup, an infomancer named Celia, but she won't be much use for a subterranean job where I can't use a lot of tech. I could use some backup, people I know won't try to stab me in the back. I'll cut you in for a full share each."

Hana rubbed her hands together and a huge grin split her face.

Alison shrugged. "And here I was, trying to avoid any

threats to my life for a few days. I guess it wouldn't hurt since it's a local thing and not some weird trip to Antarctica, and it'll be good training for Hana in a different environment. It'll be good to have a job without a lot of weird worries about who is actually the bastard pulling all the strings."

Lily nodded. "No bastards here. I've worked for this client before. She's merely a quirky collector."

"I'm just happy to go on a tomb raid," Hana all but squealed. "When I was growing up, I loved all the archaeologist series, *Tomb Raider, Indiana Jones, Ancestor's Quest*. You name it. I never thought I'd actually get to do something like that."

The half-elf chuckled and brushed some of her long gray hair behind her ears. "Don't get too excited. Tomb raids are mostly a lot of boredom punctuated by two minutes of heart-pounding stress as someone or something weird tries to kill you."

Hana shrugged. "That sounds like our usual Thursday night."

Lily laughed. "Well, then. Fine. I figure we can hit the site tomorrow night. Since I have the map, we should be able to find the bowl without spending days there. The entrance is hidden underneath a Wal-Mart and sealed with a magical artifact, but I have a key artifact—a nasty little fragment of a finger bone—that we can use to gain access."

Alison smiled. "I was going to suggest we hit Maneki tonight, but maybe we shouldn't now."

Hana eyed her with a confused look. "Don't tell me you've turned your back on Maneki. That's sacrilege."

"The Japanese place?" Lily asked. "I thought you loved it."

"I do." She shrugged. "But it's our go-to for victory sushi, and now this isn't a visit; it's a job. We'll grab some after we get your artifact." She pulled her phone out. "How about some delivery Chinese instead?"

"We can do pizza," Hana suggested. "We almost never do pizza."

Alison laughed. "Besides training Lily to be a kickass tomb raider, Mom also infected her with the same pizza snobbery that she did with me."

Hana sighed. "I miss pizza."

"No, we can. We simply have to order from a good place. It's about time I found a good place. Lily?"

She shrugged, a smile on her face. "Whatever's fine by me."

Alison tapped at her phone. "Finding some good pizza is a challenge I can handle." She looked up. "If we're going to hit the site at night, anyway, why not hit it tonight?"

Lily arched a brow. "Sure. Why not? Let's eat, arm up, and go."

CHAPTER FIVE

Alison glanced into the rearview mirror, not at the cars behind her but into the backseat. Hana sat there with a grin on her face, decked out in a ridiculous khaki safari outfit complete with a matching safari hat and knee-shorts. The *tachi* sat across her lap.

Why did she even have that outfit to begin with?

But I can't bitch too much. It's a functional outfit, complete with boots. It's not like she's wearing the sexy costume version. It simply looks like she's ready to go hunt a lion rather than find a magic healing bowl underground.

Lily fiddled with some of the pouches on her tactical vest. "ETA?"

"Only a couple of minutes," Alison replied. "Do you have any intel on other tomb raiders or mercs who might show up?"

"Nope." The half-elf lifted her phone and tapped in a few final messages to Celia. "This should be a clean job that way, but I can't guarantee anything about what's inside. I'm not here to kill anyone, but I won't let anyone shoot me either. I have a load of sonic grenades and a couple of stun batons in that box in your trunk, but I'm not sure if they'll work once we're on site."

"We always have my magic, but from everything you've said, it doesn't sound like we'll run into people."

Lily pursed her lips and nodded. "Yes, probably not any…people."

Hana rubbed her hands together in the back. "Giant spiders? Giant rats? Giant worms? Bet they aren't bulletproof."

Alison laughed. "Yeah, a lot of monsters aren't." She shrugged. "Then again, neither are most people."

Hana patted the *tachi*. "Even if they are, between this and both of you having magic knives, we're good to go. I wonder if my claws can tear into a giant spider." She stared at her hand, a thoughtful look on her face. "It might be nice to know in case we have to protect any future clients from giant spiders."

"That would be an interesting job." Alison turned into the Wal-Mart parking lot. "Where is the entrance?"

Lily pointed forward and to her left. "Just park anywhere. It doesn't matter where. The bone shard will teleport us in and teleport us out." She shrugged. "But try to pick somewhere that's not super-obvious."

"I probably shouldn't have brought the expensive sports car," Alison mumbled.

"If all goes well, this should be in and out." Lily shrugged. "I mostly wanted to come to visit you, so I looked around for an easy raid in the area. Without the map, this would be painful and would probably take weeks. With the map, it should be a matter of hours, not days."

"We'll see." Alison found a nice tree-covered, darkened spot between lights in the far corner, maneuvered the car there, and parked. "If any cops show up later, I'll tell them I was hunting a bounty. That should get them off our backs about the weapons."

They filed out of the car and moved to the back. Alison popped the trunk, and they grabbed some sonic grenades, headlamps, and wrist flashlights. Even with Hana foxed out, she wouldn't be able to see in total darkness.

Alison double-checked her gnome knives as Hana strapped the sword belt around her waist. Lily had her own enchanted dagger. They all settled on the same 9mm Glock so they could swap magazines if necessary.

With a solid pull, Alison shut the trunk and activated her car alarm. "I need Myna to teach me some sort of car thief curse."

Lily turned on her headlamp and the light cut through the overly dark parking lot. "Myna?"

"That's the old Drow woman I told you about. I told her about the AMDS, and she thinks she's got a line on how to cure it." Alison shrugged. "She made it sound like it'd be soon, but she's ancient. To her, soon probably means five years from now."

Lily snorted. "Or it could be two weeks from now. From what little you told me about her on the phone, that woman has a lot of powerful magic and experience."

"Someone that old has to know what they are talking about," Hana suggested. She smiled as her nine glowing tails popped into existence and her eyes turned yellow. Her claws extended. "I need to practice at a range with my claws out. It's hard to fire with them." She frowned and the claws retracted. "It takes a little effort to not pop them out when I change. It might be good to get more comfortable with them when I use a weapon."

Alison shrugged. "That's actually a good idea. I've mostly trained you in your human form, but you need to practice more when you're all foxed out, too, and not only in the occasional fight at the gym. I can't wait until the contractors finish the obstacle course and the tactical training room. Then we can really go to town."

Lily shook her head. "Obstacle courses and training rooms. Ugh. If I never see one again in my life, I'll be a happy woman."

Hana laughed. "I like it. I'm learning next-level ass-kicking."

Lily pulled a small fragment of bone from her pouch. "Move close to me. It'll open a little portal, but it won't last long. This artifact has enough power for two portals, but otherwise, we'll spend a day down there while it recharges."

Alison and Hana moved closer to the half-elf. The tomb raider held up the small white bone fragment, closed her eyes, and murmured in some ancient language Alison didn't recognize. Orange-pink flames erupted around them in a circle as she continued to chant.

The flames grew taller and licked at the air like a hungry animal. Alison cracked her knuckles, unperturbed. Lily knew what she was doing.

A bright line erupted from one of the flames in the front and inscribed a circle into the ground. The parking lot vanished, and they arrived in darkness. The fetid air turned Alison's stomach.

The beams from their headlamps and wrist flashlights cut through the darkness to reveal a surprisingly wide wooden tunnel.

Alison looked around for any sign of the portal, but they were at a dead end. A door frame stood behind them, but rock and dirt had blocked farther passage. Some of it spilled into the tunnel.

"Did we leave a big scorch mark in a Wal-Mart parking lot?" She chuckled.

Lily shrugged. "I hope not. The flames are only supposed to burn people if they step through them and not the ground, but I guess we'll find out."

Hana laughed and adjusted her hat as her tails swayed behind her. "Onward to the treasure?" She sniffed the air. "There is a lot of low-level magic in there."

The other two women nodded their agreement.

Lily retrieved a folded piece of paper from her pocket. "It would have been nice to do this via AR goggles, but sometimes, you have to go old school. I'll take point." She stepped forward, the map in hand.

Alison and Hana fell in behind her. The trio's footsteps echoed in the tunnel and made an occasional splash as they stepped through the small puddles here and there.

Hana wrinkled her nose. "This is one time I wish my sense of smell wasn't so good."

Lily grinned over her shoulder. "This isn't even in the top ten of worst-smelling places I've been."

"I'm starting to see that tomb raiding has its downsides." She sighed and shook her head.

Alison ran her hand along the wall. Some of the wood had rotted away to reveal dirt and rock beneath, but much of it remained in good shape with little sign of cracking or decay. A small amount of magic lined the walls, perhaps a remnant of past decades or evidence of someone newer and not picky about where they lived.

People lived and worked here once, and now it's gone, forgotten by most people above. Will some android tomb raider in five hundred years excavate the Brownstone Building and try to figure out what it all meant?

She chuckled.

"What's so funny?" Lily looked her way.

She shrugged. "I was thinking about the future."

"That's always dan—"

A click sounded, and several blades erupted from the wall. Lily spun and bent backward in an instant. The deadly projectiles missed her and thudded into the wooden wall.

The tomb raider righted herself and blew out a ragged breath. "That was close."

Alison nodded. "Do you think we should use magical shields?"

Lily waved a hand. "Save them. I didn't see that one coming, but no one's missing any fingers." She shrugged.

Hana walked over to examine the blades embedded in the wall. "Regular old-fashioned death trap. Nice. Now we need a magical death trap."

Alison frowned. "Huh?"

Her friend stared at her like she was an idiot. "No tomb raiding experience is complete without at least one magical death trap."

Lily chuckled. "Let's get going. Maybe you'll get what you want."

"So, Alison, about this Myna…" Lily began as they arrived at an intersection sometime later. Conversation had been light as everyone concentrated on watching for traps, but there'd been no other incidents. She waved to her right and proceeded that way.

Alison continued to sweep the tunnel in front of her for signs of danger. "What about her?"

"You said she's going to help you with your problem, right?"

Hana harrumphed. "I should note that Alison kicks major ass even with her virus. It's not that much of a problem."

"I'm sure she does kick ass." Lily grinned. "But no one likes to not be at their maximum potential, and you know how these Brownstones can be. Always attracting trouble."

"True enough." Hana snickered.

Alison shrugged. "I've adapted for now, and yeah, Myna said she'll help. I planned to take a trip to Oriceran anyway to talk to the Drow about it eventually, and this saves me the trouble. I also don't totally trust that the Drow won't try something, so I'm glad she might be able to help me."

Lily frowned. "Really? What's up with them? I thought you were on good terms with them. Last I heard, they hadn't messed with you since Laena was still in charge."

"Yeah. Sure, they have the Guardians now, but that doesn't mean they can't fall back into their old ways." Alison shrugged. "I'm not saying I have any particular reason to believe they'll come after me, only that the fewer people who know about my problem, the better. At least until I'm cured."

Lily nodded. "What's your backup plan in case Myna can't do anything?"

"I don't really have one. Mom and Dad are looking around quietly. Maybe I can go to Correk, but it's not like I have him on speed dial, and I'm not even sure if it's a good thing to get more people, even non-Drow, directly involved in this until I figure out more about how it happened. It doesn't seem to be contagious from what that doctor said, but from what Myna told me, this is as much a curse as it is a disease, so it doesn't hurt to be careful."

"I can have Harry ask around. His beat might be L.A., but he has a lot of contacts around the world now. Maybe one of them knows something or can point you at someone who knows who might be responsible."

Alison shook her head. "I already have a line on someone I'll talk to about that after you head out, and I don't want to drag you and Harry into this. You don't need the kind of trouble that follows me around." She shrugged. "If Myna can't help me, then I'll start worrying a little more, but thanks for the offer."

Lily looked at the smiling Hana, an uncertain expression on her face.

You're wondering why she's involved? She probably shouldn't be, but she's the one who chose to keep helping me with this. You've got your own life, Lily. Don't get too tangled up in my mess.

The tomb raider leapt toward Alison and tackled her to the ground. A glowing blue beam rocketed across the tunnel and passed through where Alison had been only a second earlier. The beam lingered for a few seconds before it disappeared. The sweet, pungent scent of ozone fought against the stink of the tunnel.

"Everyone, crawl for the next few yards," Lily commanded.

Hana dropped and complied. She didn't stand until the half-elf did.

"An actual magical death trap," Hana shouted. "Definitely the true tomb raiding experience now." She pumped her fist in the air.

Alison groaned and dusted her pants off. "I'm glad someone's having fun."

Hana blinked and pointed at Lily. "Wait a second. You actually saw the future, didn't you? Badass."

The bounty hunter nodded. "Yeah, I tried to pulse a little while looking around for actual traps." She pinched the bridge of her nose. "I was getting lazy because I didn't see anything, and I had trouble keeping myself grounded in the here and now. We'd better shield up, just to be safe."

Alison tapped at her crystal ring and the red glow fed additional light into the darkened tunnel. "This is why I always preferred bounty hunting. I hated the few times Mom convinced me to go on a tomb raid with her. I hate all this death trap tunnel crap. I like enemies you can see coming and stab."

Hana nodded and grabbed her pendant. "*Corpus meum defendat. Custodiat animam meam.*"

The jewelry glowed.

"It was my suggestion, so it's my turn." Lily reached into her pocket and pulled out a small match. She struck it against the wall, and a bright white flame appeared. She lifted the match to her mouth and popped it in, swallowed, and grimaced. "Talk about heartburn," she muttered as she pounded her chest, "but it'll keep me alive if I miss any traps." She pulled the map out to look it over before she nodded down the tunnel. "We're already halfway there."

Alison frowned. "There's one thing I don't get."

"What?" Lily folded the map again and slipped it back into a pocket.

"How do you even have that map? Doesn't that mean someone had to come down here?"

The bounty hunter shrugged. "It's based off some records from a long time ago combined with several doomed tomb raids and a few survivors. That sort of thing."

"Doomed?" Alison raised an eyebrow.

"Mostly traps and creatures. A couple of betrayals. Standard stuff."

Hana grinned. "Come on. There's nothing the three of us can't take on."

Alison considered that before she grinned herself. "You know what, Hana? You're right. Let's go."

CHAPTER SIX

They continued deeper into the tunnels. The pools grew in depth and gnawed bones appeared. Rat bones mostly, but there was at least one humanoid femur and a few other bones that looked like they might have come from dogs, cats, possums, and raccoons.

Doorways, rotted or still existing, indicated rooms— some with wooden walls, but others were carved directly into the earth instead. What had begun as a series of tunnels now resembled the remains of a small under- ground town.

A few pieces of metal or stone furniture remained and even a few sturdier pieces of wood that had survived the centuries, but whatever other treasure they might find, most of the rooms linked to the hallways were long since abandoned.

Alison poked her head into a room, this one half- collapsed. "And this wasn't part of the town around the kemana?"

Lily shook her head. "It was a separate thing entirely,

even if you could get to the kemana from the Secret Underground."

Hana sighed as they stepped past several half-chewed rats. "Yeah, this is the part of tomb raiding I could go without experiencing."

Lily snickered. "You should be happy that we've not run into piles of bodies or zombies. I hate zombies."

Alison shrugged. "Does anyone like them?"

"Necromancers do."

"Good point." Alison blew out a breath. "Are we close?"

Lily nodded. "We should be."

Several splashes echoed in the distance, but it was impossible to tell what direction they came from.

Hana frowned and looked back and forth. "there isn't a lot of room to swing the sword in here. Gun or claw time."

"It could be nothing," Alison suggested.

More splashes echoed, along with a scratching sound.

She sighed and pulled out her 9mm. "Yeah, that's something. It sounds like several somethings."

Lily's eyes glazed over as she stared into the distance.

Hana drew her gun and aimed in the opposite direction to Alison with a frown. "Here come the giant spiders?"

Alison snickered. "Something like that." She glanced at Lily who still stared with an almost blank expression. "Lily? Are you okay?"

The tomb raider didn't respond.

Alison sighed and walked over to her friend. She holstered her gun and shook Lily by her shoulders.

The half-elf blinked a few times and stepped away. She scrubbed a hand down her face. "Sorry, I got stuck looking at the wrong time. Get your guns ready." She drew hers. "It's time for some pest control."

"So it is giant spiders?" Hana's bright smile and excited voice made it sound like she was receiving a birthday present.

"I wish." Lily sighed. "I already had a vision of one of these things taking a bullet. They aren't bulletproof. Come on." She waved her pistol to motion the others forward. "We're close. Might as well get it over with."

They proceeded deeper into the tunnels, their weapons at the ready as the splashing and scratching grew louder. Faint overlapping hisses joined the other noises.

Lily paused at a corner, her gun raised and her face tight. "Some things shouldn't exist," she whispered.

Hana swallowed, her eyes wide and her glowing tails up.

Alison crept up to the corner and peeked into a larger chamber linked to three different hallways. "You've got to be kidding me."

Dozens of cockroaches skittered around a putrid mass of rotting rats, bones, and trash. That was disgusting enough, but the bright green glowing stream that filled a drainage ditch cast an eerie and unsettling light over the whole room. Even that light was only a minor detail compared to the vermin themselves.

It wasn't their green metallic carapaces that worried Alison, but their ridiculous size. The roaches varied in length, but the smallest couldn't have been less than a yard, with several closing on two yards. They scuttled and crawled all over, gnawing at the garbage, rats, and bones.

"I hate being right," Alison murmured.

Lily frowned. "About what?"

"I argued with a biology professor in my freshman year about this."

"About giant roaches?" Lily blinked.

"About how all the old rules of biology that scientists came up with didn't apply in the age of magic. He was talking about how bugs can only grow so large because of how they breathe." She released a dark chuckle. "And I said, 'With enough magic, I could probably make a giant cockroach that would do just fine.' Now, it's like the universe is punishing me for being mouthy."

Hana took a quick look herself and made a face. "The giant spiders would have been epic; these are just disgusting. I wish we had brought a few frag grenades."

Lily nodded. "We're probably close to the bowl now. According to my contact's information, it enchants water to turn it into a kind of healing liquid, which she even described as green and glowing."

"The artifact has leaked into the water here and mutated roaches?" Alison sighed. "Of course it has. We're lucky it didn't produce rats the size of elephants."

"It probably changed the roaches first, and that's how it worked out. They've kept the area clear of other creatures that might get changed with extended exposure." Lily shrugged. "But we don't know how long it's been leaking. Still, it doesn't matter. We've got to get past those things and find the bowl, which means we'll probably have to clean them out."

Hana made a face. "Maybe they'll run. Or we could use the sonics?"

Alison shook her head. "They don't really hear in the

same way. It'd probably simply piss them off, not knock them out." She shrugged. "I could channel some magic into an explosion, but they'll probably charge us the minute we head around the corner." She glanced at the red and white light mixing on the wall and was surprised the roaches hadn't reacted to that already.

Lily's face grew tight. "I suggest that on three, we all come around the corner and see if they react. If they don't, fine. If they do, let's do what we need to. It's not like we can let these things wander around. They might get out of the Secret Underground and attack someone."

Hana and Alison nodded. Neither woman's face suggested that they held even the smallest enthusiasm for the task before them.

"Three..." Lily began. "Two...one."

The women darted around the corner, their pistols aimed and ready. The giant pests all jerked toward them and their hissed cacophony was deafening.

"So much for them running," Alison muttered.

Several roaches leapt toward them, but their wings didn't move.

Thank God they can't fly.

She opened fire. Hana and Lily joined her.

Their bullets ripped through the first few mutated roaches and sprayed bright green ichor everywhere. The rest of the roaches leapt or charged now as more poured out of holes in the wall or emerged from the small stream.

As disgusting as the creatures were, a 9mm bullet fired from an Austrian handgun worked as an effective insecticide. The loud reports of the guns echoed all around

Alison, deafening her and drowning out the hissing of the charging roach horde.

Her gun clicked empty but the horde still charged.

Screw it. It's not like these things can get through my shield.

She holstered her gun and yanked out two knives as the insects approached. Lily drew her dagger a second later, and Hana extended her claws as the scuttling mass moved closer.

We killed tons of those things, and they're still coming.

Many of the ones they'd shot still writhed on the floor.

Alison narrowed her eyes. The horde might turn her stomach, but they were simply giant bugs in the end.

The next line of roaches reached the trio. Alison slashed away and her blades produced an audible crunch as she ripped into two roaches. Lily ducked and stabbed as she gutted enemy after enemy.

Hana growled and leapt into the mass. Her claws tore into the creatures with equal ease as her friends' magic weapons.

The hissing and scuttling grew quieter as the crunch of the dying roaches and the grunts of the women overcame the earlier noises.

Her breathing ragged, Alison pinned the last surviving roach with her boot and sliced it into several pieces with quick movements of her knife.

The three women jerked their heads back and forth, looking for any more reinforcements. Although a few bodies continued to twitch in the darkness, no brave new roach rose to attack them.

Hana slumped against the wall, her outfit stained. Her pendant had protected her from harm but apparently, not from needing a good, long shower. Alison hadn't fared much better, though her skin, still glowing red from the ring, was spared.

"I take it all back." Hana groaned.

Alison sheathed her knives and drew her pistol once more. She ejected the magazine and reloaded the weapon before holstering it. "Take what back?"

Lily stepped toward the stream.

Hana gestured to a dead giant roach. "Tomb raiding is absolutely disgusting. We're only lucky these were giant roaches instead of giant zombie roaches."

Alison winced. "Yeah, good point."

The half-elf followed the stream that headed toward one of the connecting hallways.

Hana shook her head and set off after the tomb raider. Alison took one look around before she followed.

Lily crouched near a wide hole in the far wall. The green liquid flowed out of the hole. "According to the information and the map, the bowl was supposed to be in this room." She pointed toward the center of the carved-out chamber. The roach feeding pile sat there as if to mock them.

Alison groaned. "Please tell me we don't have to dig through *that*."

"No." Lily shook her head and nodded at the water. "It's clearly flowing from the hole into the drainage ditch, which means the bowl is through the hole." She shined her light into the aperture. It went several feet before it curved and the flow of green glowing liquid seemed confined to a narrow channel on one side. "There are no rooms on the map that way." She stood and shrugged.

Alison frowned. "I could try to blow my way through with magic."

Lily shook her head. "We've seen plenty of half-filled rooms where the ceiling has collapsed, and who knows how well they were even supporting this place against earthquakes before the destruction of the kemana. If we start blowing things up, we might bury ourselves. I won't die in some roach-infested hole."

"We can't fit in that hole," Alison pointed out. "It's decent-sized, and none of us are all that large, but we're still too big to crawl through a hole. We'd need a willen or a gnome or someone like that."

Hana sighed and started unbuckling her sword belt. "Or an animal that's a little smaller."

Alison nodded. "I guess, but what's your plan? Fly down to L.A. and grab Dad's geriatric dog?"

Hana lowered the sword belt to the ground and unbuttoned her jacket. "No, you can have a cute young fox do it." She winked but grimaced a second later. "But I won't go into any old tunnels or sewers or anything for a long while after this."

Lily laughed. "See, I told you turning into a fox was cool."

Hana shuddered as she finished shedding her equipment and clothes. She heaved a great sigh, and all nine tails wrapped around her body. A golden light illuminated the room and cleared a few seconds later, leaving behind a red-orange fox with nine non-glowing tails.

The fox looked from Lily to Alison before she rolled her eyes and scurried toward the hole.

"You're a true tomb raider now, Hana," Lily called.

"We can order pizza for a week," Alison offered. She threw a hand over her mouth to hide her snickering as her now four-legged friend entered the small hole.

Several long moments passed before the light scurrying sound of the fox beyond the hole grew quieter.

Lily turned to Alison. "It's still not too late to give up all this security contractor crap and join me as a partner in the glorious giant roach-filled world of tomb raiding."

Alison laughed. "Yeah, I think I'll stick with the vicious killers and assassins. Even a Kilomea is lovable compared to these guys." She gestured toward a pile of nearby roach corpses.

"It's good to have you watching my back, though." Lily shrugged. "I always looked forward to you coming home for summer so we could train together or even do an occasional job when Shay could convince James, but you did your thing in school. And now, there's no such thing as summer vacation, simply all ass-kicking, all the time." She released a wistful sigh. "Sometimes, I open up my eyes in the morning and I forget I'm not a teenage tunnel rat."

"I know what you mean." Alison shook her head. "With everything that's happened these last few months, it's been hard to process. I'm only twenty-five. I spent the first fifteen years of my life thinking I had a weird way of seeing, and then my bio-dad betrayed my mom, and I found out I was a Drow Princess, and then James and Shay…" She sighed. "I'm still wrapping my head around it all."

Lily patted her on the shoulder. "It's okay not to have all the answers, Alison. Don't think that Shay does simply because she acts confident. When I first met her, she wasn't much older than you, and your dad? Well, he's the master of ass-kicking and barbecue, but he's clueless when it comes to a lot of other things."

Alison laughed. "Yeah, I know, but I love him anyway because he tries so hard."

Scurrying from the hole caught her attention, and she turned toward it. A few seconds later, Hana crawled out of it, a small clay bowl in her jaws and the fur around her muzzle stained green.

The fox padded to Lily and set the bowl down before she backed away. Another golden flash almost blinded Alison and a crouched and cranky-looking naked Hana replaced the cute four-legged animal.

Hana wiped some green liquid off her face. "When I get home, I'll take a five-year shower, assuming I don't turn into Giant Hana first." She shuddered and stood.

"Not loving your first tomb raid?" Alison smirked.

Hana marched to her clothes. "I think I'll stick with the more glamorous life of security contracting. Let me get dressed, and let's get the hell out of here."

CHAPTER SEVEN

Hana smiled as she lifted the tuna sashimi with her chopsticks and plopped the fish in her mouth, the fatty slice almost melting inside. Fighting a room of giant cockroaches and scurrying through some dark smelly hole to grab an artifact was worth it for victory sushi the next evening. She waggled her eyebrows at Lily and Alison who sat across from her at a table in one of the private rooms at Maneki.

She was grateful for the private room. The main dining room was packed and every table was full. Some of that noise still penetrated into the private room, although the copious sake, tea, sushi, and sashimi helped her to not care.

Maybe only the sake, considering she'd already polished off a cup. A pleasant warmth spread throughout her body.

This is what I'm talking about, Hana thought to herself. *Victory sushi and some good friends. Plus, Lily's awesome. I wasn't sure if she'd be awesome or too up her own ass. I could never tell given the way Alison described her.*

"I'd murder ten men for this sashimi," she announced. "Maybe even more. It's so damned good."

"Have all you want," Alison replied with a smile. "After all, you got the bowl in the end. Lily's right. If I tried to blow through, we would have been digging ourselves out for days."

"Or dead," Lily suggested.

"That too!" Alison laughed.

Hana smiled. It was good to kick back and relax with no worries about assassins or evil billionaires. Merely a bunch of friends sitting around and having a good time.

Lily took a sip of warm sake, her pale cheeks already red. "You seriously saved me a lot of time, Hana. I've already booked my flight out for later tonight, and the bowl will be in the hands of the client by tomorrow morning. That job went well. Textbook. I almost forgot what it was like to work with a competent field team. Knowing you guys had my back made it far easier for me to concentrate on the traps."

Hana swallowed her fish. "Was it really that big a deal? Only a few traps and some giant roaches. They weren't even bulletproof. I think next time, I'll just reload and keep shooting because that was seriously disgusting, but it was also kind of easy compared to some of the assholes we've had to deal with around here."

Lily chuckled. "Kind of easy? That's why you and Alison are such good backup. It doesn't matter that bullets worked on those things. Your attitude is what matters. I've worked with some partners who broke and ran the minute anything weird showed up, but you two stood there shooting away and then started ripping giant cockroaches to shreds like you do it every day."

Alison snickered. "It was a lot easier to handle them than assholes in power armor. At least there weren't any roach wizards."

Hana nodded her quick agreement. "It's the first time I've needed to go four-legged for a job with Alison. I used to...never mind."

Yeah, probably not best to tell them how I used to go four-legged so I could help keep a lookout in the bushes for scumbags doing scummy things.

Lily nodded and turned to Alison. "This whole thing reminds me of that time Shay forced you to do that tunnel training. Remember that?"

Alison rolled her eyes. "Oh, yeah, the whole 'We need to make sure you're comfortable in case you need to hide somewhere for a long time.' Part of her whole thing about me not being a prissy princess, even though I'd already gone through a lot of her and Dad's training by then. I think she enjoyed some of that way too much."

The half-elf laughed. "Yeah, she never forced me to do that kind of training, but I was a tunnel rat, so I guess she figured I didn't need special training."

Hana furrowed her brow. "You mentioned that before. You said something about tunnels under L.A.?"

"Yeah, before I met Shay and Alison. A bunch of us—half-magicals, some runaways, some abandoned. We all had powers, but they weren't all that reliable. We lived in the abandoned nuclear tunnels under L.A. as our home for several years." Lily sipped some more sake. "Of course, we went all over, subway tunnels, whatever we could use.

Simply trying to survive day to day. I wasn't thinking much about the future at the time. When you don't even know where your next meal is coming from, worrying about your career seems like a waste of time."

Alison nodded. "Until you bumped into and helped Mom out. Luck or destiny, your call."

Lily laughed. "Yeah, I didn't know what to think about her at first. I thought she was merely someone else trying to screw me over, but you know, she offered an opportunity, and I decided to take it. I never thought I'd end up a tomb raider." She shrugged. "I don't know. I was a stupid teen, and I only wanted to make sure I didn't leave my friends and Harry. I'm glad I didn't, but I wish I had decided to commit to Shay earlier."

"The weird thing is how Mom kept you secret for a while." Alison picked up her own cup of sake and took a sip. "Like you were her hidden love child or something."

Both women laughed as Hana finished munching on more tuna.

Alison set her cup down. "I know I've said it before, but I still have to admit I was a little jealous of you at first, Lily. At that point, Mom was still forcing me to call her Aunt Shay, and then you showed up out of the blue. I was worried you would steal her from me." She laughed. "I know that sounds silly, but I was a stupid kid who'd lost her first mother, and I didn't want to lose a second one."

Hana furrowed her brow as she listened to the conversation. Alison hadn't mentioned most of this to her when she'd talked about Lily before.

Lily finished off her sake and blew out a long breath. "I didn't see Shay that way. I merely wanted to use her, get something out of her. I never thought that it'd turn into something more than helping her out for a few jobs." She shook her head. "I was jealous of you, too, you know. I was living in tunnels, worried about where I would get my next meal, and you had James and Shay looking after you. Plus, you have to admit you were a little spoiled originally."

Alison laughed. "Dad and Mom and the guys at the agency beat that out of me."

"It's not a big deal. I mean, you were still dealing with being blind back then. It's not like I ever had to deal with that." Lily picked up her chopsticks and hunted around the plates in front of her for a few seconds before picking up a cucumber futomaki slice. "And I had all my friends, and I had Harry."

Hana hid her frown by downing some shrimp maki.

Okay, I need to calm down. Of course they're going to talk about a bunch of stuff I've never heard of. Lily has known Alison for years, but I've only known her for months. It's not like I'm going to know everything there is to know about her because I'm her roommate.

Jealousy is for losers. Alison saved my life. She's given me an honest job, and a nice place to live.

Alison smiled. "Does he ever talk about you settling down? Quitting the tomb raiding lifestyle. I'm sure Mom could give you a few tips about going into semi-retirement."

Lily waved a hand and snorted. "Nope. I think he finds it hot." She laughed, her face even redder than before. "I think I've got another ten years of raiding in me. I don't think I'll become a college professor like Shay, though."

"I managed to not exactly follow in my parents' foot-steps." Alison shrugged.

Hana shoveled more sushi in her mouth. Lily was a tomb raider who could see into the future. She'd defeated the traps like nothing and even saved Alison.

Alison let her take the lead. She didn't give her a big speech about needing to protect her. She simply trusted that Lily could handle whatever they ran into because she knows her and respects her. Because they're old friends.

Hana swallowed her sushi as she pondered what it meant to have an old friend. She couldn't honestly claim she had friends in her old life, only acquaintances and occasional partners.

Would Lily and Alison like to hear about the time me and Sasha conned two cops into raiding a donut shop? Or about the time I covered for Elijah? I don't even know what he was doing. I still don't. I might have helped him steal from an orphanage for all I know.

It's not like Elijah would have saved me from the Eastern Union. Sasha never let me stay with her. And Travis left town the second things got hot with the Union.

Hana stood and blinked a few times. The other two women looked up. She'd lost track of the conversation and so didn't even have a smooth lie to offer them.

"I've got to use the ladies' room." Hana motioned to the table. "I'll be right back. You two carry on...carrying on?"

A slight frown appeared on Alison's face, but she nodded in silence.

Hana pulled the paper screen door open and stepped out of the private room. She closed the door behind her and took a deep breath, her hand over her heart before she walked toward the bathroom. She didn't need to go, but it'd be too obvious something was wrong if she didn't.

Alison's my only real friend. Everyone else is a mark, a competitor, or someone who helped me to screw someone else over. What kind of person has only one real friend when she's twenty-two? What does that say about me?

Hana stopped in front of the ladies' room door and leaned against the wall. When they'd first met and Alison still had her soul-sight, her friend insisted that Hana had a good soul, and that was one of the reasons she'd helped her out and even let her stay with her. Could it have simply been a line?

I spent my entire life preying on others. Alison's been protecting people since she was fifteen.

Hana looked down the hallway and sighed. She slapped her cheeks and looked up.

"I can be a better person. I just have to take the opportunity."

CHAPTER EIGHT

Alison yawned as she stepped into the lobby. A stubborn headache remained despite the gallons of water she probably guzzled once she'd returned home last night. The festivities might have produced even more lasting effects if Lily hadn't had to jet back to her client that night. They'd packed as much fun as they could into a few hours, then took a Currus back to the condo.

Lily had already arranged private transportation to her plane, and that was that. A tomb raid and a visit from an old friend done in days.

It was good to see Lily again, but also kind of weird. So much has changed these last few years, even these last few months. It feels like almost another life.

Reflection would have to wait. Alison still had a witch to interview—or maybe threaten and interrogate. The witch's reactions would determine that.

"Alison," called an excited voice from behind her.

She blinked and turned around to find a middle-aged man in a crisp dark suit smiling at her. There was something familiar about him, but she couldn't quite remember who he was.

Alison stared at him for a moment. "Can I help you?"

"It's me. Ryan." His smile grew. He gestured toward the elevator. "I live in two-oh-eight. We chatted when you moved in."

"Oh, yeah, Ryan." She rubbed the back of her neck and gave him a sheepish smile. She vaguely remembered now, but when she'd moved in, she hadn't paid much attention to anyone other than the workers helping her move her boxes. She shrugged. "Sorry, it's been crazy. Work, work, work."

Ryan nodded quickly. "Of course. I know management at a pet food company probably isn't as exciting as being a security contractor, but I can sympathize when it comes to being overworked."

Alison blinked. "Wait. You're a manager at a pet food company? What company?"

"Golden Beak." Ryan smiled. "We specialize in bird food."

Alison let out a sigh of relief. "Oof. Good."

The man stared at her for a moment, obviously trying to keep a smile on his face, but confusion crept into his eyes. "Do you have a problem with other kinds of pet food companies?"

"It'd take a while to explain. I had a case recently involving a pet food company." Alison laughed and shrugged. "It got complicated, and I wanted to make sure I hadn't brought work home by accident."

Ryan gasped. "I won't deny there are some shady operators in pet food production. We at Golden Beak pride ourselves on quality ingredients for our feathered friends. We never cut corners, and we don't use any genetically or magically modified ingredients." He winced. "Not that magic is bad, you know, but maybe we shouldn't use it in our bird food without more tests. No offense." He chuckled nervously.

Alison waved a hand. "I don't run a pet food business, so no offense taken, and when I use magic on the job, it generally does involve hurting someone." She shrugged. "Hey, it's been great chatting, Ryan, but I was kind on the way to something."

"Yes, yes, of course. How rude of me. Just…" He looked around and licked his lips before he leaned closer. "I wanted to ask you for a favor."

Oh, crap. Please don't hit on me. The last thing I need is some guy twice my age lusting after me in my condo building.

Alison kept a small smile on her face. "What?"

"I'm a huge fan of your father. Before my promotion at Golden Beak a few years back, I used to be a volunteer moderator on one of the larger James Brownstone fan forums out there, Low and Slow Ass-kicking. But I don't have the time anymore. Too bad, you know? I know he's keeping things lowkey, but I still like to read about new tidbits that have to come to light—the agency, barbecue competitions he's won, that kind of thing." Ryan chuckled and turned a little red. "Oh, I just thought about the name and how it must sound. I know it's a bit on the edge, but, well, you know, he's your father."

"That name does kind of fit him." Alison chuckled. "What's this about exactly? What favor did you need?"

Ryan placed his palms together and gave her his best

puppy-dog eyes. It'd be cute on a kid but was pathetic on a grown man. "I'd kill for a signed picture. If he has some sort of fee or something, I'll gladly pay it. I've looked around a lot, and I can't find sites selling legitimate officially sponsored Brownstone merchandise, not even barbecue stuff. I'm surprised he's not licensing stuff. He'd make a killing."

"Yeah." Alison shrugged. "Dad banked a lot of money in bounties even before he opened the agency. He doesn't really need cash." She sighed. "Look, I'll ask him about it, but I can't make any guarantees. Fair enough?"

Ryan's eyes lit up and he grinned. "Thank you so much, Alison. Thank you."

She held up a hand. "Like I said, no guarantees. Dad values his privacy, and it's not like he listens to me."

"Simply asking is enough. I should let you get on with whatever you're doing. Have a great day."

"You too." She waved before she turned and strolled toward the lobby doors. As she stepped outside into the crisp February air, she sighed.

Huh. I don't know if that was less awkward than if he'd hit on me.

Alison's phone rang with a call from Hana when she was a few minutes away from her building.

She activated speakerphone before answering. "What's up?"

Hana yawned on the other end. "Where are you, girlfriend? I woke up and you were gone."

"Oh, I'm on my way to check on the witch Vincent told me about." She pulled her Fiat onto the 99. "She lives in Kent, so I'll stop by and say hello. I checked with Tahir, and he has a positive thermal trace of someone inside her townhouse right now."

Her friend sighed. "Why didn't you wake me up? This sounds like a charm situation, not a punch them through the window situation."

Alison laughed. "I'm not punching anyone through the window, and this is a witch who'll already be off-balance by me showing up. If you try to charm her, she might pick up on it, and then it'll lead to me to having to punch someone through the window."

"I used to con people for a living. I can be convincing without using the magic, too, you know," Hana scoffed.

"Sure, I know. But I figured that toward the end of the night you were drinking more sake than either Lily or me."

Hana didn't reply for several seconds. "You and me normally don't tend to drink like that. I guess I wanted to take my opportunity."

"You're right. We don't. Things have been busy, and I've been worried about keeping a clear head. Plus, I've never been that much of a party girl. I figured it was kind of a special night. Lily visiting, and us helping her with the tomb raid and all. Anyway, the point is, I thought you could use the rest, and since I didn't need you this morning, I figured I'd let you sleep off the hangover."

Alison frowned for a moment as a black SUV appeared in her rearview mirror. She'd had far too much trouble with those in recent months, but the vehicle changed lanes and passed her. She doubted anyone planning to assassinate her would bring their two young kids along in the backseat.

"I don't get hangovers. Or at least I never have." Hana chuckled. "I don't know if it's a fox thing or not. There are no other foxes around to ask. I'm fine. I could have come along, but...I guess, if you don't need me there, that makes sense."

"Yeah. I've worked you hard between the job and training. We don't have an active job, and this witch lead might not turn up anything, so I have no problem with you taking a day or two off." Alison smiled. "And you had to fight a bunch of giant cockroaches and effectively crawl through a sewer to help out my friend, so I owe you a little time off."

"That makes sense," Hana replied quietly. "Okay, um, I think I'll go grab some breakfast or something then. Call me if you need me."

"Sure, I wi—"

Hana hung up before Alison could finish the sentence.

Alison glanced at her phone.

Is she really okay? Something seems a bit off. I really must be working her too hard. I know she wants to improve, but I have to remember I've been doing this a long time, and she hasn't. She's probably more tired than she's admitting.

Alison shook her head and sighed.

———

Hana sipped at her chai tea and leaned back in her chair. People filled every table in the Starbucks, many taking selfies with their phone. An inordinate number of

Oricerans filled the store, mostly elves and gnomes but a few other species as well, including a single Kilomea waiting patiently to order his drink. All the humans stood well away from the huge Oriceran.

She didn't understand why the magical underground trains that ran to each Starbucks remained a secret, albeit in some cases an open one. With the portals to Oriceran fully open and magic an everyday occurrence, it didn't make much sense that the magicals would continue to cling to the idea that some small part of their world remained hidden. The government knew.

Maybe everyone yearned for a time when being a magical was something far more special, and so they all agreed, even subconsciously, to pretend that the train needed to remain a secret. The world still needed wonder.

Hana sighed and took another sip of her drink. She wasn't there to take the train. It was always there and she could have taken a trip anytime she wanted.

There was no point in leaving Seattle. She understood the city and the flow of the people. She even understood how she fit in with them. At least she used to.

That's why she'd come to the Starbucks at Pike Place. As the original, there were also tourists there, and their interactions with the Oricerans were always interesting. Technically, it was actually the second location, even if it was still the first store. She didn't know enough about the history of the train lines to know if it took a few more stores before they were established.

A muscled young man in a UW sweater sauntered up to a red-headed Light Elf woman sitting at a table and reading a weathered tome. He leaned over and murmured something into her ear. She stared at him until he grimaced and walked away.

The best way to learn how to manipulate people was to watch them. Hana had spent years in places like the coffee shop, watching and listening.

Training. Exactly like she now did with Alison, but training of a different skill. It wasn't so different being a con artist. She had to size up targets, marks, and evaluate their relative risks.

I'm learning how to fight everyone from power armor-wearing soldiers to dark wizards. Although I've tried to stay away from fights my entire life, it's like I look forward to them now. What does that mean? Am I cocky because Alison's always around to bail me out if I get into trouble?

But she doesn't always need or want me around, does she?

"I haven't seen you here in months," a man's voice murmured behind her. "You too good to hang around the old haunts? Not only that, it used to be I couldn't even sneak up on you. I could have taken your purse and been out of here before you even knew what was going on."

Hana set her cup down and turned. She recognized the attractive man with his slicked-back dark hair and black leather jacket. Travis grinned at her, his teeth as white as ever. A lot of women found him charming. Even she had once before she'd learned enough to see through him.

She snorted. "You always were a sneaky bastard who liked to take things that don't belong to you. Were you a Willen in another life?"

Travis snickered. "Maybe I was. Not all of us were blessed with magic, Hana, so I've had to work with the gifts the good Lord gave me."

"I don't think anything or anyone divine had anything to do with your life choices." Hana motioned to the chair across from her. "Besides, why are you complaining about me not being places? Last I heard, you skipped town and were going to Baton Rouge to escape the Daimyo."

He dropped into a seat with a snort. "He's not a problem anymore, is he? Ever since your little sugar momma killed him."

Hana rolled her eyes. "The bastard had it coming, and Alison gave him a chance to surrender. Am I supposed to care about that guy dying? He was a waste of a human being."

Travis held up his hands in front of his chest. "Look, I'm not complaining. I was in deep to that guy, and yeah, I did run because I would have ended up in Elliot Bay otherwise." He sighed and shrugged. "I feel bad about what happened. I heard about the way things went down with you and him, and I'm the one who introduced you to that bastard's operation." He shrugged. "But like I said, he's not a problem anymore."

He looked her up and down, a faint look of concern on his face. The expression didn't sit well on him.

Hana frowned. "What?"

"It's true, then? You're Brownstone's pet fox now?"

"I'm her friend and her employee," Hana spat back. "She helped save me from the Daimyo and has given me a well-paying job. She didn't run off to Baton Rouge to leave me to become a sex slave for the Eastern Union."

Travis sighed. "Yeah, I deserved that, but you have to understand, Hana, I didn't have a choice. I'm not a Drow princess. I'm not even a magical. There wasn't anything I could do, but you—I figured you're a nine-tailed fox. Even without your magic, you could con a bum into giving you his last dollar. I knew you'd be okay."

"I almost wasn't."

He smirked. "But you are." His smirk vanished and was replaced by a sympathetic smile. "You say you're Brownstone's friend? Seriously?"

Hana crossed her arms. "I know I'm her friend. She's even let me be her roommate."

Travis shook his head and patted his chest. "We used to be friends. I got you out of jams, and you did the same thing. That meant something. We had each other's backs."

"Meaning what, exactly?" Hana took a deep breath, her heart already pounding. "I have Alison's back, and she has mine, and not only for shady crap."

"Come on. Friendship's about having things in common, the same interests." Travis shook his head. "Alison Brownstone is the daughter of a celebrity. It'd be one thing if she was only going around and beating down gangs. I could respect the power, but I've heard about the building she's remodeling."

Hana shrugged. "So? She's running a business and she needs an office. What's wrong with that?"

"What kind of twenty-five-year-old woman rolls into Seattle and can start dropping that kind of cash on remodels?" Travis snickered. "Think it through, Hana. She's not only a little rich girl; she's an actual princess. She might pat you on the head and say you're great now, but you have to accept that deep down, she thinks she's better than you. She's not a real friend. You're simply some entertaining toy she's slumming with as she gets used to Seattle. It won't be long until she kicks you out so she can hang out with her real friends."

Real friends? Like Lily?

"Screw you, Travis," Hana replied. "You don't know anything about her."

"I know enough. I know she's not a true friend to you like me or any of the people who really had to come up on the streets. We know what you went through. She doesn't."

Hana scoffed. "Friends? We were never friends, Travis. Merely two pieces of garbage helping each other screw other people over. Most people call those accomplices."

Travis' eyebrows lifted. "Oh? Is that how it is? The little princess has filled your head with tales of how you'll be a better person? Will she take you to meet billionaires and to little parties?"

"I have met billionaires," Hana groused. "And I'm not impressed, by the way."

"Of course you have." Travis snickered. "But we can't run from our true natures. If you were such a good person, you wouldn't have used your looks and powers to con people."

Hana frowned and averted her eyes. "I had no choice. I had to survive."

"Bullshit. Everyone has a choice. But it was easy. Fuck. It was fun." Travis chuckled. "I'm not saying I'm better than you, Hana. I'm saying we're the same, and I understand you in a way that some rich celebrity princess never will, no matter what bullshit lines she feeds you. We've both done shit we're not proud of. Do you think hanging around Alison Brownstone and wagging your tails for her will turn you into a better person?" A dark grin crept over his face. "Now that'd be some impressive magic."

Hana stood, her knees weak. "I always had rules. Lines I wouldn't cross."

"All lines get crossed. It's only a matter of when. Maybe it wouldn't have happened when you were young and hot. Maybe it'd be when you were old, and even the charm magic didn't work as well. Shit, maybe it'd happen the first time you charmed the wrong person and they threatened you." Travis shrugged. "The way I heard it, you were looking for some other woman to whore out to the Daimyo in your place." He grinned. "Is that what you tried to do with Brownstone? Did you pick the wrong woman?"

Hana dug her nails into her palms. The pain felt cleansing. "I didn't...I stopped before I even knew who she was."

Travis sneered. "How convenient for you. What would have happened if that woman didn't turn out to be Alison Brownstone? How long would have you held out? How long would your precious rules have kept you in check?"

Hana hissed. Her eyes turned vulpine, her tails appeared, and her claws extended. "Go to fucking hell, you bastard."

Silence swept over the coffee shop. Everyone now looked her way. The Kilomea from the line glared at them, and a few people, both human and Oriceran stood as if preparing to intervene.

Travis smoothed a hand over his jacket. "I think this proves how close to the edge you were. I'm not saying this to be a hater, Hana. I'm simply telling you that you should get away from Brownstone and back to your real friends before it's too late."

Hana snatched up her tea and threw it in Travis' face. "I hope you get magical chlamydia, you son of a bitch."

Travis chuckled and wiped the tea off his face.

She stormed toward an exit and the crowd parted to let her through. A few people took pictures with their phone and murmured among themselves.

After she threw the door open and stepped outside, Hana reverted to her human form. Blood trickled down her palms from her earlier tight fists.

He's not right about me. I'm not that person anymore simply because I occasionally charm a guy for a free meal and wipe his memory. It's no big deal. I don't even do it that often anymore.

Hana made it halfway toward the pier when her stomach knotted.

"I can stop anytime I want," she whispered to herself. "Can't I?"

CHAPTER NINE

Alison pulled her Fiat up to the address Vincent had given her. A row of identical gray townhouses with attached garages stretched down the block and only willows and dogwoods broke the monotony.

She stepped out of her car and looked around, then narrowed her eyes on the carefully trimmed lawn. Faint magic tingled her senses.

So that is what she does with her powers?

Alison chuckled and headed up the narrow concrete walkway that led to the porch. She knocked lightly on the door. There was no reason to go in hard unless she expected resistance.

After a few moments, the door opened, and a tired-looking woman in an apron stood on the other side, flour on her face and clothes. "It's really not a good time." The woman looked Alison up and down. "Whoever you are."

"Alison Brownstone." She smiled and shrugged. "I'm looking for Madison Vance."

The woman's hand twitched, and she glanced over her shoulder.

Alison smirked. "Left your wand in the kitchen, I'm guessing?"

"You can't take me in. I've done nothing wrong. I've never committed a crime, which means I've got no bounty on me." Madison folded her arms and frowned. "So you have no reason to even be here. You're harassing a law-abiding citizen."

"I'm not a bounty hunter," Alison replied. "I have a license, but I'm a security contractor, and this isn't even about that. It's...a different matter."

The witch took a deep breath and looked over her shoulder again.

Don't run. This doesn't have to be a big deal, Madison.

Alison shook her head. "I simply want to ask you some questions. I'm not here to fight you or take you in."

Madison frowned and sighed. She motioned inside to her worn couch. "Ask your questions then. I won't necessarily answer, though."

She headed toward the couch. The living room was as boring as the neighborhood, with a modest TV on the wall and a coffee table that had seen better days. A light blue vase on the coffee table added a touch of color, but whatever help Madison provided Chesterton hadn't elevated her to the Mercer Island elite.

The witch closed the door and moved to sit on a recliner. "I've done nothing that should have you even sniffing my way. So why are you here?"

"Huh. You really don't know, do you?" Alison folded her hands in her lap. "Why are you so nervous then?"

Madison laughed nervously. "Are you serious? You're Alison Brownstone. Everywhere you go, death and destruction follow. Exactly like your father."

"We both only take down people who have it coming." Alison took a deep breath. "Like I told you before, I'm not here to bring you in. I simply want to ask you some questions about some work you did for Derek Chesterton."

Madison's eyes widened. "What? How do you even know about that? That was confidential work."

Time to push forward with a little gamble.

"Because I'm Alison Brownstone, and I always find out." She leaned forward and forced a smile onto her face. "I know you did work for him." She narrowed her eyes. "Curse work."

"I...signed a non-disclosure agreement. I can't talk about any of the work I did." Madison swallowed and rubbed her hands together.

"I'm very good at keeping secrets," Alison murmured. "And you know what I think? I think you want to tell me deep down."

"What the hell are you talking about? Why would I want to do that?"

Alison shrugged. "Because you know something was off about the whole thing. You know they were hiding something from you, too."

Madison looked down. "I signed an NDA."

"Do you know any truth detection spells?"

The witch nodded.

Alison pointed toward the kitchen. "Go get your wand and use one, then. I'm willing to swear right here and now under a spell that if you tell me the truth, I'll make sure no one ever knows where I got it from."

"You can't guarantee that." Madison shook her head. "Someone could torture it out of you."

She laughed. "Seriously? You were terrified when I showed up because of who I am. No one will capture me. They might kill me, but they won't capture me."

"And I can use a truth spell?"

Alison nodded.

Madison sighed and slumped forward. "I won't even bother if you're willing to go that far, but I want to be clear. I didn't work for Derek Chesterton, at least not directly. I was recruited by a company to help them with some research. They wanted specific and rare curses performed on animals. They told me it was part of an experiment to evaluate if certain types of magic are carcinogenic from basic exposure." She furrowed her brow. "The whole thing was odd because they'd never give me any information beforehand. I'd show up, and there'd be an animal, usually rats but also some rabbits and even a goat and a few monkeys. They asked me to perform different kinds of spells and curses, really odd stuff. In some cases, the animals had already been enchanted, but the researchers wouldn't tell me about the magic on them." She threw a hand up. "I tried to explain how I might not even be able to accomplish what I tried to do if I layered my spell on top of others, but they didn't care. They even told me not to worry and that it was all part of the experiment."

That matches up with what Tahir found in the memo. It's not like a witch would have been happy to work on an anti-magic virus. Maybe they layered curses on genetically engineered viruses until they got what they wanted?

"They might have simply been idiots who didn't know a lot about magic so didn't know how to set things up." Alison shrugged.

"I thought that at first, but then they started asking for very specific spells—in many cases, specific kinds of curses. There's no way they didn't know what they were asking for." Madison stared at her hands. "That's when I started to worry that there was something important they weren't telling me." She looked at Alison. "Even without that, I realized early on that something was odd. The research schedule was very erratic. I started to think it was maybe some big technomagic company trying to cover their ass and prove that something they were working on wasn't a cancer threat. I didn't understand why they needed to test so many curses, but I also didn't want to ask too many questions. They paid me a lot of money, and it's not like these spells are ones I get much opportunity to use. It was…interesting work." She snorted. "I know someone like you might wonder why a witch needs to specialize in curses, but you have to understand, I studied those spells to help protect people. I thought I might be doing that at first, helping a company figure out a way to protect people."

Alison ran her tongue along the inside of her cheek. The resources and methodical effort put into the virus was outstanding. Based on what little Tahir had turned up, it was obvious that Madison wasn't the only magical working on the project.

They must have tested it, too. Not only on animals but on magicals. Otherwise, how would they know if it worked?

She almost snorted when she realized she'd almost forgotten what the memo said. They were testing it on magicals, including her.

"I see," Alison murmured. "But something happened, didn't it? Something that pushed you off the project?"

Madison nodded. "I started to ask more questions. I was curious, but I also needed to know more. I tried to explain to them that the more I knew about what they specifically tried to evaluate, the better I could refine my magic to help them. I approached the main researcher, cornered him in the hallway, and asked him point blank to give me more information. I offered to sign even more NDAs if that was the problem. But he still refused to give me more information."

She frowned. "There's one thing I don't get. When I asked you about working for Derek Chesterton, you reacted with disbelief that I knew. You told me you didn't work for him directly, but it seems to me like you knew this research was being funded by him."

"I…overheard his name mentioned a couple of times," Madison explained. "When they didn't think I was paying attention. I tried to ask if he was funding the research one day." She shrugged. "The next morning, I was told they no longer had need of my services and reminded me I'd signed the NDAs. They sent my final payment immediately, and I figured I'd leave well enough alone. The last thing I wanted was a billionaire coming after me."

"Trust me. It's pretty damned annoying." Alison pulled out her phone. "Even if you didn't deal with Chesterton directly, you went somewhere for the experiments. I need the company name. Maybe your main contact. I'll take it from there. No one will ever know you were involved, and on top of that, everything I know suggests you were far from the only magical working this project. It'd be hard to trace it to you."

Madison stared at Alison, her lips pursed. "Prometheus Testing Services. The head of the project, at least the one I worked for, was Doctor Ajit Patel."

That should be enough for Tahir to point me in the right direction.

Alison blew out a breath and hopped up. "Thanks. I'll leave you alone. Unless it's by accident, you'll never have to see me again." She turned to leave.

"Miss Brownstone," Madison called.

"What?" She turned back.

"The project…the fact you're looking into it. It's something terrible, isn't it? It's got nothing to do with cancer testing, does it?" A mask of fear covered Madison's face.

"Don't worry about the details. It's best if you don't know. Safer." Alison smiled and opened the door. "I'll promise you one thing. I'm going to take care of it. All of it."

I'm finally making progress. It's time to rattle a few more cages.

CHAPTER TEN

A lison folded her arms and tapped her feet as she stood in front of Agent Latherby's desk.

This guy really needs to get a chair.

The PDA agent gave her a tight smile from his desk. His shaved head was stunningly shiny, practically a mirror. Alison half-wondered if he used a spell on it.

He folded his hands in front of him. "I didn't expect you to show up so abruptly, Miss Brownstone." His tone dripped with annoyance. "I'd prefer it if you didn't do that. It's not like I sit around all day awaiting your arrival with bated breath."

Alison snorted. "I wouldn't have had to if you hadn't blown me off. You're the one who forced me to do this."

"Oh?" Agent Latherby leaned back in his chair. "What are you talking about?"

"It's been over a month since I sent you that memo we found." She shrugged. "You said you'd get back to me, and you haven't. And you also haven't called me in for any jobs. That kind of makes me think you're ignoring me on purpose. I took a big risk sending you the memo to begin with. I'm not an idiot. I know you can read between the lines."

"Yes. I can." He inhaled deeply and let the air out slowly through his nose. "I understood immediately who the Dark Princess is. It's impressive to me that you've accomplished as much as you have, and you're not even at your full power. But are you really so concerned about me knowing your little secret? It's not to my advantage to spread such information around. It's only to my disadvantage."

Alison pointed to a picture of the President hanging on the wall. "My theory is that Chesterton is behind it, but it's not like the government doesn't have the resources to do it. The government has screwed with my family several times over the years, and so let's say I don't trust them not cook up some anti-magic as a weapon." She snorted. "To be clear, I'm not saying this project was created to target me, only that I have no reason to trust anyone in the government."

Agent Latherby chuckled quietly. "You trust me well enough."

"And I'm questioning if that was a good decision." She shook her head. "You may be a government stooge, but you're also a wizard. Whatever the original point of this project, it's as much a threat to you as it is me or any other magical, so I'm banking on simple self-preservation along with some vague sense that you actually give a crap about protecting people."

"Such a stirring evaluation of my personal character." Agent Latherby frowned. He withdrew his silver wand from his jacket to set on his desk. "Yes, I'm a wizard, but I'm also a member of the PDA first."

Alison narrowed her eyes. "Meaning what?"

"I told you before, Miss Brownstone." He offered her a thin smile. "We exist to protect the country from all enemies, foreign and *domestic*." He picked up his wand and slid it back into his holster. "I'm well aware of your family's history with the government, and I'm also well aware that not everyone in the government is enthused about the return of magic even three decades out. It might very well be a government faction, and so I've been careful with your information. I don't want to push it up the chain in case it is a government faction, rogue or otherwise, but to be honest, if it'll help put your mind at ease, I doubt it is."

"What makes you say that?"

He chuckled. "Because I've read a lot of government documents in my career and documents written by contractors for government consumption. I know what they sound like. I know how they're written, including classified documents. The document you sent me doesn't read like a government document or a contractor working for the government."

Alison nodded slowly. "Okay, fair enough, but what about Chesterton, then? Is the PDA going to let some asshole billionaire sit around making biological weapons?"

"No, we most certainly won't," Agent Latherby replied. "But the PDA is still a branch of the government, and we can't go after private citizens without some direct proof of wrongdoing."

"Are you kidding me?" She threw her hands up. "You're going to sit and do nothing? Right now, this whole plan is still in the test phase. For all we know, they're getting ready to dump it into the water treatment plants in every city in the world or sprinkle it from planes. However the hell it works."

The PDA agent gave her a bland look, clearly unimpressed with her predictions. "The subtlety employed by the people behind this suggests nothing so grand anytime soon, and there's little that can be done for the current victims, but I'll have you know that we're doing something. We're monitoring Chesterton. Your encounters with him and his cat's paws are enough for that, but we've been hampered by having to be careful with our investigation. It's not only this office involved in looking into him. Even if we've had trouble collecting evidence and witnesses willing to testify, his indirect links to Jacobsen Associates are already of interest."

Alison nodded and some of the tension seeped from her body. "Good. All I wanted was for someone to look into this crap. I'm doing it myself, but, yeah, like you, I have to be a little subtle about it."

"I'll let you know one important thing. Chesterton is obviously scared."

"Scared?" She furrowed her brow. "Why do you say that?"

"You haven't noticed yourself? He's been unusually quiet. He's not made a single public appearance since your dismantling of Jacobsen Associates. We're taking our time, Miss Brownstone, watching him and preparing. When we go after him, we need to make sure it's for the final kill. If we give him any room to maneuver, he might lawyer his way out, bribe his way out, or simply run and hide somewhere. Money lets you do that. He can buy himself enough wizards to hide from us." Agent Latherby frowned. "Trust me. I share your frustration, and I can assure you, Derek Chesterton will be going down, one way or another."

"I don't know if I'm willing to wait. This guy's not only an asshole; he's a billionaire asshole who is testing biological weapons on people." Alison shrugged. "Including me."

"So you believe."

"Yeah, so I believe." Alison locked eyes with Agent Latherby. "Is this where you tell me to back the hell off?"

Agent Latherby chuckled. "No, this is where I remind you that self-defense goes a long way in Seattle." He glanced down at his watch. "Now if you'll excuse me, Miss Brownstone, I've got a meeting to attend."

She nodded slowly. "I'll be in touch."

"So will I."

Hana sighed as she walked down the street, her hands in her coat pockets. She'd wandered up and down the area near Pike Place for hours, watching tourists and trying to identify the pickpockets, con artists, and other people who used the area as a hunting ground like she had before meeting Alison.

The encounter with Travis replayed constantly in her mind. She wanted to find fault with what he said, but the more she thought about it, the harder it became.

How many people had she conned over the years? She'd lost count. Half the reason she now walked around was to test her self-control and see if she could be around so many marks without wanting to con any of them.

Hana had tried to tell herself in the past she wasn't hurting anyone seriously, merely borrowing a little cash or getting a few favors. She'd tried to pick targets who looked like they could afford to lose a little money, but it wasn't like she checked in on them later.

A few months of helping Alison out doesn't make up for everything I did. I told myself it was about survival, but would it have been impossible to find someone to take me in, even if I am a nine-tailed fox?

She sighed and stumbled toward a wall and away from the dense river of people and drones that choked the land and sky around her. Movement caught her attention, and she looked up.

Someone in dark clothes ducked around the corner.

Huh? What was that about?

Thuds and shouts followed. Hana grimaced. Even at a distance, she recognized the sound of fists meeting flesh.

"Damn it," she mumbled. "It's not my business, but no way I can walk away now."

After another long sigh, she jogged around the corner.

Four men in dark suits with gold chains around their necks stood around a man crouched on the ground. Travis' head was bleeding.

The men turned toward Hana.

One of them smirked at her. "Move along, sweet thing," he ordered, a faint Russian accent underlying his words.

"Run, Hana," Travis groaned. "Eastern…Union."

The man kicked him in the head. "Shut your mouth, asshole." He sneered at Hana. "If you're a friend of this asshole, let this be a lesson to you." He crouched beside Travis and lifted his head by the hair. "You're gonna fucking die here. You thought you could run from the Eastern Union and live?"

Hana blew out a breath and shook her head. She should leave. Travis was scum, and this was scum cleaning up other scum. But she couldn't bring herself to leave.

Alison could have said the same thing about me. Even if she had her own reason to kill the Daimyo, she didn't have to hire me or let me move in with her. She could have left me to the Eastern Union's revenge.

Hana shook out her hands. "Walk away right now, and there won't be any trouble."

The gangsters all laughed.

"Get a load of this bitch." The crouching gangster rose and cracked his knuckles. "Don't think I won't beat your fucking face in because you're a woman."

Hana snorted. "To quote a good friend of mine, I'll give you one last chance to walk away."

The gangster stomped toward her. "Okay, bitch, now you've pissed me o—"

Her lightning-fast throat-punch sent him to the ground gasping. Her soft boots weren't the best gear for kicking, but a few quick blows to the head still dazed him.

The three other men stared at her, shock on their faces.

Hana's tails appeared, and her claws extended. "You picked the wrong little bitch to fuck with," she shouted.

Two of the thugs went for their guns.

She bounded toward the nearest man and slammed her knee into his face. He fell with a crunch and she pushed off his collapsing body and raked the hand of one of the men who fumbled for his gun. He screamed and dropped his weapon.

A quick spin sent her foot into the side of his head and her fox speed added power to the blow. He dropped with a grunt and clutched the side of his head.

The last man managed to get his gun out, but she ripped it out of his hands a second later and left deep gouges in his hand.

Hana bounced back and emitted a low growl as the four men all moaned. "Apparently, you assholes don't get told anything. I'm Hana Sugimoto and I work for Brownstone Security." She pointed a clawed finger at Travis. "He's a friend of mine, so unless you want to bring me and Brownstone Security down on you, you'll back the fuck off. Understand?"

Wow. I really channeled my inner Alison there.

The men all rose and several gritted their teeth in pain. They fled in the opposite direction without another word.

Hana glared at them until they turned the corner. She retracted her claws and released her tails.

Travis pushed himself to his feet. "Damn, Hana...I always knew you were fast, but every time I saw you use your powers, you used them to run away." He winced and touched a bruise on his face gingerly. "Thanks. After everything I said to you earlier, I wouldn't have blamed you if you left my ass there to get beaten or worse. I'm worried, though. Like I said, those guys were Eastern Union."

Hana snorted. "So? I'm not the same woman I once was. I'm not afraid of them. They should be afraid of me."

Travis managed a chuckle. "Yeah, after what I saw, definitely. Damn, it was a little..."

"What?"

Travis looked away. "A little hot. There's something about a badass woman taking a bunch of guys down that I like." He shrugged. "What can I say? I always thought you were hot, but now, you're so much more confident and badass. I think that's why I was such a little bitch to you earlier. You passed me up, and I was jealous." He hissed and slumped against the nearby brick wall. "Damn. They fucked me up."

Hana fished a healing potion out of her purse and held it in her palm. "Here, take this."

"Shit. Do you have any idea how much this is worth?"

She laughed. "It's not a big deal. We've got a whole box of them. Take it. Okay. I didn't save your ass so you can die from internal injuries a few hours from now."

Travis alternated between looking at the potion and her eyes before he snatched it. He yanked the cap off and downed the contents.

"This shit tastes awful." He made a disgusted face.

Hana shrugged. "It's supposed to heal you, not taste nice."

The lacerations on his head sealed themselves, and the bruises faded.

"Damn," Travis murmured as he touched his face. "The pain's all gone."

"So are the wounds. That's magic for you." Hana smiled.

"I owe you big time, Hana. More than big time after the way I treated you earlier." Travis rubbed the side of his nose. "I was a complete asshole, and I don't know what to say other than I'm sorry. I was a dumbass."

Hana shrugged. "Hearing you say you're an asshole and a dumbass is pretty satisfying."

"Yeah. I gave you all that shit, and you saved my life. Damn, I'm such a fucker sometimes. Can I at least buy you dinner this weekend? It's the least I can do."

"Dinner?" Hana considered it for a few moments before nodding. "Sure, why not?"

This doesn't have to mean anything, but there's no reason to turn down a little fun time. I made him eat his words in the end. Maybe this could be something useful, not only for me but also for the company. Alison helped me out, so maybe I can help Travis out. We could use him as an informant or something. That would work.

And there's nothing wrong with a date, even if I don't want to go somewhere. Tahir's not biting, so it doesn't hurt to be reminded that men actually do find me hot.

Hana grinned at a sudden thought.

Maybe Tahir's not biting because he doesn't think there's any competition.

"Let me give you my number, Travis. Assuming you don't get your ass beaten by this weekend, I'd love to go out on a little date with you." She shook her finger. "This doesn't mean anything, though. Just so you know."

Travis eyed her for a moment. "You've got someone?"

"It's complicated."

He chuckled. "It always is."

CHAPTER ELEVEN

When Alison entered the condo that evening, Hana bounced around the living room like a crazed raver. It took her a few seconds to notice the earbuds. She stepped into the room and waved her arms until her roommate finally noticed her and stopped her mosh pit of one.

Hana plopped out her earbuds and smiled at her. "Productive day?"

"You could say that." Alison hung up her jacket before taking a seat on the couch. "I've got a lead on the AMDS research. I've sent the information on to Tahir, and he's looking into it. I also bothered Latherby, and he let me know they are looking into Chesterton more."

"Wow." Hana sat on the couch beside her. "You did have a productive day."

Alison shrugged. "How about you? I've been worried about you, but it looks like you're okay."

"Worried?"

"Yeah. I grew up half my life with bounty hunting and

combat training and all that craziness." Alison smiled. "Sometimes, I worry I'm working you too hard."

Hana blew a raspberry. "I'm fine, but I'm not saying I didn't enjoy a little time off. Um, by the way, I happened to run into some Eastern Union guys and kicked their asses, and I name-dropped the company. In my defense, they were beating someone up at the time, and I wanted them to be scared."

Alison chuckled. "Maybe next time, tell them who you are and who you work for before kicking their ass, but I'm not worried about them. If we're lucky, they might leave town. I don't think so, but it's always a possibility."

"Here's to hoping. Oh, and I have a date this weekend." Hana grinned.

Alison blinked. "A date? You went and talked with Tahir?"

"No, it's...not with Tahir. It's with the guy the Eastern Union was beating up. Somebody I used to know in the old days. I think..." Hana sucked in a breath. "I think I need a few dates that aren't complicated, you know?"

"I see." Alison sighed. "I won't tell you what to do, but make sure you're not setting yourself up for disappointment."

Hana winked. "I never set myself up for disappointment." She placed her hand on Alison's shoulder and locked eyes with her. "You said earlier that you sent some information for Tahir to look into."

"I did. Yeah. Why?"

"I want to go with you when you talk with him. Knowing Tahir, he'll probably have something within a day or two." Hana pulled her hand away. "Pretty please?"

Alison snorted. "Fine, but keep whatever games you're playing low-key. I need him focused right now."

The next evening, Alison eyed Hana as the fox smiled at Tahir who sat at his computer desk. She didn't like the hungry smile on her friend's face.

This is going to end badly, isn't it?

Alison sighed and shook her head. She'd worry about her friend's love life later. They weren't there for a friendly visit. She didn't want AMDS-related information going out over the phone, even with Tahir securing it, so that necessitated a face-to-face meeting. He increasingly preferred face-to-face reports anyway, probably so they could see his expressions as he bragged about how good he was.

"Prometheus Testing Services," he intoned and swiveled in his chair to face Alison. "They aren't what you think."

She frowned. "What do you mean?"

Tahir nodded toward his center screen. "Chesterton doesn't own them and has no controlling interest in the company at all."

"No way. He has to own them." Alison shook her head. "The witch said she overheard them mention his name."

Tahir nodded. "Yes, and that may very well be the case. Everything I could find on short notice, which did still include some deep dives, suggests the company is a subcontractor that helps with patient testing on sensitive research when the clients lack some of the necessary in-house resources. They've been around for decades and are well trusted across a variety of industries." He shrugged. "To be clear, they've worked openly for companies controlled by Chesterton in the past, and I've found some evidence of more recent hidden work, but they've also worked for AMS."

Alison blinked. "As in Scott's company?"

"Yes, but not only his company, virtually every major technomagic company and many biotech firms who are exploring magical research." Tahir swiveled back toward his screen and tapped something on his keyboard. "That seems to be one of their selling points—the fact that they have a lot of experience doing clinical patient testing involving magic."

Hana watched the two in silence and the same hungry smile remained on her face. She'd never looked more like a fox, even on four legs.

"Wait." Alison pinched the bridge of her nose. "So these damned bastards are probably on Chesterton's payroll, but we don't have a good way to prove it. Is that what you're telling me?"

Tahir continued typing and didn't bother to look her way. "I'm still trying to penetrate their systems fully. For one thing, I've not been able to find any evidence that an Ajit Patel has ever worked for the company in any manner. I'm doubtful that they could have run extensive testing on the virus, especially if it involved magical resources, without leaving some evidence in their systems. I simply need more time." He frowned and stopped typing. "It pains me to admit it, but their systems are surprisingly hardened, including with magic."

"It's fine, Tahir. You've already made some progress.

Even if we can't one hundred percent tie Chesterton to the research, we know his money was sloshing around in the general area." Alison shrugged. "That means we're at least heading in the right direction."

Tahir nodded curtly. "I suppose. I'll continue looking into things. I've also not established any connection between the Prometheus systems and the server I found the memo on, but that server's already been taken down, which means Chesterton's people probably know I've penetrated it."

"We're getting there. We simply need to keep pressing forward. Latherby told me Chesterton is lying low, which means he's worried. I don't care if he's worried more about the PDA or FBI than me. We can take advantage of that." Alison stood. "But there's no point in bothering you for now. We'll leave you to your work. Thanks for all your help as always, Tahir."

He scoffed. "This is a puzzle that needs to be solved. I'm as interested in finding out the answer as you are, but it will probably take a few days."

"Take the time you need. It's not like Chesterton's going anywhere, and he's obviously afraid to send anyone after me for a while."

Hana stood and stretched her arms toward the roof. "So you'll spend your weekend cracking systems. Sorry for that."

Tahir looked her way. "Why would you be sorry? I enjoy a good challenge."

"Oh." Hana shrugged. "You're so hardworking. It makes me feel bad about going on a date this weekend. That is assuming you don't find some super-incriminating evidence right away."

"We'll see." Tahir cleared his throat and returned to his typing. "Enjoy your date."

Disappointment spread over Hana's face.

I told you to not get your hopes up.

Alison let Hana stew in silence for the first ten minutes of their drive home before she finally shook her head.

"Whatever happened to being direct?"

Hana frowned. "What do you mean? Direct about what?"

"Tahir. I thought you were going to be direct with him, but now, you're playing games." Alison sighed as she changed lanes, moving in behind a large Andercarr delivery van. "I get that some of this is you wanting to get that thrill of manipulation or whatever, but if you're really interested with him, be honest. That's what I've done with Mason, and it's working out."

Hana snorted. "Tahir's a little denser. A little more of a challenge."

"I'll back you if this is serious. But I don't want you to twist yourself up in so many games you forget the original goal. I'm not trying to be a bitch about this. I only want to see you happy."

A vulpine smile took over Hana's face. "Don't worry. I know exactly what I'm doing, and this will help me judge if I have a shot. It was easy to tell Mason was into you because he couldn't take his eyes off you at the gym, but

Tahir's a different kind of guy, and I get it. Some guys don't even understand they're interested until they see someone going after the woman they're attracted to," she whined. "Trust me. This will work. It's a great plan."

"And what about the guy you're going out with?" Alison inquired. "Is he in on the plan?"

Hana nodded. "Yes. I made it clear this date's nothing romantic. Don't sweat it. I'll simply have a little fun this weekend, and when it's all over, Tahir will finally see me as a woman."

Alison chuckled. "I don't know what to say other than good luck."

"That's all I need." Hana rubbed her hands together. "This will be great." She glanced at Alison. "Assuming we don't have to go smash Chesterton's head in first."

"Don't worry. I promise to wait until Monday if we need to." Alison grinned.

Hana gave her a thumbs-up. "You're the best."

CHAPTER TWELVE

Mason smiled from across the table. He picked his wine up and took a sip. "So, that's when I told the client, 'Look, we can either fly out in the helicopter, or we can sit here and die.' This is all while the mercs are opening up with machine guns, and I'm pushing my magic to the limit."

Alison nodded as she chewed a bite of her lobster risotto. Sweet and succulent.

"The idiot keeps arguing with me. All the while, I'm seeing more reinforcements coming. These guys really wanted him dead." Mason laughed. "I'm still not sure to this day whether I should have been impressed the guy wasn't freaking out about the dozens of mercenaries shooting at us or that he was so afraid of getting in a helicopter while we were taking lead. We were lucky they didn't have any explosives."

"No offense, but I'd be afraid of getting in a helicopter with someone who didn't know how to fly one," Alison pointed out after swallowing her food. "Even if the guy suggesting it was handsome and funny. It's about picking where you want to die."

"I know how to fly." Mason shrugged. "I'm a licensed helicopter pilot."

Alison blinked. "Huh? You are? Since when?"

"For a long time. Years."

"How did that never come up before on our previous dates?" Alison stared at him like he'd grown wings. "What other secrets are you hiding?"

"I never mentioned it because I didn't really think it'd be the kind of thing that would impress you." Mason chuckled. "And it's not like I own one. It's merely a useful skill to have for my job. I ended up learning how to fly 'copters after an early job. I was with a client in one. The pilot got hit by a sniper. I had to bring the 'copter down myself, and I…mostly did a good job." He shrugged. "Some quick spell work saved me and the client, even if I didn't escape unscathed. At least I brought it down in the middle of a city. Cops showed up, both SWAT and AET, and took down the hitmen coming after my client. After that incident, I wanted to make sure I could at least fly a helicopter. I thought about getting a fixed-wing license as well, but it's been hard to find the time. You know how it is."

"No, because I don't know how to fly a helicopter." Alison grinned. "Well, aren't you full of surprises, Mason. Do you also drive race cars?"

"Don't I wish." He took another sip of his wine. "I've merely picked up a lot of skills that help me with my job. You never know what will happen on a job."

"Don't I know it." Alison shook her head. "Stupid pet food guy."

"I saw on the news they've indicted him for over thirty different charges. Don't worry. He's going away. I hope he already paid you."

"Yeah, I know. The DA contacted me the other day." Alison rolled her eyes. "Fortunately, the idiot's going to plead, so I won't have to testify." She shook her head. "That's what I get for not being careful. What about you? Besides idiot clients, have you ever been screwed over?"

"Yeah. It happens." Mason shrugged. "And I don't have all the support staff that you do, so I have to rely a lot more on public knowledge of the potential client and instinct, but sometimes it fails me, or sometimes I realize the guy I'm guarding is a piece of crap who is better off dead and I regret taking on the job."

Alison nodded slowly. She took a sip of her chardonnay. "What happens then? You let someone take them down?"

"If someone's honest with me and I took the job with full knowledge of who and what they are, I protect them. It's rare that I take on pieces of crap unless there's some compelling reason they need to live." Mason frowned. "Like they are going to roll on someone else or something like that. Mostly, though, if I find out someone's total garbage, I'll give half their money back and walk."

"It sounds like a good way to make enemies. do you have any? At least any who survived?"

Mason nodded. "Sure, but it comes with the territory, doesn't it? I won't be the perfect bodyguard who'll defend anyone and everyone simply for a paycheck."

"Good." Alison set her glass down. "I wouldn't want to date someone like that. I worry about it myself. I get that not every client can be a saint, but it's still hard to know where to draw the line. It was easy for my dad. When you're bounty hunting, pretty much everyone you go after by definition isn't a good person. There are far fewer moral questions that way."

"Can I ask you something about that? Not your dad, but bounty hunting." Mason gave her a questioning look.

"Sure. It's not some big secret."

Mason leaned forward and curiosity shone in his eyes. "Why didn't you become a bounty hunter? You've talked a little to me before about not following in your parents' footsteps, but it's not like you became a doctor or accountant or something. There are career paths you could have chosen that would be way different."

Alison ran her finger around the rim of her glass. "Yeah, I still ended up in a job where I kick a lot of ass. Is that what you're getting at?"

"Basically." Mason shrugged. "I'm not saying there's anything wrong with it, but why not do what your dad did? It would have been easier. You would have that full Brownstone reputation to back you up."

Alison sighed and shook her head. "Like I said, fewer moral questions, but I guess it's about how you view the world. One way to help the world is to stop evil, to obliterate it, small or big. That's my dad, you know—the Granite Ghost, the Scourge of Harriken. Few men have personally taken down as many scumbags as he has. My experiences, though, with my mom—my birth mom, you know—early on made me think about evil." She stared at her unfinished risotto. "Walt, my bio-dad, sold her out. Sure, he got what was coming to him, but removing evil didn't bring my mom back. The dark wizards I dealt with in my time at the school and after...defeating them didn't heal their victims or reverse the damage they'd done." She winced. "Do you really want to talk about this? It'll get awkward, because...well, you know..."

Mason nodded. "I'm not jealous of Tanner. He's not here with you. I am. I don't know the guy, and I've got nothing against him, but I'm also not worried about him."

"I've taken down a lot of dark wizards since my time at the School of Necessary Magic," Alison murmured. "But it doesn't reverse what they've done. It only stops what they might have done." She stared at Mason. "I don't simply want revenge. I don't only want to stop future pain. I don't want other people to have to go through the kinds of things I did. Protecting people is a way to do that. The best of both worlds. I take down scum before they can hurt people. At least, that's the idea."

"You never thought about joining the PDA? Although maybe I shouldn't be the one to talk given what I ended up doing for a living."

Alison smiled. "I simply don't trust the government. There are many good people in the government, but there are too many moving parts and too many snakes. I'm too stubborn to want someone else telling me what to do. I figure running my own security company is the best compromise. I can still protect people but on my terms. If I don't like a client, I can tell them to go to hell."

Her phone buzzed and her gaze flicked to her purse, but she forced her eyes back to Mason.

He nodded toward her purse. "Go ahead and check it.

We both aren't the kind of people who should ignore our phones."

"Sorry." Alison gave him a sheepish grin. She pulled her phone out and checked the message. It was from Hana.

Hope you're having fun, girlfriend. I'm having fun. Do everything I would do and more!

A winking emoji and wine glass emoji followed.

Alison rolled her eyes. "It's only Hana. She has a fake date tonight."

Mason laughed. "Fake date? How does that work?"

"Long story. I'm not sure how much of it involves her genuinely being concerned about something versus simply liking a lot of drama in life." Alison tapped out a quick response of "okay" before she dropped her phone back into her purse. "But she's fun. It's good to have a fun roommate."

"Is she a roommate who'll miss you if you don't come home tonight?" He raised a brow suggestively.

Alison sighed. "No, but..."

"But?"

"I'm still not ready for that. If that's okay." She shrugged.

Mason chuckled. "You're worth waiting for, A. I'll wait as long as you want."

Her cheeks warmed. "Thanks."

Hope you really are having as good a time as I am, Hana.

Hana's head thundered, and she blinked her eyes open into complete darkness. She couldn't remember what had happened.

Memories trickled in. A date with Travis. They'd talked about the old days and some of their more outrageous stunts.

Wait. What the hell? Why can't I see anything? Where am I?

Her arms and legs wouldn't move. It took a few seconds to realize her wrists were handcuffed behind her back, and her legs bound with something cold and smooth.

She hissed and struggled. Her tails popped into existence and provided some small light.

The illumination revealed that she lay on her side on the floor. Several metal chains were wound around her legs.

Light filled the room and pain spiked in her throbbing head. She squinted for a few seconds before she closed her eyes.

A door clicked open behind her.

"I'm really sorry about this, Hana," Travis' voice said.

Hana rolled onto her other side and forced her eyes open. Her blurry vision barely made out her date standing in the open doorway.

"What the hell is going on, Travis?"

He shrugged. "I owe the Union too big a debt. I thought I was free and clear, but then a guy tracked me down in Baton Rouge. I thought he would waste my ass right then and there, but he told me I could be free and clear if I helped them out with a little problem. With you."

Hana barked out a harsh laugh. "You really are a son of a bitch. I'm glad I never slept with you, even back when I thought you were hot. But I'm sure I would have been disappointed anyway by certain...things."

Travis snorted. "It's your fault, you know. They're not even pissed much with your debt. It's Brownstone. She's humiliated them and made them look weak."

"So the hell what? If they're so pissed at Alison, they should try to take her out. Then they can see how weak they really are." Hana spat at Travis but couldn't reach him.

"You don't get it, do you? A lot of people thought she wouldn't be as tough as her dad, but she's even worse. She's got all that magic." He shook his head. "They're too afraid to go at her directly, so why not a two-for-one? They get someone who owes them something, and they hurt Brownstone and make Princess Bitch understand that she doesn't run Seattle."

Hana tried to stare at him, but her vision still swam. "What the hell did you do to me? This isn't about drinking too much. I drank way more the other day and was fine."

Travis walked closer and crouched beside her. He stared at her tails. "I didn't know how much to use. I put it in your drink when you went to the bathroom but worried I might have put in too much. You're not human, so I couldn't get by with the bare minimum."

"You're such a little bitch, Travis. You drugged me on a date?" She laughed but that only hurt her head more. "You're right, and I was an idiot. I deserve it. I got conned and bought it all. The well-timed beating after the initial toying with me, making me question everything. You're better than I thought."

He smirked. "I don't have tits and magic, Hana. I've had to make sure all my skills are even better."

Hana rolled onto her back. "Congrats, Travis. You beat me. Probably because I'm a con artist deep down."

"What do you mean?"

"Come on. We both know the most important truth when it comes to cons. It's way harder to con an honest person. The best cons take advantage of greed. In my case, I got greedy by wanting to believe I was a better person than I was." Hana sighed. "Look, I've been in this exact position. I did the right thing. You still can, too."

Travis stood and sneered at her. "Are you still trying to feed me that bullshit? Look what doing the right thing got you. Sure, you got to play at being Brownstone's pet for a while, but it made you soft. Made you weak."

"Weak?" She snickered. "Who's the weak guy now? You're the one who drugged me, and you're only talking shit because I'm handcuffed and in chains and still drugged. I'll tell you what Alison taught me. She taught me to give everyone one last chance, and when they blow that chance, to kick their asses. I'll kick you so hard you end up in Canada, you son of a bitch."

Travis slammed his foot into her side. Pain spiked through her, and she hissed. He dropped to one knee and lifted her by her hair to glare into her face.

Hana's stomach swam. The drugs made it impossible to focus. Something poked at the back of her mind, a solution, but she couldn't focus.

"I win, you arrogant bitch," Travis screamed and spittle blasted from his mouth. "It doesn't matter that you're a magical and I'm only a normal human. I win, and you lose, and I'm not hiding behind someone else. The Union probably won't even whore you out. They'll probably send you to Brownstone piece by piece to make a point."

Hana let out a quiet chuckle. "You dumbass. You called me Alison's pet. Haven't you heard what Brownstones do to people who hurt their pets?"

His face twisted into a mask of hatred. He yanked a syringe from his pocket. "They only let you wake up because I wanted you to hear it from me." He slammed the syringe into her neck and injected a cold liquid into her. "Nighty-night, Hana. If you're lucky, you'll never wake up."

She groaned at the fire in her neck. "You better run back to Baton Rouge before I wake up. I know one piece I'll remove from you. A very tiny piece."

Travis stood and snorted. "You should have stayed on the streets. Maybe then I would have had your back. Too bad you picked the wrong side." He spun on his heel and stormed toward the door.

"I'm…gonna…enjoy…" Hana slurred.

The darkness overwhelmed her.

CHAPTER THIRTEEN

Alison stopped the treadmill at the gym and stepped off. She wiped the sweat from her face with her towel before she frowned at an empty treadmill beside her. Her roommate hadn't come home last night.

It wasn't her place to dictate her friend's love life, even if she thought Hana hooking up with some guy her friend didn't care about to make Tahir jealous was a terrible idea.

She could have at least sent me a text.

Alison walked to a water fountain to take a drink, still frowning.

Why didn't she send me a text? Even if she decided to stay over at her temporary boy toy's place, I would have expected twenty thumbs up and winky face emojis, and a few lewd messages.

The cool water poured down her throat but didn't quench her burning worry. Alison finished her drink and walked to a bench. She sat and pulled her phone out to check for voicemails or texts.

Nothing.

I'm being overprotective. Hana's a big girl and a nine-tailed fox. She was getting along fine before I came along. Wait. Not really. Damn it.

Alison sighed. Was she being overprotective like her dad? Maybe. Was that so bad? She wasn't so sure.

She dialed her friend and held her breath as the phone rang. One time. Two times. Three times. After a few more rings, it went to voice mail.

Hi! You've reached Hana. I'm off doing something awesome and fun right now, but I'll get back to you. Or send me a text. Maybe we can do something fun together.

Alison frowned and tapped in a text.

You should have sent me a text saying you weren't coming home last night. Just let me know you're okay. And don't bother telling me I'm being overprotective, I already know.

She stood and slipped her phone into the pocket of her sweat pants before heading toward the weight machines.

Five minutes and many triceps-targeting reps later, her muscles burned but her mind remained stubbornly focused on her friend.

For every action, there is an equal and opposite reaction.

Vincent was right. Physics or crime, the statement was true. Alison had pissed off a significant number of dangerous organizations in Seattle, and it wasn't impossible they might screw with her friends to get at her. It wasn't like she could protect everyone all the time.

she swallowed and texted Tahir. She didn't want to admit she was worried simply because Hana hadn't come home, so she came up with a suitable excuse.

Progress?

He responded less than five seconds later.

Ongoing. Don't worry. I'll contact you when I have anything.

Thanks, Tahir. You're doing great.

A text to Ava followed.

About those paint questions. I'll leave it up to you.

Ava responded almost immediately.

Very well.

She released a sigh of relief. Those responses cut down on the possibility of some more general conspiracy against her friends, which in turn lowered the chance that anything other than a steamy night in the sheets happened to Hana.

The fox already admitted to Alison before leaving for her date that she found Travis attractive, and they'd had some chemistry from the old days, even if they never hooked up. But she'd also said that Travis wasn't a magical and not all that tough.

If anyone jumped them, it'd be on Hana to defend them.

She did take her gun, but she didn't take her pendant. A wizard or power armor ambush would be too much.

Alison wiped down the triceps machine and moved to the bench press machine. Her stomach churned the entire time.

She lay back on the bench and took a deep breath. Too many people she cared about in her life had been hurt. It didn't matter if she was the Dark Princess. That wasn't always enough.

Alison sat up and shook her head. If she tracked Hana down and nothing had happened, she'd look like an obsessive idiot, but if she ignored her instincts and her friend was hurt or worse, she'd never be able to forgive herself.

Hana has never stayed away for the night since she moved in without at least sending me a text. That has to mean something.

"Screw it. Obsessive idiot it is."

Alison dialed Tahir.

He answered with a snort. "Patience, Alison. I'm working on it. Bothering me won't speed up the process."

"This isn't about that. It's about me obsess…me worried about Hana."

"Worried about Hana?" Tahir replied, the irritation gone from his voice. "What about her?"

"She went out on a date last night, remember? But she also never came home. No messages, nothing. Tell me I'm an obsessive idiot."

He didn't respond for several seconds. "Behavioral pattern changes are always a cause for further investigation. Let me see if I can track her phone. One moment."

Alison rubbed the back of her neck and sighed. "Okay."

She waited as the only thing she could hear was the faint clack of his typing and his breathing.

Tahir broke his relative silence with a grunt. "This is concerning."

Alison stood. "Concerning? What do you mean?"

"I'm assuming the restaurant she ate at was the Gilded Duck?"

"Yeah, she mentioned probably going to that place." Alison walked toward the front door of the gym. She'd survive without a shower.

Tahir muttered something under his breath. "I pinged her

phone there and hacked a traffic drone to go to the coordinates. They lead to an alleyway a few blocks away. The sensors on the drone are too limited for me to look for thermal traces, but I think it's in a small garbage can in the alleyway."

Alison tossed her towel into the dirty towel bin. "I'm going to my car. Lead me there, and I'll check things out. Good thing I keep a receiver in the car. It's time to do this more efficiently."

Alison stepped into the alleyway, still in her sweats and T-shirt and her hair a mess. A small whirring drone hovered a few feet off the ground near a small garbage can, its rotors creating a small updraft and pushing a few stray wrappers through the alley.

"That's the can," Tahir explained through her receiver. "That's where the phone probably is."

As far as Alison was concerned, this was now an official rescue operation. Although she didn't have her full gear, she did have her gun, a few spare mags, and her ring. Combined with magic and Tahir's support, it would be enough. It would have to be.

Alison pulled the lid off the garbage can and frowned. Hana's phone, the pink sparkly case unmistakable, lay inside with a few pieces of torn plastic and worn paper on top of it.

She grabbed the phone and gritted her teeth. "Check the police and hospital reports. See if you can find anyone matching her description being brought in."

"On it," Tahir replied. "What will you do? Go to the police? Vincent?"

"No." Alison held up Hana's phone. "She loved this thing. She always has it on her. It's not as good as having a hair or something, but I can still set up a good resonance tracking spell off it."

Tahir inhaled deeply before he released the breath slowly. "Given the available evidence, it's not unreasonable to assume she's been taken. If that is the case, they might have the ability to use anti-tracking magic."

Alison frowned as she turned and marched back toward her Fiat parked in the front of the alley. "I'll go buy some water and try the spell. For now, stick with checking the police and hospital reports. If the spell fails, we'll figure out where to go from there."

"And what…if it's the worst-case scenario?" Tahir replied, his voice almost a whisper.

"Then whoever's responsible better run to the World in Between before I get to them," Alison growled. "Start prepping some tactical support drones just in case."

Hana kept her breathing shallow and quiet when she next awoke and didn't open her eyes. She lay motionless, listened hard, and tried her best to ignore the spike of throbbing pain in her head and her stomach.

Underestimated me again, asshole.

The few times she'd tried drugs in the past, they didn't last as long for her as they did for the humans she knew—if they worked well at all, even dust. Combined with her hangover resistance, she'd long suspected she had some sort of enhanced metabolism but never cared enough to explore the implications. Mostly, it was simply fun to know she could drink a lot and not worry about the next morning.

It wasn't like she ever expected an acquaintance to drug her and turn her over to the Eastern Union.

Despite the pain in her head and her stomach, none of the oppressive heaviness she'd felt in the Two Worlds Security conference room was present, which meant no magical nullifiers. She fought to stop herself from smiling.

I need to surprise them in case they're watching.

Her captors placed too much faith in the drugs. They knew what she was, and that meant they knew they had to keep her unconscious to prevent her from escaping.

Hana allowed herself a grin and let her eyes open. Her glowing tails emerged and wrapped around her. Even though she could feel muscles, skin, and bone stretching, rearranging, and shrinking, her shift to her four-legged form brought no pain, only excitement. Her heart sped up.

Her smaller paws came free of the handcuffs. The chains dropped to the ground, but she struggled and wriggled to get out of the dress that covered her fox body. The seconds ticked by as she finally emerged from the pile of cloth and chains.

Heavy footsteps approached.

They were watching, after all.

She shifted to her humanoid form again and waited in front of the door, her tails rigid behind her and her claws out. Her head continued to pound, but her murderous rage helped her focus.

The door flew open and the dim light of the hallway spilled inside, but it was practically daylight to her eyes.

Two thugs with guns stood on the other side.

Hana leapt toward the closest one and swiped at him with her claws. She ripped his throat out before he could even shout. His blood spattered on his surprised friend.

She grabbed his arm and shoved it up as he fired several rounds. Her claws slashed back and forth several times and shredded the top layer of his shirt and jacket to gouge into his chest. He screamed and stumbled backward.

Hana yanked the gun out of his hand and whipped it around to aim at him. Her claws made it awkward to handle the weapon, but she didn't retract them before she fired several rounds into the wounded Eastern Union man.

She inhaled deeply. The metallic smell of blood hung thickly in the air.

After a moment, she dropped the gun and rushed back into the room to grab her dress. She wriggled back into it, her glowing tails passing right through the material, but left her heels on the ground.

These assholes won't get a free peep show as I kill them all.

Hana snatched up the two guns from the fallen thugs and looked back and forth in the lushly carpeted hallway connected to the room. Small alcoves lay several feet apart, each containing vases and small sculptures. She didn't know much about art, but they all looked expensive to her. A few more side doors stood on either side, all labeled as storage rooms. Soft lighting filled the area.

With a shrug, she picked a direction at random and started down the hall, wishing she had the shield pendant.

She'd not brought it along because she was on a date and it clashed with her blue-clinging dress.

After a few more feet of walking, Hana couldn't decide if it was lucky or foolish to not have brought the artifact with her. If she'd worn the pendant or even brought it in her purse, the Eastern Union would now have a new and powerful tool.

Hana took a few deep breaths and did her best to ignore her head and stomach.

Okay. I can do this. I'm somewhere the Eastern Union controls, and I have no shields and no phone, but I've got claws, speed, and two guns and whatever else I can take off the bastards I kill.

Wait. Phones!

Hana hurried back to the dead men and searched their pockets. No phones.

"Assholes. Why can't you cooperate?" She frowned and shook her head. Her stomach gurgled at the motion. "Fine. I'll do this the hard way."

CHAPTER FOURTEEN

Hana emitted a low growl as she encountered another hallway. The damned building didn't seem to have any windows or fire exits from what she had seen.

Hope finally appeared in the form of a windowed door at the end of the hallway, a glowing green **EXIT** sign directly above it. Stairs, she assumed. Without windows, that might be her only escape path. It'd at least get her away from the current floor.

Hana glanced at the door plaque directly across from her. It read "Golden Room."

She'd already passed the Diamond Room, Platinum Room, and Silver Room. Quick checks of each of those rooms revealed no more Eastern Union thugs, but she did find expensive leather couches, recliners, and massive televisions, along with small refrigerators filled with wine bottles and plush beds in corners.

Hana began to get a sense of where they'd taken her, which didn't help her head.

The Platinum Room also included a holographic

projector that currently displayed a buxom blonde pole dancing with her top off. The Silver Room's television was a feed of the storage room she'd been held in—a feed that now displayed nothing but two dead thugs right outside the door.

What's my best move? If those idiots from the Silver Room were the only people keeping an eye on me, I simply need to find a place where I can get out of this damned building. Up or down the stairs? If I go to the first floor, there are bound to be more guys, but none of these stupid rooms seem to have a phone. Maybe the roof? If I get up there, maybe I can jump to another building or climb down the side.

Though it still felt like someone pounded a drum inside her head, her stomach at least had stopped churning a few minutes prior.

The headache only fueled her anger. She'd use it empower her revenge against any Eastern Union she ran into on the way out.

She jogged toward the stairs. Polished chrome elevator doors stood to her right and her reflection startled her for a second. The elevator would be an easy way down but getting trapped in a target box wasn't a good plan. The stairs at least provided somewhere to dodge under fire. She wasn't sure how long it'd be before the dead men's buddies discovered she'd killed them.

If I grab a phone, I can call the cops, but who knows how quickly they'll come? And that's assuming I can even find one. Maybe the Eastern Union's paid off the local precinct. I need to get the hell out and then call the cops and Alison when I'm free and clear. At least if she shows up, the AET will probably come, and if the AET was corrupt, they would have killed her when she took down the Daimyo.

Hana threw the door to the stairwell open. A large black number on the brick informed her she was on the fourth floor. The stairs only ran down. So much for her roof option.

"Damn it," she mumbled.

Hana bounded down the stairs and reached the third-floor landing when voices floated up from several floors down.

"What do you think they'll do with that fox bitch?" a low voice asked. "You think they'll make her work here? Or sell her off?"

"Is that who they have up on the fourth floor?" another man replied. He scoffed. "Is that why we had to send all the girls away? That's some bullshit."

"Yeah." The first man grunted. "Boss said he didn't want the girls getting freaked out, but he said it'd all be figured out within a couple of days. I don't know. Ask him. I do what he fucking tells me to."

"The fox bitch is the one who helped get the Daimyo killed, right?"

A dark chuckle followed from the second thug. "I don't know about that. The way I heard it that was all Brownstone, but the bitch works for Brownstone now."

The first thug groaned. "Shit. If she works for Brownstone, she's dangerous. We should have killed her when we had the chance, not brought her here."

"It seems like a waste. She's got a nice body. I'd like to spend a little time with her in the Platinum Room."

Hana rolled her eyes as she could almost hear the waggling eyebrows from the scumbag.

The second thug snickered. "She'd probably bite it off. You can't trust them shifters. Too dangerous."

Not a shifter, asshole, but yeah, you should have killed me when you had the chance.

"I wouldn't want to dip my wick in any magical," the man continued. "I don't care what they look like. You can't trust that shit. You might have some fun, but then it shrivels up and falls off the next day. But how they gonna stop her from going all beast mode or whatever the fuck shifters can do?"

"Nah, it's fine," the first thug replied. His voice drew closer and both men's footsteps grew louder. "They drugged her ass. She won't wake up for days. It don't matter how magical some bitch is, if she's asleep, she's just another bitch, and at least then, she'll keep her mouth shut."

Both men laughed.

Hana gritted her teeth and tried to decide whether to continue down or try to find another set of stairs on the opposite side of the building. The men obviously didn't realize she'd escaped, which meant there was no general alarm. Every man she killed would increase her risk of discovery.

Okay, let's keep it quiet for now. No one heard the gunshots earlier. Maybe a lot of these rooms are soundproofed, or I simply got lucky. I won't complain.

She opened the door to the third floor and closed it gently before she jogged down the hallway and looked for another set of stairs. As she approached a corner, she passed more elevator doors.

There were no stairwell doors on the other end of the hallway, only a vending machine selling soda.

"Man, I was getting somewhere with Denise, too," a man's voice came from around the corner.

Hana skidded to a stop and flattened herself against the wall. She raised the gun in her right hand.

"You kidding me?" another man replied. "She gets paid to convince men they're rocking her world. She's playing you, bro. Getting somewhere? You don't have enough money to get anywhere with Denise. Have you seen the hourly rate they charge for her?"

"That's bullshit. The boss should give us free time with the girls. We work hard. We shouldn't have to pay for some tail." The thug snorted. "I think I got more free chicks when I was still in Viktor's gang. What's the point of joining up with the Union if I get less pussy?"

Yeah, the world won't miss you two.

Hana raised one of her guns and spun around the corner. Judging by their faces, the two Eastern Union men hadn't fully registered what was happening when she opened fire. She continued to pull the trigger as their bodies jerked with each hit. Some of her shots flew wide, but most struck her targets. The assault didn't end until her gun clicked empty.

She dropped the weapon on the ground and tossed the gun in her left hand into her right. Marching forward, she kept the weapon aimed at the downed thugs, but they were already dead and a pool of blood formed beneath them.

"Not the cleanest shooting, but not bad," Hana

murmured. "Maybe a little overkill. I need to work on accuracy under pressure." She pinched the bridge of her nose. The loud gunshots hadn't helped her headache.

The new door-filled hallway dead-ended with a vase on a stand at the end. She had no reason to believe there would be windows in any of the rooms.

Given what she'd seen and heard, the building served as some sort of Eastern Union brothel, which might explain their aversion to windows, especially if they catered to any high-end clients. They would make it too easy for a drone to spot someone or use a laser to pick up voices. But that still didn't explain why they didn't have any fire exits.

Being a gangster doesn't make you fireproof, assholes.

Their reasoning didn't matter as much as the implications of their choice. Everything pointed to her having to take the stairs to the first floor to escape.

Hana took a deep breath and her heart pounded in time with her head. She snorted.

What am I scared of? I'm not the fox who has to run from a fight anymore. I'm drugged, and I'm still kicking ass. I've got claws and I've got guns. Alison's turning me into a badass.

She grinned as she remembered what Lily said.

I've worked with some partners who broke and ran the minute anything weird showed up, but you two stood there shooting away and then started ripping giant cockroaches to shreds like you do it every day.

Hana headed toward the stairwell. Alison hadn't only trained her how to fight better. She'd trained Hana how to approach fights. Her experience the last few months had pushed something out of her head that used to live there full-time rent-free—fear.

"I'm Hana Sugimoto," the fox murmured to herself. "And I'm a badass. It's about time I showed these assholes that."

She threw the stairwell door open, eager to kill the two bastards from before but didn't hear or see them. Lucky them.

Hana bounded down the stairs and reached the second-floor landing in seconds before she continued to the first.

She approached the first-floor door and laughed.

"Bring it on."

Hana flung the door open and grimaced. She'd hoped the stairs were close to the front, but she was at the end of another long hallway.

"Why did you assholes make this place such a maze?" She rolled her eyes and jogged forward.

CHAPTER FIFTEEN

Alison stared down at the needle floating in the water bottle before she lifted her head and glanced across the street. The tracking spell performed decently, even if she'd had to take a few more turns than she would have liked. Her current destination screamed suspicious, which only reinforced in her mind that she'd found Hana.

A large man with a buzz cut and wearing a suit and tie stood near the front of a single dark red door. A matching dark red awning hung over him. Dense bushes hid the rest of the narrow but long four-story building. He continued to look at his phone and didn't seem to notice the red Fiat Spider parked across the street from the building.

Not the best guard in the world, is he? That's fine by me. It doesn't look like this will involve a lot of power armor and railguns.

"This is it," Alison announced. "I'm sure of it. Wherever the hell here is."

"According to city records," Tahir replied through her earpiece, "the building is some sort of private club registered to a non-profit I've never heard of, and none of my searches have turned up any reports of police or hospital reports that are likely to be associated with Hana. I've got searches still going."

"That makes sense. My spell led me here. She's here."

"Does that spell track her body regardless of whether she's still alive?"

Alison's face tightened. "She's still alive."

"That's not what I asked."

She snorted. "I don't care. We're focusing on saving her. I merely need to make sure I don't hurt the wrong people before that."

Tahir sighed. "I understand."

Alison stared at the man playing with his phone. An obvious bulge indicated a not-so-concealed weapon, but that would be expected from any security guard. Beating down some rent-a-cop who didn't know what was going on wouldn't be fair.

"And do you think this place actually is some private non-profit club?" She narrowed her eyes and studied the guard carefully. "From what I can see, it's damned suspicious, but I might be a little biased at the moment. Anything you can tell me from your drones?"

"I haven't had enough time to dig into the non-profit," Tahir responded. "But I'll tell you one interesting thing. Whoever built this building went to a lot of trouble. I have two drones flying around, and I can't see any windows. I don't get any real thermal signatures either, other than surprisingly high levels of exhaust heat out of a few key spots."

Alison frowned as she considered that. "Meaning what?"

"Meaning when they built this building, they specifically wanted to make sure you couldn't use thermal cameras to figure out anything inside, and I'm not even picking up many EM signals on different frequencies. Whoever owns this place is very, very concerned about people spying on them. I doubt they've done it because they are really concerned about people learning about their charity budget."

She tucked a gun into the waistband at the small of her back and draped her T-shirt over it. "Too many things stacking up. That's good enough for me to at least attempt entry. You keep digging into the club records." Alison threw her door open, stepped onto the sidewalk, and slammed her door shut. She took a deep breath and jogged across the street directly toward the phone-obsessed guard.

His head jerked up at the last movement, and a confused expression crossed his face. His gaze roamed her for a few seconds before he snorted in disgust.

"You look like you rolled up from the gym," the man explained. "Have you even looked in a mirror lately?"

"You're not so hot yourself." Alison shrugged. "So what? Is this the part where you tell me to smile more?" She nodded toward the door. "Whatever. I need to go in there. I have to ask a few questions and pick up a friend of mine who's stranded in there."

The man snorted. "This is a private club. Invitation only, and we don't need some college girl who just got done with lacrosse practice ruining the atmosphere. I don't know who told you about this place, but forget they told you anything. You aren't what we're looking for."

Oh. Is that what this place is? Wait, what did he just say?

"Lacrosse? What are you—" Alison looked down. Her t-shirt was a UCLA women's lacrosse shirt from her college days. She didn't play, but she had a few acquaintances who did. She folded her arms. "I don't need your money. I've got more than enough money to qualify for your little club. Now let me the hell in."

The guard shook his head. "Private club, Lacrosse Girl. Invitation only and men only. Now get out of here before you make me mad."

Alison unfolded her arms and shook out her hands. "Let me make this a little clearer. My name isn't Lacrosse Girl. It's Alison Brownstone. I know for a damned fact you have a friend of mine in there, and you'll let me go in there and get her, or people will get hurt, starting with you, asshole. This is me being an obsessive idiot. People like you won't like it when I'm an obsessive idiot."

"Obsessive idiot? What are you talking about?" The thug's face twitched. "Wait. Did you say Alison Brownstone?"

She nodded. "That's me. Alison Brownstone. The Dark Princess and kicker of asses."

Despite this tight face, the guard couldn't hide the fear in his eyes. He pointed to the street. "You better get out of here before I call the cops. You have no business here, Brownstone."

Alison laughed. "Go ahead call the cops. The only reason I haven't called them myself is because I'll enjoy kicking all your asses too much. Let's make this easier.

Who owns this place? Give me the right answer and my friend and I walk away."

"Fuck you," the guard snarled. "This is a private club, and you're trespassing. You think you can go into any place because you're Alison Brownstone? Fuck that, Dark Princess. Fuck that, too. This isn't Oriceran. You're not shit here. You're not Princess of Seattle. Go back to where you were born, bitch."

"I was born in LA," Alison snorted. "And, yeah, I'm nothing but a security contractor with a lot of magic and a bad attitude when I'm annoyed—a bad attitude that tends to come out in me beating down criminals." She narrowed her eyes.

Should I wait for Tahir to figure out who really is running it? Nah. Good people don't kidnap women off the street. Screw this guy and screw whoever owns this place.

Alison locked eyes with the guard. "Last chance. Whatever you're thinking you can do, you're wrong. If you know who I am, then you know what I can do. Didn't you see what I did to Jacobsen Associates online? They were ready for me. Are you?"

His breathing grew shallow as he didn't take his eyes off her as his hand jerked toward his jacket.

Alison whipped her Glock out and shoved it in his face before he managed to draw his own weapon. "I didn't even need magic. Too slow. You're a terrible guard, by the way."

He swallowed. "Please don't kill me. I don't know shit about what goes on inside. I only guard the door."

"You're probably lying through your teeth, but I won't kill you if you don't make any sudden moves." She raised her left hand, placed it on the side of his head, and murmured an incantation. Her hand glowed.

His eyes widened. "W-what are you doing?"

"Don't worry, I won't kill you. I simply don't want the cops or reinforcements here too soon." Alison laid her hand on the side of his head. "Nighty-night."

The man's eyes rolled toward the back of his head and he collapsed in a heap.

Alison tapped her crystal ring three times. Her shield sprang to life and red light bathed her skin. She walked to the door and grabbed the handle, but it wouldn't budge.

She looked around for a locking mechanism or keypad but saw nothing.

"Two options," Alison murmured. "Blow it open or unlock it?"

"Didn't you just tell that guy you didn't want the police showing up?" Tahir replied through her earpiece. She'd almost forgotten about him.

"Good point. Unlocking it is."

Alison traced the unlocking glyph over the door with her finger as she uttered the incantation. Yellow light surrounded the entire door, and it clicked open.

She grasped the handle and took a deep breath. "So, from what you said, I won't be able to chat with you on the inside, Tahir."

"That's accurate. Should I contact the police after a certain period of time?"

"No," Alison replied. "I don't know who's on the other side of that door, but fancy privacy is not the same as being tough. I want Hana free and resting, not dealing with a million cop questions right away."

Tahir snorted. "You're sure about the authorities? It's not only your life at risk. It's Hana's."

"I'm sure. That guard was pathetic. Whoever is running this place is someone with a lot of money but who is used to being able to intimidate people. That guy was about to wet himself once he realized who I was. Maybe I should show up to more places in my sweats to surprise people." Alison threw the door open to reveal a velvet-heavy monstrosity that passed as a lobby. Dark, thick carpet smothered the floors, and a keypad-secured door led to some stairs. An elevator filled much of the back wall right beside another keypad-locked door and a desk.

The man who sat at the desk leapt to his feet and his eyes widened. He blinked several times before he sat slowly and his gaze cut to a television across the room before it returned to Alison.

You were watching TV instead of paying attention to your job? Pathetic.

"Talk to you soon, Tahir. And don't worry, I'll bring her home." Alison stepped inside and closed the door behind her. A cold smile took over her face. "I'm Alison Brownstone, and I believe you have a friend of mine. Don't waste my time with a big speech about how you don't know anything about it."

The man swallowed, and his hand drifted below the desk.

Alison snorted. "A gun won't get through my shield, and I really, really doubt you have anti-magic bullets in there. If you shoot me, it might give me a reason to shoot you. Just tell me where my friend is."

The man took a deep breath, licked his lips, and his

mouth twitched. "This isn't like the Daimyo's place. You don't know what you're walking into, Brownstone."

"Daimyo?" Alison rolled her eyes. "You're Eastern Union? Are you kidding me? What, are you trying to see if you can push me into wiping every last one of you assholes out?" She pointed at the man. "I'm only here because you assholes took my friend. Turn her over, and I leave. Don't, and I go through as many of you as it takes until I find her."

The man grinned. Something clicked beneath the desk. Yellow lights flashed in the corner.

"That was your big plan? An alarm?" Alison snorted. "Good. I want everyone coming for me. It makes things easier."

"Fuck you, Brownstone." The man leapt up and over the desk, a large serrated knife in hand. Alison didn't even bother to dodge as he brought the weapon down on her chest. The blade and his arm bounced off, and he stumbled backward. The knife fell and embedded itself tip-first in the thick carpet.

Several distant gunshots sounded from the back of the building. They seemed to come from behind the door to the left of his desk.

"Nice try." Alison frowned and stomped toward the door.

The thug looked between his knife and her a few times before he scrambled to his feet and rushed toward the exit.

"Good choice," Alison shouted before she performed a quick unlocking spell on her destination door.

These bastards went through all the trouble of protecting themselves against all kinds of spying but didn't spread some cash around for a witch or two to help them secure their place against magic. Idiots.

Alison threw the door open to reveal a wide hallway. Six suited men, all decked out in layers of chains, aimed guns at her. They opened fire but the bullets bounced off her red, glowing skin and dropped harmlessly to the ground.

She took six careful shots and planted a round in each man's head. Additional echoing gunshots confused her as she swept her weapon back and forth, seeking another target before she realized it was deeper in the building, just like she'd heard before.

What the hell is going on? If they are executing Hana, it wouldn't take so many shots.

Alison rushed forward. She kicked doors open on either side of her. Nothing but small offices.

She continued down the hall and kicked in the next pair of doors. One entry revealed a breakroom with several tables and a few vending machines. The other room was a janitorial closet jammed with vacuum and mopping bots, and only a couple of sad actual mops leaning against the back corner.

Another gunshot sounded, closer this time. Alison sprinted down the hallway. She wasn't sure if it was Hana or someone else, but for the moment, anyone going after the Eastern Union was an ally.

CHAPTER SIXTEEN

Alison barreled through the doorway at the end of the hallway with a grunt. Another loud gunshot sounded, and a man screamed. This time, the sounds were much closer.

It has to be Hana. She's okay. I've been training her for months. She knows how to fight and how to take people on.

Two men ran around the corner, their suits covered in blood and terror written on their faces. They didn't carry any guns, most likely because something had ripped deep gouges in their hands. Blood dripped from their wounds as they looked over their shoulders.

Those look a lot like claw marks.

A glowing blur appeared and tackled them both. Nine glowing tails waved in the air.

The men's screams died in their throats as a Hana shredded their necks. She bounced up and wiped her claws off on her already bloodstained dress. She sniffed at the air a few times and frowned.

Hana stared at the dead men, her face locked in a scowl

and her back to Alison. "Whoever you are, run. I don't want to kill you, but I will if I have to. I've been drugged, locked up, and chained, and I'm really pissed off about it."

Alison snorted. "I didn't track you halfway across town only to run, Hana, and you'll need a lot more training before you can win against me, let alone when I use magic."

Hana blinked and spun toward her. Relief spread across her face. "Woah, Alison." She swayed and stumbled against a wall, blinking several times. "Damn it. I was being so badass, and then you had to see that."

Alison rushed to her friend. "Are you okay? Did you get hit? Damn. I don't have a potion on me, but I have one in the car."

"I'm fine," Hana replied. She took a few deep breaths. "At least they didn't manage to hit me, but they drugged me with something and it's still messing with my head a little. I thought I could power through it, but I'm dizzy as hell after all that ass-kicking." She laughed. "It's like I saw you and I relaxed, and it hit me all at once. Damn it. And my stomach is messed up again. I guess now that the adrenaline is wearing off, I'm kind of screwed." She grimaced. "It's a good thing you showed up to save my ass."

Alison glanced over her shoulder. "Yeah, a good thing, but you did a lot of the heavy lifting yourself. The way you took those two guys out was straight Brownstone."

Hana managed a grin. "How did you even know I was in trouble?" She shook her head. "I'm not even sure how long I was out. I didn't even have my phone to send up a Brownstone signal."

"I figured it out because I'm an obsessive idiot. I couldn't get a hold of you, and you never called me or sent me a message saying you were staying over at your date's house, so I got worried." Alison grinned and tucked her gun into her waistband. She offered her arm to her friend. "And I decided to check up on you in case you'd ended up in some trouble. You know, like ending up captured by the Eastern Union."

"You're a lot of things, but you're not an idiot," Hana took the offered arm and groaned. "I wonder if this is what a hangover feels like. I feel like crap."

Alison shrugged. "Massive headache and a stomach that wants to empty itself?"

"Yeah." Hana nodded, then grimaced and obviously regretted it. She rubbed her forehead. "Definitely."

"That sounds like one to me. Sorry. Welcome to the club."

Hana winced. "No fun is worth this. I don't get people."

"We can worry about that later. For now, we have other things to worry about." Alison glanced back and forth, looking for more thugs.

She slipped her crystal ring off and put it on Hana's finger.

"Aww, girlfriend, proposing so soon?" Hana winked. "But we've not even known each other a year. And what would Mason say? He'll be so jealous."

Alison smirked. "You can't be that messed up if you're still cracking jokes. Activate the shield. I want to make sure you're okay if we have to take anyone else on. Between all the people you've killed and the people I've already taken out, I'm not sure how many are left. If they're smart, they'll leave us the hell alone."

Hana tapped the ring, and the red glow appeared.

"Sorry about all of this. I might have been able to clean up my own mess, but I'm still damned happy that you're here."

Alison helped her walk down the hallway. "What the hell happened? Did the Eastern Union ambush you after your date? I figured they had to get to you fast. You're drugged and foxed out, and you've killed a lot of them, so for them to take you down the other night, they must have surprised you."

"Not exactly. I did get surprised, but not in the way you're talking about." Hana sighed. "I got conned, Alison. Conned like a dumbass tourist from small-town Bumfuck Nowhere. Travis, my date, was in on it from the beginning. He worked my insecurities and then worked my ego, and next thing I know, I'm all chained up and drugged in some Eastern Union brothel, and he's talking about how they'll use me to get to you."

Alice grimaced. "So it's my fault."

"No, it's his fault and the Union's fault. You're the one saving me. They're the ones who hurt me."

Alison glowered. "We'll have to have a little chat with Travis soon so he understands the error of his ways."

"You think?" Hana managed a grin. "I'll show that asshole who won and who lost."

"Let's get you out of here first." Alison smiled. "And I'm glad you're okay, but it looks like you were almost out even without me."

"Only because I have the best teacher in the fine art of kicking gangster ass," Hana replied. "It's too hard to get out of this place. It's like a maze, and they don't have any windows. Otherwise, I would have smashed through the first window I saw and ran."

"Tahir says they've got the entire building shielded. Not with magic but in the way they've built it. They don't want anyone to know what's going on inside."

Hana's breath caught. "Tahir knows about this?" Embarrassment flavored her voice.

That's what you're worried about right now?

Alison nodded. "Of course he does. He's the one who traced your phone. I tracked you using a resonance spell on the phone after he led me to it. That saved me time. Otherwise, I might have had to go back to the condo and look for hairs on your pillow or something."

"And I might have run out of juice." A warm smile crept over Hana's face despite the unfocused look in her yellow eyes.

It's a good thing I got here when I did. She's right. I wonder how long she could have kept up her escape with a bunch of drugs still in her system.

Alison led her friend into the lobby and out the front door. "We're almost out of here. My car's parked right across the street."

"Oh, give me a break," she shouted as soon as they stepped outside.

Suited men crowded the street. Most held pistols or rifles but a few carried melee weapons, including a man with a sparkling ax. Tension lined their faces. The men all aimed their weapons at Alison and Hana, but no one fired.

Tahir cleared his throat over the reestablished link. "Should I contact the police now?"

"No, Tahir," Alison barked. "This has to be solved by us, right here and now, or I'll have to spend the next year destroying Eastern Union groups all over the damned world. This is where I'll make my damned stand."

Hana glanced at Alison and sighed. "Too bad I didn't have a receiver handy. I wonder if I could have contacted him even through the shielding."

"What about Hana?" Tahir responded, oblivious to her talking. "I can see you from a drone, remember. She's obviously in no condition to fight. There's a time and place for revenge, Alison. You have to consider her safety."

"She's got the shield."

He snorted. "And if they're using anti-magic bullets?"

"She'll be fine. I'll kill every one of those men before I let them hurt her." Alison sighed. She shimmered as a summoned shield appeared around her. "And this isn't about revenge. This was a rescue operation and it still is."

"I'm sorry," Hana murmured. "I was doing so well, but now it's hard to concentrate or even see. I think I pushed myself too hard and it's all caught up with me."

Alison sat her down in front of the door and turned toward the men. "Don't worry. You did what you needed to. I'll take it from here."

Hana responded with a shallow nod.

Alison took a single step forward and shrugged at the gathered Eastern Union men. "No one's fired yet. That's a good sign. Congratulations on having self-control. If you had fired, you would have forced me to respond and you'd all be dead in probably less than a minute." She gestured at her outfit. "As you can see by my clothes, I really wasn't thinking I'd have to break into an Eastern Union club and rescue my friend today. I'm tired, cranky, and extremely pissed off that I had to, for a lot of reasons that I don't think I need to explain."

The man with the ax stepped forward. "You're outgunned, Brownstone. These men have anti-magic bullets, and this ax is magical. We'll win. Surrender."

Alison snorted. "It's kind of obvious the sparkly ax is enchanted. Here's the thing, though. If you thought you could win, you would have already attacked me, which makes me think you don't think you can win, and that's not a crazy thought. It's smart." She pointed her thumb at Hana. "She's not as powerful as I am, and you pumped her full of drugs, but she still killed a bunch of your guys. I've already killed several of your guys, and I'm only getting started and not drugged. And did I mention I'm pissed?"

She extended a shadow blade from her hand. The gangsters all stepped back but didn't drop their weapons. No one fired either.

That's right. Be afraid, assholes.

Alison pointed the blade at the ax wielder. "Do you know why I've not killed every last one of your assholes for daring to kidnap my friend already?"

The man stared at her and his hands tightened on the ax handle as he shrugged.

"Because I found my friend alive." Alison nodded toward Hana, who pushed herself to her feet. "And the more of you I kill, the more I have to talk to the police. It's annoying, and it's a waste of my time. As it is, I'll have to talk about what happened here, and that's also annoying." She swept the gathered men with her glare. "I would have thought after what happened with the Daimyo, you assholes would have figured it out. He was geared up in a major Eastern Union stronghold. I stared him down with all his guys surrounding me, and I killed him, and then I killed every last man who messed with me on the way out." She laughed and strolled back and forth, adding a little swagger to her step. "Basically, every time the Eastern Union goes up against me, you lose badly and men die. The thing is, it's not even like I hate you guys. The Daimyo had to die because he was former Harriken, and the Harriken and the Brownstone family have some history. Well, they did, until my dad annihilated them because they were too damned stupid to learn to back the hell off. The question is, are you that stupid, too?"

The gathered men all exchanged nervous glances and a few swallowed. Some murmured quietly and one man crossed himself.

Oh, come on! I wish Dad was here. He'd lose it over that.

"I'm not in Seattle to clear out every last piece of crap gang out there," Alison scoffed. "I don't have the time. I've got better things to do. I have to keep telling everyone. I'm not in town as a bounty hunter. I'm here to run a security company." She flared her nostrils. "But if the Eastern Union keeps coming at me, I won't have any choice but to keeping killing people until you finally get the point—or maybe I'll simply follow my dad and become the Scourge of the Eastern Union. But if that happens, that's on you, not me. Now, if you don't want to die, it's easy. Step one, get the hell out of my way right now. Step two, you need to go back to your bosses and pass a message along for me."

The ax wielder frowned but he seemed thoughtful. He lowered his weapon to his side. "What message?"

"If the Eastern Union doesn't want to meet the same

fate as the Harriken, they'll stay the hell away from me. Not only me but anyone associated with me. My friends, my employees, my family. The delivery driver in my neighborhood. Any busker I smiled at for more than a few seconds." Alison glared at him. "Because this is the Union's last chance. Next time any of you assholes so much as sniff in my direction, I will spend the next six months systematically tracking down and annihilating every last Eastern Union member and building on the west coast. You know I have the power to do so, and you know the cops and the PDA won't stop me. Why would they? I'd make their job easier."

She punctuated her sentence by flooding magic into her back and extending a pair of shadow wings for dramatic effect. The magic produced only the faintest strain in her body. Her previous magic use had been minor, thanks to the ring, and no one had even challenged her shield. If they wanted to fight, she could wipe them out, even if they did have anti-magic bullets.

Alison shrugged. "Or I can kill you all and carve that message into that ridiculous lobby. Your choice. Your lives."

Several of the men lowered their weapons. Others frowned and glanced around, anger and confusion on their faces.

Alison cut through the air with her shadow blade. "I don't care how things worked before I came to town. I'm here now, and that means the rules change. If you don't like it, you've got two options—kill me or get the hell out of town, because nothing's changing until I get bored and move, and that won't happen for a while. This is a Brownstone town now. Let's say it's the start of the reign of the Dark Princess. Get that through your heads before I have to put one of my shadow blades through your heads."

She extended another shadow blade and pushed magic toward her feet. If a fight started, she'd need to disrupt their attack before they could take too many shots at Hana.

"Let's go, guys," the ax wielder shouted. "This shit isn't worth it."

"But what about the Daimyo?" another man with a rifle shouted. "What about the artifact she stole? You saw the pictures just like I did. That bitch thinks she can do what she wants to us."

"She can." The other man pointed his ax at him. "Fine. Go the fuck ahead. Take her on. I won't throw my life away. She's too strong. We can't win."

"What about our rep?"

"Rep doesn't mean shit if you're dead." The ax wielder snorted and walked away. He dragged his weapon behind him and his head slumped forward.

Most of the men fell in behind him, all headed toward several parked cars and SUVs lining the street. A handful of men remained, their rifles still aimed at Alison.

Their fingers and faces twitched for several seconds. Alison layered shadow magic into her shield and prepared to strike.

The holdouts lowered their weapons and sighed.

One of them shook his head. "People will come at us. They'll say we're weak."

Alison let the energy she'd gathered at her feet slowly leak away and her wings dissipate. "Then do what I've done. Do what my father did. Kick their asses until they understand. That's not my problem. That's yours."

The gangsters nodded, a glum look on their faces as they turned and followed the other men.

Alison kept her shields up but released the swords before she hurried to support Hana. "Tahir, you still there?"

"Yes, what did you need?" he replied.

"Please tell me you were recording that. I want you to splash that around the dark web for me. I think that, combined with the Jacobsen stuff, will cut down on a lot of crap in the future." Alison sighed. "I'm glad I did plays back in school. I needed a little inner actress power there."

Tahir chuckled. "I was recording. The drones won't have good audio, but I can use the audio from our comms."

Alison blinked. "You record our comms audio?"

He scoffed. "You never know where you might find evidence. You might pick something up in the background. I don't keep it for long, but I don't ignore obvious resources."

"Okay, that's good to know for the future. I'll try not to say anything embarrassing." Alison led the exhausted-looking Hana to the car. "I'm taking her home so she can sleep the drugs off. Thanks for your help in tracking her down. Keep an eye on those Eastern Union guys and make sure they don't suddenly grow their balls back. No fight means Hana's safe."

"I will."

Alison helped her friend into the passenger seat before she headed to the other side. "Are you okay?"

Hana snickered. "I'm okay, but I have a killer headache

and I feel like I'll throw up. Sorry in advance if I puke in your nice car."

"Don't worry about it. I have a spell that can take care of that."

"You have an anti-puke spell?" Hana eyed her with disbelief.

Alison shrugged. "There was a short period in college where I hung out with a party crowd."

CHAPTER SEVENTEEN

Alison sat on her couch and thumbed through messages from Ava the next morning when her roommate crept into the room. The woman's face was pale and her hair in dire need of taming, but her loose shoulders and smile warmed Alison's heart.

Hana yawned and tied off her white silk robe before she headed to the couch.

"Please tell me I didn't sleep for a week," she groaned as she sat. She smacked her mouth. "I'm thirsty, but at least my headache's gone and my stomach's fine. I'm not super-hungry, though."

Alison shook her head. "I got you into bed and you fell asleep right away, but you slept through the night. I gave you a healing potion in case it might help and used a little healing magic on top of that, but it seemed the best thing for you was simply a lot of rest."

"Yeah, I feel like a new fox." Hana lifted her arm and sniffed her armpit. "Ugh, but I smell like a dead one. No, I smell like I've slept with those fish they throw at the market. Between this and the tomb raid, it's my month to stink."

Alison smiled. "A little shower or a long bath will take care of that." She sighed. "There's something I wanted to talk about before you do."

Hana nodded and her smile faltered. "About how the hell I screwed up so badly you had to charge in to save my admittedly beautiful ass? And, yeah, I did a good job, but we both know if you hadn't shown up, I would be toast."

"It's not about screwing up." Alison frowned and shook her head. "It's about your attitude. I understand questioning yourself. I've done it my entire life. When I first found out my heritage, I hid it, even at the School of Necessary Magic. I was ashamed that people thought I might be evil and from a race that used a lot of dark magic. Even as I got older, I questioned myself, but I realized that it's okay to have an occasional question as long as you don't let it paralyze you." She shook her head. "What happened, Hana? How did you of all people get conned? You told me yesterday that it was about playing on your insecurities."

Hana groaned and let her head fall back on the couch. "It's going to sound so lame when I say it aloud."

"You're my friend, my roommate, and my employee." Alison shrugged. "I'm not my dad. I can't simply grunt and say, 'Suck it up. Keep it simple. Eat some ribs.' I want to know what's going on with you. I'll always have your back, and I'll carve through however many bastards I need to rescue you, but I need to know how you got there so I can help make sure you're ready next time."

"I..." Hana shrugged and sighed. "It kind of started with Lily."

"Lily?" Alison frowned. "What about her? Did she say something? Everything she mentioned to me about you was positive. I thought you hit it off."

"It's nothing against her. She's awesome. I mean she sees into the future. How cool is that?" Hana sat up. "Giant mutant roaches aside, the raid was awesome, like a dream come true, and Lily was a badass, but then we had our victory sushi. I just...I don't know. Got jealous, maybe? You have all this history together. Old friends from way back, all these funny stories you can share about each other and Shay." She looked down and picked at her nails. "That wasn't a big deal at first, but then when you told me to take the time off, I went to the original Starbucks, and I ran into Travis, right?"

Alison nodded. "The bastard who sold you out."

"Exactly, but I didn't tell you what happened with all of that to begin with—how I ended up on a date with him."

"I thought it was after you beat up the Eastern Union guys and saved him."

Hana nodded. "Yeah, but there was more to it than that. I didn't want to tell you before." She rubbed her arm fretfully. "Maybe if I had, you would have seen through all of it. He gave me a speech at Starbucks about how I was a sell-out, street scum who tried to rise above her place, how a rich princess like you would leave me behind eventually, and how we couldn't be real friends. That kind of thing."

Alison shook her head and frowned. "But I didn't grow up that way. Even if I had, it wouldn't make sense. It's not like everyone at the School of Necessary Magic had some elite background or heritage, and, come on, my dad might be famous, but he's also not exactly a stuck-up guy. His best friends are cops, ex-Marines, and former gang members."

Hana moaned and rubbed her temples. "I know, I know. This isn't about you. It was never about you. It's all about me. Travis didn't simply tell me that you'd leave me behind. He fed me a line about how I was scum, a criminal at heart, all that stuff, and I found myself asking if that was true. If I was simply a user, a parasite feeding on people and hiding behind you." She tapped her forehead. "It's because I let him get in here. Let him make me feel weak. Since I've been around you, I've felt strong, like one of the good gals, you know? Then he set up this fake Eastern Union beat-down, talked about how he found me hot. It's working the contrasts, heightening them to make it easier to push someone onto one path." She rolled her eyes. "It's Manipulation one-oh-one. I've not done that type of con, but I've relied on the same psychology in the past. That's what's so annoying, and the whole, 'Oh, Hana, you're so hot' thing made it even worse, especially since I've questioned myself on that lately."

"It's not like you have trouble getting guys even without your powers, Hana." Alison shrugged. "You've simply been focused on Tahir." She smiled and patted her friend on the arm. "Look, I don't care about your past. I told you before I've seen your soul, and that's true. I know the kind of person you are deep down, and whatever sins you think you committed in the past are nothing compared to the kind of dark place my mom came from or some of the things my dad's had to struggle with." She sighed. "I want you to know that I've been honest with you about everything since we've met, and I'll continue to be honest with you. I also trust you." She gestured around the living room. "I trust you to have my back in a fight and trust you to live with me. Yeah, occasionally, I worry about pushing you too hard, but that's on me. I've not always been able to protect people in the past even with all my powers, so it's something that is always there, but that doesn't mean I don't trust you. I don't trust myself. Understood?"

Hana smiled. "Thanks, girlfriend. I know it's really needy, but I think it helps to hear you say that." She laughed. "I also never realized how overprotective you were. I mean this wasn't like with the Daimyo. You were going to kill all those guys not because it was personal but to save me."

Alison shook her head. "You've got it all wrong. It was personal because they screwed with you." She frowned. "Though I did something that might annoy you."

"What?"

"I had Tahir hack your phone so I could get the information on that Travis guy," Alison explained. "I went back and forth on whether I should simply kill him, but it might be hard to explain or justify to the police, but I wanted him to pay for what he did to you."

Hana nodded slowly. "What did you do?"

"All our street informants, along with Tahir and even Vincent, are now making it very clear that Travis isn't allowed in Seattle anymore, and if he comes back, we will end him." Alison shrugged. "Tahir arranged a one-way ticket for him to Laramie, Wyoming, sent him a message, and then zeroed out all his accounts."

Hana laughed. "Laramie? Why Laramie?"

"Travis doesn't strike me as a Wyoming in February kind of guy." Alison smirked. "I'm sure he'll slither into some hole and talk about why he can't come back to Seattle. That's another way of building my rep and making sure that asshole has years to reflect on his poor choice in screwing you over."

Hana laughed and clapped. "You do realize what this means, don't you?"

"What?"

Hana lifted her chin in an attempt at faux regalness. "Princess Alison has exiled a man who offended her from her lands on pain of death."

Alison tilted her head and nodded. "I suppose I did." She stood and stretched. "Why don't you take a shower, and we'll go grab something nice to eat? After that, we need to make a little stop over at Tahir's. He sent me a message about thirty minutes ago saying he wanted to chat."

Hana hopped up and saluted. "Operation Sexy Clean Fox will now commence, ma'am."

———

Tahir sat in his chair, his fingers steepled as he looked at the two women who sat on his couch. "I exercised some autonomy that I stand behind, but I should admit that it had the potential to backfire."

Alison glanced at Hana before she nodded at Tahir. "What do you mean?"

"It took me a while, but I finally managed to hack the club systems, including cameras. I scrubbed the images of you and Hana, but I passed along a number of other incriminating images from the past few days. I sent that, along with some other files, to Seattle PD's vice squad." Tahir gave her a thin smile. "Incidentally, there's a councilman and a few CEOs who will probably soon be in trouble. A few other people of stature as well."

"Why did you do that?" Alison replied. "Did you see something that suggested my threats weren't working?"

Tahir focused on Hana. "Because the Eastern Union needs to understand your power goes beyond violence. They need to understand that we could destroy them on every level if so inclined, even if they crawl into the shadows." Anger crept into his voice, and his hands twitched. "Many gangsters fancy themselves warriors of a sort. They crave a glorious battle, even one that will lead to defeat, but they are businessmen in the end and they need to understand that their end might not be a brave battle against the Dark Princess. Instead, they might find themselves penniless and powerless, another pathetic loser on the street and no better than the people they lorded over."

Alison sighed and nodded. "I understand why you did what you did, but it's like you said. It could have backfired. Next time, check with me. I want the Union to understand that if they stay out of my way, I'll stay out of their way. I don't want a war if I can avoid it."

"I know." Tahir gritted his teeth. "But I've also watched the chatter about them. The word is that all Eastern Union in the entire Pacific Northwest, including those in British Columbia, have general 'avoid Brownstone Security at all cost, even if mildly provoked' orders. There's even some talk that they might cede their territory in Seattle entirely, with the expressed logic that it's not a profitable environment and that any organization that rises too high in this place will be cut down by you anyway."

"The Brownstone Effect." Hana grinned. "Yeah, those assholes better run."

Alison scratched her chin. "Okay, that works." She chuckled. "If they leave, that's fine by me, but if they stay out of my way that's fine by me, too."

Tahir stood, his fists clenched. "It's not satisfying enough. It doesn't feel that way to me. Maybe you should have killed them all there and made your point in blood."

Alison stared at the red-faced man for a moment and shrugged. "If we can get what we want without killing, it's always to our advantage."

"They hurt Hana." He took a deep breath and released it slowly. "They should be hurt in turn."

"Sure, Tahir," the fox responded, "but Alison and I *did* both kill a bunch of guys in the club. It's not like they got away with it. We hurt them."

He dropped back into his seat, a scowl still carved on his face. "Regardless, this incident proves we have some security holes we need to fill. We need some sort of dead man's switch system to send out an alert, a check-in system. We're Brownstone Security, and this won't be the only time someone targets one of us when we're alone." He sniffed disdainfully. "I propose a system that requires active interaction by the employee at certain time intervals. Perhaps once every twelve hours so you can sleep without trouble. I'd suggest a verbal passphrase delivered into the phone. If it's not delivered every twelve hours, an automated alert is sent out and everyone knows to start looking for the potentially missing person."

Alison sighed. "You know, a day ago, I would have said you were being too paranoid, but I think it's a good idea although I won't force anyone to do it."

Hana shrugged. "I'm fine with it. It's not like I'm not on my phone every hour anyway. Given how Ava is, I'm sure she'll agree. She probably has some secret spell they used on her in the PDA to do something similar."

"Okay." Alison nodded at Tahir. "You start working on something."

He spun in his chair to face his keyboard. "I will. I'm also continuing my dives against the Prometheus systems with greater vigor. This latest incident only reinforces in my mind that we need to handle this threat dangling over us before someone more worrisome than arrogant gangsters comes at us. I trust you can see yourselves out?"

Alison stood. "Yeah. Just keep doing what you do, Tahir." She nodded to Hana. "Let's go. There's somewhere we need to be tonight, and I want to make sure you're not tired."

"There is?" Hana blinked. "Where?"

"You'll see." Alison grinned. "I'm not telling you until tonight, though."

CHAPTER EIGHTEEN

Hana glanced continually at Alison from the passenger seat, her brow furrowed in irritation. "Okay, this is pure torture. You can't drop some mysterious tidbit like that in the morning then refuse to tell me all day about what will happen. It's unfair. I think I'd rather still be chained up by the Eastern Union than suffer through a minute more of not knowing."

Alison smirked. "What? Our little fox can't handle a few secrets? There are a lot of secrets in the security business, Hana. Get used to it."

"I'd hit you with my purse if you weren't driving, you know." Hana harrumphed. She looked at her forest green halter dress and chuckled. "I can figure a few things out, though. You told me to dress sexy and flirty, and you've even got a dress on. At first, I thought this was about us going and talking to someone about Prometheus Testing Services. That we were supposed to be seducing some scientists tonight." She gestured to Alison's backless black scalloped dress. "But seduction doesn't really seem a

Brownstone thing to do, and it's not like I'd need this dress to charm someone or you threaten them. I have my pendant in the purse, and you have your ring, but you didn't arm up otherwise, so this isn't about us rattling the Union or anything either."

"Yeah. It's not about a job or the Eastern Union. There's no way I'd make you work a job so soon after what you went through." Alison looked into the rearview mirror and puckered her lips. "This is a surprise girls' night. This is me being spontaneous and helping out my roomie."

Her lipstick didn't look great in the mirror, but it'd looked better in her bathroom lighting. She frowned at the implications concerning the club lighting. After a moment, she decided she wouldn't worry too much.

Mason wouldn't be with them tonight, so she had no one to impress other than her friend. Hana was sensitive to the effort, though, and dressing the part would be part of making the girl's night a success. They needed to be two friends having a good time, not two security contractors who happened to live together.

Hana worked her mouth a little, her lips pursed. "I don't know if I like mysterious Alison versus straightforward Alison. She's kind of creepy." She shuddered.

Alison laughed. "Ouch. I've been called a lot of things in my life, but no one's ever called me creepy before. Thanks for that, Hana." She turned at an intersection and slowed. Their parking lot was coming up.

"Hey, wait." Hana looked around. "I know this neighborhood. I used to come here all the time a few years back. It's not like I hated the area, but I kind of stopped hanging out with a lot of people who came here." She smiled. "You're taking me to Café Artemis, aren't you?"

"You figured it out. See, I'm not that mysterious." Alison shrugged. "I had Tahir help me score some tickets. Cold Fusion is playing there tonight. They're more light rock than metal, but you didn't seem to mind that band we saw last month."

"No, no, I love Cold Fusion. The lead singer is too damned yummy. The bassist isn't so bad on the eyes either." Hana exhaled a contented sigh and leaned against the window. "Yeah, some live music with my girl is exactly what I needed. Are you sure you don't have some telepathy spell?"

"Not like that, anyway."

Hana chuckled. "It's been a rough few days, and it'll be a nice time to recharge my batteries before we have to kick down some doors in a lab and fight some mercenary assholes."

"I'm glad you like the idea." Alison turned into the parking garage and the entry bar lifted and allowed her Fiat through. Café Artemis was still a couple of blocks up the road, but they could handle the walk, even in their questionable heels. "I tried to decide whether we should go to a huge concert, but in the end, I figured a smaller venue would be nice, more intimate, and more fun. A nice way to blow off steam."

A huge grin spread over Hana's face. "Yes. This is great, girlfriend."

Alison winked. "Good, let's have a great time tonight. You never know who will come after us tomorrow."

They joined the stream of people leaving Café Artemis after the end of the concert. The heat of the wild night and packed club still clung to their bodies. Neither woman even buttoned up their overcoats as they stepped into the chilly February air.

"Three encores!" Hana clapped her hands together. "That was ridiculous. I thought the band would pass out. Did you see how much they were sweating?"

"Small club, bright lights." Alison smiled. "Fun, nice fun concert, no tricks, no fancy magic. Sometimes, it's good to simply enjoy the sound."

"Or enjoy the sights," Hana replied. "I'm pretty sure that lead singer was coming onto me." Hana grinned after they'd walked a few more yards. "Did you see the way he looked at me?"

Alison laughed. "Maybe. I think he made eyes at every woman in there, and he worked the crowd hard. Yeah, it was pretty warm in there, but I don't think he took his shirt off to cool down, and that crowd was a little woman-heavy compared to the last concert we went to."

"Scrumptious abs." Hana licked her lips. "And scrumptious voice."

"I figured a little eye candy might help relax you." Alison shrugged. "He's no Mason, though." She shrugged.

Hana rolled her eyes. "You've already got it bad, haven't you?"

"No, I wouldn't say I have it bad. I merely find the man I'm dating, who happens to be a buff professional bodyguard and life wizard, very physically attractive among his other positive traits. I won't apologize for that." They arrived at the corner and waited for the walk sign to change.

Hana laughed. "I'm not saying you have to apologize. I'm happy for you. I want you to have it bad." Her smile faded slowly. "I also wanted to ask you about something from earlier."

"Sure," Alison responded. "Go ahead."

"Tahir seemed really mad earlier. Like straight-up angry." Hana shrugged. "I've never seen him like that before."

Alison nodded. "Yeah, he was pissed. Furious by his standards. I half-expected him to send a bunch of rocket-armed drones to that club and level it."

The silhouette of a man appeared on the walk sign, and the women stepped off the curb.

"It's weird, you know," Hana replied with a shrug. "He's normally so calm. He acts annoyed and smug all the time, but forget rocket-armed drone. It was like he was ready to go down to the club and tear it apart with his bare hands."

They crossed the street and continued up the sidewalk.

"Of course he was," Alison replied. "I went down to tear that place up myself, but that's because of my kind of training. I'm sure that as much as he's used to sitting in his chair, it still had to frustrate him, especially since he couldn't even communicate with me when I was in the building. Someone he cares about was kidnapped and threatened."

Hana's breath caught. "Cares? You sure it's not that he's mad about the agency getting threatened? A blow to his male pride, even indirectly?"

Alison turned to look at her friend. "I don't get it, Hana. Why are you so scared of him? I get why you had concerns over everything that happened with us, but this is more your realm. I thought you'd be more confident by now. I'm not saying you should infiltrate his building and assassinate him. I'm saying you should ask him out. He likes you."

"I guess because it might mean something. Something real, and that scares me." Hana tucked some dark hair behind her ear. "Realizing you're my first real friend has also made me realize I've never been in a real relationship before. Yes, I've messed around with guys, but messing around with some guy isn't the same thing as a relationship. It was simply a fun way to spend some time, so it didn't mean anything when it was all over. No real risk. So with Tahir, it's not only about it being awkward at work, it's about what happens if someone I like genuinely thinks I'm not worth going out with. That thought hurts." She chuckled. "Even when you're as sexy and awesome as I am."

Alison shook her head. "The way he acted earlier wasn't like an angry colleague. I don't need soul sight to see that. He's into you. Come on, Hana. You're a badass sexy woman who could carve through a bunch of Eastern Union assholes even while drugged. Plenty of guys in Café Artemis were eyeing you, not only that singer. I hate that you doubt yourself. I feel like it's my fault."

"No, no, no." Hana sighed. "Well, kind of. I won't lie. You're a rich Drow princess who is practically a force of nature. That can be intimidating, and sometimes, yeah, it's hard to measure up. But without you, I'd still be a con artist and probably doing awful things for the Eastern Union to pay my debt back. Being around you has made me a better woman in every way, and I'm grateful every day that I met you. I hate to think what my life would be like if I'd never met you" She smiled. "All this crap with the Union has only made me want to train harder and faster, but you're right, too. I need to stop being a wimp. If I can fight through a bunch of thugs while drugged, I can ask Tahir out. And you know what? So what if he says no? If he does, then he doesn't know what he's missing, and I'll continue the hunt." She gestured to her body with her hand. "And he'll be missing out on all this."

She raised her hand for a high-five.

Alison high-fived her with a smile. "You've got this, Hana."

CHAPTER NINETEEN

Hana took a deep breath and knocked on Tahir's door. Showing up mid-morning wouldn't be too outrageous, even if she'd not bothered to call ahead. She rubbed her hands together and wondered if that had been a mistake but quickly quashed the thought and smiled.

She'd expected a twisting stomach and a racing heart, but she instead found herself relaxed, calm, and focused.

I need to get this done, or I'll always find excuses why I shouldn't. It's time to kick love's ass like it's some gangster son of a bitch.

She frowned, already questioning her own choice of metaphor. Not exactly love poetry.

If he says no, he says no, and I move on knowing that at least I tried.

Tahir opened the door, an annoyed look on his face. "You didn't tell me you were coming. I prefer it when people tell me they are coming."

Hana shrugged. "Surprise!"

"I don't like surprises." A faint look of triumph entered

his eyes. "But I wasn't surprised. I'm never surprised. I knew you were coming before you even entered the building. Perimeter alerts are useful for that sort of thing."

"Paranoid much?" Hana grinned.

Tahir shrugged. "A healthy paranoia keeps one alive."

"You make even Alison look carefree, and that takes some effort." Hana tilted her head to glance past him. No problem with making sure he was alone. "Now that I'm here in a non-surprising way, may I come in?"

Tahir stepped back and gestured inside. "I was in the middle of the investigation, but if you've come all the way here, I assume it's for a good reason and not for idle chitchat."

"Idle chitchat? It depends on who you ask, I guess." Hana entered the apartment and shrugged before she moved to the couch. "I think it's important, but you know, it's all a matter of opinion."

"So is all of life." Tahir rubbed his eyes and headed back to his desk. He eyed his coffee mug with longing. "Do you need anything? I just made a fresh batch of coffee."

"No, I'm fine. I wanted to talk to you about something, and it doesn't really involve Alison—at least not directly— so I figured I'd come alone." Hana sighed. "It's not a secret, though, or anything. She knew I was coming. No surprises there. Just to be clear."

Okay, now I sound like a nervous idiot.

Tahir dropped into his seat and took a sip of coffee. "If you want to keep secrets from Alison, that's your business, although we're both linked to her now in our own ways, and it's to our advantage to be as honest as possible accordingly.

The incident with the Eastern Union should be a stark reminder of that. Even if we were to walk away from her tomorrow, we might still be at risk without her protection."

"True enough." Hana nodded. "And I'd say it's to our advantage to be as honest as possible between all of us."

"I suppose. Depending on the circumstances." Tahir set his mug down. "Life is a puzzle to be solved, but there isn't only one way to do that. Many things become clear with enough time and effort."

"Sure. That's something I've thought about a lot lately. Not, you know, life as a puzzle, but life in general. Past, present and future." Hana shrugged.

She unbuttoned her red overcoat, although she'd not glammed up for her visit and had selected only an Atlantis and Doom band shirt, black jeans, and ankle boots. Not that the tight T-shirt and jeans didn't flatter her form. A girl had to use a little ammo when going after a man, especially a clueless man.

"Reflection is critical to improvement," Tahir replied. "We can't avoid future mistakes if we don't understand why we've made past mistakes. All mistakes are learning opportunities. I am talented, sure, but I've only achieved this level of skill through iterative self-improvement." A thoughtful look passed over his face before it vanished as quickly as it had appeared.

Hana stared at him for a moment, enjoying his handsome features but also curious about the slight discomfort on it. He wasn't as comfortable and confident at that moment as he tried to project.

"I've made so many mistakes you could fill the bay with

them. What about you, Tahir? Do you have a ton or three of regrets?"

"Mistakes? Yes. Regrets? No." Tahir snorted. "Despite my calls for honesty, for now, I'll only note that there's a reason I'm so careful. I'm not like you, Hana. People are tiring to me. Hard to understand. Machines and code, even involving magic, are understandable. It's simply a matter of applying the right techniques and getting the expected outputs. People are too…chaotic. It makes them fascinating but frustrating. Dangerous, even. I've learned that the hard way."

"Yes, I'm probably better with dealing with the average person than you, but even as a former con artist, it's not like I always know what to expect. That's what makes people so fun. You never do know how they might react. Alison could have killed me for the crap I pulled on her when we first met instead of helping me." Hana sighed. "But, yeah, if I could predict people's behavior all the time, I wouldn't have ended up in the mess with the Eastern Union. So I'm still learning the lesson."

Tahir took a deep breath and exhaled slowly. "I suppose that's true, but it's as I said, you merely need to learn from your mistake. Reflect on all aspects of the experience from beginning to end and mentally game out strategies for the future. You're a talented and intelligent woman. I'm sure you won't make the same mistake twice."

Hana grinned at him and tilted her head as she nibbled on her lip. Her heart pounded, and her palms grew sweaty. So much for calm.

"I did learn a lot of things from my mistake, including how I need to be direct sometimes, even when it might be uncomfortable. That leads to a better understanding between people."

"That's a good lesson. It certainly works for Alison." Tahir shrugged. "Her friends and enemies both know where she stands."

Hana stood and made her way around the couch until she stood in front of Tahir's chair. "I need to move forward. That's the big lesson. The most important one. The past is the past, and I can't change it, but I can change my future. I can choose the kind of woman I want to be and the kind of people I want to be around, even if they're different than the kind of people I used to spend time around."

Tahir nodded. "It all sounds very reasonable to me."

Hana leaned closer to him. Her breathing grew shallow and their faces were only inches apart. "I've thought for a while that maybe you were simply playing games."

"Games?" Tahir furrowed his brow. "In what context?"

"With me. Let's go out sometime. You and me. Not with Alison. A date. Or three. You're smart and talented and handsome." Hana laughed and shrugged. "And a wizard. You have many positive qualities, and I'm very attracted to you. Every time we come over here, I try to think of how to impress you. Changing my outfits, my jokes. I'm used to manipulating people, but I don't want to manipulate you. I simply want to get to know you, and you me."

Tahir blinked a few times and shock suffused his face. "What?"

Hana laughed and shook her head. "Is it really so hard to believe that I want to go out with you? I tried to lay hints for you. As much as you like your little puzzles, I like my games, too, but I've realized that I thought about this the wrong way. I'm not a machine, and I don't necessarily give the expected outputs, so I'm making it easy for you."

"I…" Tahir looked down for a few seconds. "I didn't understand that you felt that way. Yes, your manner is often flirtatious, but I thought that was a habitual default and not directed at me in particular. I've even seen you flirt with Alison on occasion, so it was hard to understand that…" He shrugged.

"Understand this, then." Hana leaned forward and planted her mouth on his. She half-expected him to push her off, but he opened his mouth to hers and placed his hands on her waist.

The kiss continued and warmed her body until, finally and reluctantly, she pulled away, her breathing ragged and shallow.

"Does that make it clear enough for you?" she whispered.

Tahir nodded and blinked. "Yes, very. I also want to make it clear right now that I've always found you appealing, both physically and in terms of your personality."

Hana sat on the edge of his desk, crossed her legs, and grinned. "That's such a you way of describing me. I'm glad to know this hasn't been one-sided."

"I can guarantee nothing." Tahir shrugged. "I'm bad with people. You may grow tired of me quickly."

"All I want is for you to try." She hopped off the desk. "But I also understand I'm distracting, and you've got work to do. So, let me give you a hint. Let it sink in for a few days and maybe figure out a place we can go, or if you want to stay here and watch movies, that's fine, too. I'd suggest my place, but who wants to have a date when their boss is in the other room." She winked.

Tahir chuckled. "Indeed."

Hana sashayed over toward his door, every part of her still warm and her confidence threatening to explode like a nova. "You've made a smart decision, Tahir."

A subtle hunger entered his eyes. "I always do."

Hours later, Tahir remained hunched over his keyboard. As thrilling and surprising as Hana's visit had been, she was right. He did have a job to do, and if he wanted to have a relaxed time with the beautiful woman, he needed to help Alison defeat the powerful enemies that threatened her. Finding the truth of Prometheus Testing Services would be key to that.

A window popped up on his left monitor with the results of his last directed search for his main topic of interest, Ajit Patel.

Zero matching expressions found.

Tahir narrowed his eyes. The mysterious Ajit Patel remained stubbornly absent from every server and record he'd cracked, and the level of resistance within the Prometheus servers was ridiculous. He'd had an easier time cracking DoD and NSA servers in the past.

No one erected a high wall and complicated locks unless they had something important to protect. He refused to let Prometheus beat him. If he couldn't brute-force his way through their defenses, then he would need to find out a way to burrow under them.

"What are you hiding?" he murmured. "I won't let you beat me."

Another alert window popped up, this time on his right monitor.

Trace detected.

Tahir snorted. "You won't win. Not against me. I won't let you."

He moved his mouse and clicked to upload a file. It was gibberish to normal systems, powerful magical glyphs expressed numerically. He continued to tap away and a golden metal rod embedded under his keyboard glowed—his wand.

You have no idea who your opponent is. I'm not some fool poking around to prove myself.

A progress bar appeared in his left monitor as he continued to focus on his central monitor and selected additional spell scripts to upload.

Tahir murmured a few additional incantations, and he clicked on an icon. A Mercator projection of the Earth popped onto his right monitor and displayed connected white lines marking the enemy server trace. A few seconds later, the path became erratic, the trace now reflecting nonsense as a result of his spell.

"Yes, go bother some script kiddy in Reykjavik, you fools." Tahir grinned as he returned his attention to the current server he was hacking.

A few minutes of typing and another spell script later, he'd penetrated the system and accessed a high-level directory.

An abrupt, loud alarm sounded from his speakers.

Multiple windows popped up on the right, but the top window contained the most important message.

"What?" Tahir shouted.

65536 traces detected.

White lines coated the world map.

Tahir hissed as his fingers flew to enter a command for a batch upload of rerouting and defensive spell scripts. A bright glow enveloped his entire keyboard. He didn't even need a detection spell to know the counter-attack was magical in nature and would need a massive magical response.

Damn it. I got sloppy. I underestimated them.

Sweat dripped down the side of his head.

His heart thundered as the next few minutes passed with a flurry of more typing and alerts and some fatigue crowded his mind. Magic wasn't an unlimited resource, after all.

New alerts popped up, proof that his countermeasures were working.

32768 traces detected.

16384 traces detected.

8192 detected.

By the time the trace count dropped to 256, Tahir could make out actual countries on the map again. The seconds continued to tick by until he released a sigh of relief at the message he wanted to see.

0 traces detected.

Tahir took a deep breath and shook his head. "I'm glad Alison and Hana weren't here to see that. I do have a certain image to maintain."

He chuckled and cracked his knuckles. It was like he

told the beautiful nine-tailed fox. All mistakes were learning opportunities. The enemy hadn't won this round.

Thirty minutes passed without any new attacks. He stopped and narrowed his eyes as he found an address reference in a stray Prometheus configuration file to another offsite server, along with a single comment.

#Scrub A.P. refs.

"I'll never feel bad about my poor commenting in my code ever again," Tahir muttered.

It was time to dive into a new system and find Ajit Patel.

CHAPTER TWENTY

Alison gritted her teeth as she pushed the bench press bar up and set it on the rack. Her spotter loomed over her with a goofy grin on his face.

"What's with the look, Mason?" Alison chuckled. "Am I making a weird face when I bench? I have to push myself to improve."

"Nah, you look fine, A. I just like seeing you being intense. The last woman I dated was allergic to anything close to strenuous exercise." Mason offered her a towel. "And it's always interesting to think about how much power you have, but you're still in the gym hitting the treadmill and weights."

Alison took the towel and wiped the sweat off her brow. "A well-conditioned body is magical all on its own. I've known plenty of humans who could take magicals out even without artifacts simply because of superior training. I like to keep every tool available to me. I never know what I'll need on a job."

"I agree. I'm the same way, even if it's fun every once in

a while to use a spell and do some ridiculously impressive lift." Mason flexed his already impressive unenchanted biceps. "One thing I've found in the bodyguard game is that things can escalate depending on what you use, so I don't always rely on magic, and that means, weirdly enough, I can take some attackers down before they use something even worse." He grinned at her. "Then again, I'm not able to make a bunch of guys walk away simply by yelling at them. Your little speech to those Eastern Union guys is all over the net, you know, and not just the dark web, either."

"That was the idea, and I didn't yell at them." Alison stood and shook her arms out. "I gave them a well-reasoned explanation why it wouldn't be to their benefit to keep after me or people close to me. Contrary to what everyone in this city seems to think, I don't like mowing through tons of guys if I can avoid it, and I'm not actively interested in cleaning up Seattle. I'll leave that to the police and feds."

Mason chuckled. "Sure thing, A. Keep telling yourself that."

"I will, thank you very much." Alison walked toward the water fountain. "Self-preservation is a basic animal instinct. So the more I can get people to realize I'm the alpha bitch around here, the less trouble everyone will have. I can't keep a low profile simply because of who I am, so I don't have another choice."

"This is why I like being a bodyguard. It's way simpler when you only have to worry about protecting a single client or small group than all this underworld politics crap." Mason winked. "Even if you weren't half-Drow, your hair would be white by now from the stress."

Alison rolled her eyes and stopped in front of the fountain. "You've probably been waiting weeks to use that joke, haven't you?" She leaned over to sip some water.

"A few jokes about hair aren't over the line," Mason snapped. "I forgot to tell you. I got a new job with a new client. Massive pay increase from the last guy, more flexible schedule, too. Not as many erratic night shifts."

Alison finished her refreshment and eyed him. "Someone hires a bodyguard but doesn't care if he's around? Doesn't that defeat the point? What, will he text you if he's under attack?"

"Nah. It's not like that. I can't reveal the client right now because of an NDA, but he has a large security team already. There's nowhere this guy goes without a couple of guys already watching his back. He wanted to supplement his team with a few more wizards and witches." Mason shrugged. "I'm even kind of surprised that he brought in outside security because of how big his existing security team is. This is probably my most high-profile direct client ever, but I won't start the job for a few weeks. I half-wonder if the guy's a little spooked by something recently."

Could it be...

Alison groaned. "Please, please, please tell me you're not going to work for Derek Chesterton." She threw a hand up. "And before you say anything about your NDA, let me make it clear that I haven't told you one-tenth of the crap I've dealt with in regard to that guy. He's a total son of a bitch, and the world would be better off without him."

Mason shook his head. "Not Chesterton. Come on, A. There's a good chance the guy tried to have you assassinated. I might not be the best boyfriend in the world, but

I'm smart enough not to work for someone trying to kill his girlfriend. Things would get awkward on date night."

"That's a low floor, but I'll accept it." Alison shrugged. "But I needed to be sure. He might be quiet right now, but I anticipate trouble with him again soon. Maybe even huge trouble." She headed back to the weights area.

Mason trailed along. "You should be careful with that guy. You're not the only one to have heard bad things about him. I'm guessing if he didn't own half of Seattle, he'd probably already be in prison."

"I can handle him." Alison snorted. "I've snapped the strings of every little puppet he's thrown at me, and he's too much of a coward to come at me directly."

"All I'm saying is that you don't have a handsome body-guard with you all the time." Mason grinned. "So keep that in mind."

"Don't worry about me." Alison pointed to the bench. "Get down there and start lifting. They might be useful for your job, but they're also useful for my appreciation."

Mason slid onto the bench. "Your wish is my command, princess."

Alison stared at her phone and tried to work up the will to make a call. Some problems could be defeated with a good gun or sword. Others needed magic. A few took nothing more than an angry speech. This situation couldn't be resolved by any of those weapons.

This is stupid. Dad's going to laugh at me, but if I can get him to agree, it'll make my life easier and I could use a little of that. If I can threaten an entire criminal organization, I can make one stupid phone call.

Alison licked her lips and looked from her couch at the TV hanging on her wall. Another delaying tactic.

Why did I even buy that thing? I almost never use it. Maybe I should replace it with a nice painting or something.

Alison sighed. It was time to stop stalling and face the challenge head-on. She took a deep breath and dialed her dad.

He answered with a grunt after the second ring. "Hey, Alison. I wasn't expecting you to call, not that I'm complaining."

"Hey, Dad," she replied and forced as much cheerfulness into her voice as possible. "I need a favor. It's not a big deal, and it doesn't involve you kicking ass or anything."

"From what I've heard, you don't need me to kick ass," James rumbled. "Mack told me the other day that some cops in Seattle called him. They wanted to talk to him about his experience 'handling a Brownstone' and how to best get you to do what they wanted." He snorted.

Alison laughed. "That makes it sound like we're wild animals."

"Yeah. Don't get me wrong. From what Mack said, these cops like it that you're there. They like it that you put the fear into the criminals and those pieces of shit infesting the city. I think you're doing a good job. It took me years before the police fully trusted me. Mack helped a lot with that, but there were a lot of days, especially early on, when I thought AET was gonna railgun my ass when they showed up. They hated my ass for a long time."

A loud bark sounded in the background.

"Quiet, Thomas," James shouted. "I'm talking to Alison. We'll go walking later. Go eat some more."

Alison smiled. "For such an old dog, he's still energetic."

"Yeah, he does all right. I think he forgets he's not a young pup a lot of the time, but he's a Brownstone through and through, able to stare down any other four-legged fuckers who think they're gonna start something. Forget the dog, though, you said something about a favor. What did you need?"

"Like I said, it's not a big deal. It's just kind of…stupid."

"Stupid? How?"

Alison closed her eyes and let out a long sigh. "I need a signed picture of you. Preferably one that has some sort of cool inscription that really captures your…I guess you could say captures your essence."

"My essence. What the hell does that even mean?" James grunted. "What do you need that for?"

"There's a guy in my building. He's a big fan of yours, Dad. He used to be a moderator on a fan forum and every-thing. Low and Slow Ass-kicking, he called it. Heard of it?"

James grunted. "I don't pay attention to those sites, I never have. I'm not gonna be a dick to people, but I didn't ask to become famous, and I don't care about fans. I only want people to not annoy me." His already low voice threatened to descend to infrasound. "And who is this guy? Shay said something about you dating some wizard. Whom I haven't met yet."

"I am dating a wizard. His name is Mason, and he works as a bodyguard." Alison laughed. "And of course you haven't met him yet. You don't live in Seattle and I've only been dating him a couple of months. I think subjecting him to the full James Brownstone overprotective dad treatment that early in the relationship is a bit much."

James scoffed. "If he's too much of a pussy to stand up to me, then he's not good enough for you."

"I'm sure you'll meet Mason eventually if our relationship goes anywhere." Alison rolled her eyes. "And according to you, no man will ever be good enough for me. You never change, Dad, and the picture has nothing to do with dating this other guy. Your fan is not even a friend of mine. He's someone who lives in my building. Since I live in a condo building, I thought it might be nice to get on the good side of my neighbors, and I figured this would be an easy way to do it with one neighbor. I promise I won't give him your number or anything, and I made it clear I might not even be able to get the picture."

Thomas barked again in the background, followed by Shay yelling something.

"Fine," James muttered. "I'll do it, but make it clear to this guy that it doesn't mean he gets to bother you for more shit from me. You're not some Brownstone Memorabilia vending machine."

Alison laughed. "Don't worry, I will. Thanks, Dad. This will help."

"What am I supposed to write? You said an inscription? Like what? What's supposed to be my essence?"

Alison furrowed her brow for a few seconds before enlightenment struck. "Maybe something like, 'May all your sauce be as godly as Jessie Rae's and may all your enemies get their asses kicked.' He'll love that. It's so…you."

James scoffed. "Fine. I'll think about something like that and have Shay look it over. You need anything else?"

"Not for now, Dad. Thanks again. Give her my love."

"I will. Talk to you soon." James grunted.

She ended the call and smiled. It was nice to have a problem that didn't require ass-kicking or murderous threats to solve.

Alison sighed as she settled into the seat of her Fiat. Her stomach rumbled. The cruel reality was that Maneki was only open for dinner that day, which meant she'd have to hit up somewhere else with only great food instead of mouthwatering food.

Her jaw tightened as she sensed magic. Alison threw the door open and leapt away from the vehicle. There was no way she wanted to trash two Spiders in under three months.

She layered a shield around her body, summoned a shadow blade, and prepared for the attack.

No fireball or lighting blast came. No monstrous demon ripped into her car or her. A semi-translucent shadow appeared and formed into Myna over a couple of seconds. Wisps of her floated away as if she weren't solid.

Alison sighed. "What did I say about portaling to me without contacting me first?"

Myna tilted her head. "I'm not here, though. This is a mere projection. I am contacting you first as you requested."

Alison released her spells and rolled her eyes. "I need a magical bell for you."

"Perhaps, but your surprise and reaction does highlight

deficits in your defenses." Myna frowned. "After I finish with this ritual to cure you, I will work with you to better secure your living area, building, and vehicle with defensive glyphs. Even simple alarm spells might be enough to thwart the machinations of your many enemies. As your skill with them grows, you'll have less need of me."

Alison nodded. "I can't disagree with any of that. It's something I've thought about myself. But let's focus on the here and now. Okay, so you're contacting me. What's up?"

The image of Myna disappeared, and a dark portal appeared. Shadows leaked from it to form the actual Drow wise woman.

Myna inclined her head. "I require blood and hair."

Alison blinked. "Huh?"

The ancient Drow pointed a bony finger at Alison's head. "Your blood and hair. The ritual. I've gathered the materials and knowledge necessary to initiate it except for your blood and hair."

Alison stared at her, not believing what she was hearing. "You're saying you can cure the AMDS?"

"Yes. I believe I can. It's a difficult ritual, and it'll require me to spend some time in seclusion so I can properly prepare all the materials and initial spells. I require your blood and hair for it to work, though, as a focus for the magic." Myna's face hardened. "The ritual won't work without it."

"And this doesn't require like a living sacrifice or anything, right?" Alison frowned.

"No, there will be no...death associated with this magic. That's not why it was created so many centuries ago. Quite the opposite, I can assure you." Myna frowned. "But I can't guarantee this will work, Alison, only that I can attempt it. If it does work, you will be free to access your greater potential, but even then, you would benefit from more training."

Alison blinked several times. "Sure, fine. I...honestly don't know what to say. I thought it might take years to solve this and require me to talk to dozens of doctors and visit all over Oriceran, ask for help from the Great Library, that sort of thing. Thank you, Myna."

The old woman bowed her head. "Then I'm glad I could be of some small service. If I accomplish nothing else in my time with you, this will allow me to leave living existence satisfied that I've done something useful with my meager years."

Alison plucked a few hairs from her head and held them out. "I'm guessing you don't have a syringe to draw blood?"

"I've no need of such crude human tools." Myna reached into a small pouch hanging from her waist and pulled out an open rectangular glass vial made of opaque black glass. "I will draw the blood with magic, if you don't object."

Alison shrugged. "Do what you need to. I'm not that squeamish."

Myna raised her hand, and a dark tendril shot from her finger and pricked Alison's arm. Blood welled from the wound. A thin line of blood crawled over the tendril and flowed into the vial. A few seconds later, a frigid touch struck Alison's arm, and her wound closed.

A shadow crept out of the inside of the vial and formed a barrier on the top. Myna slipped it into her pouch.

"You will not see me again until the ritual is complete, failed or otherwise," she declared. "Is that acceptable to you, or do you need me for other matters?"

"No, curing my condition is the single most useful thing you could do for me." Alison nodded. "Again, thank you very much. I only wish there was some way I could repay you."

"You've given the end of my life meaning," Myna replied. "That is payment enough."

Another dark portal opened and consumed her.

Is it really almost over? It's hard to believe, especially since I was only now getting used to the idea of it being a long-term problem.

Alison shook her head. She shouldn't get ahead of herself. Myna offered no guarantees. There was no point in getting worked up until the completion of the ritual.

She scowled. "Damn it. She didn't even tell me how long it might take. For all I know, the ritual won't be complete for years. That couldn't be it, though, could it?"

If her full power was going to come back soon, that meant she'd be able to better handle the people coming after her and the man responsible.

Alison grinned. Tahir and the PDA's progress continued, but if the final battle was coming, it was time for a few other players to pull their weight.

CHAPTER TWENTY-ONE

Alison folded her hands behind her back as she stared at an elaborate oil painting covering almost an entire wall in yet another of Scott's many receiving rooms. In the painting, a muscular man lay chained to a rock, his face contorted in agony as an eagle ripped into his side.

She frowned.

Very funny, universe. Thanks for the coincidence.

Scott stepped into the room and closed the door behind him. He fluffed his tie, still as glyph-covered as she'd ever seen it, before he offered her a smile. "I'm sorry for the wait, Miss Brownstone. Some matters came up requiring my urgent attention."

Alison nodded toward the painting. "Kind of creepy."

"You don't recognize the imagery?" Scott gestured toward the painting, faint disappointment in his eyes.

"No, I do. Prometheus, right? The Titan who created humanity. He also stole fire from the gods to give to humans, allowing the beginning of technology and civilization." Alison shrugged. "But Zeus didn't like that, so he punished Prometheus, chained him to a rock, and let an eagle peck out his liver each day, only for it to regenerate so the torture could continue for eternity. The poor bastard was supposed to have dealt with that punishment for a long time until, at least according to some legends, Hercules finally freed him." She shuddered. "How messed up is that? You got to love those ancient Greeks."

Scott chuckled. "Indeed. One wonders with everything we've learned how much truth there might be in the legend."

"You think Prometheus was real?" Alison arched an eyebrow.

"Atlantis was a myth until it wasn't." Scott walked over to the painting with a tight smile. "I'm not saying literal Greek gods and Titans existed in that sense with total power over humanity, but consider how both Oriceran and Earth magical authorities behaved before the portals reopened. Perhaps Prometheus was a powerful Oriceran who wanted to give more magical power or technological knowledge to humanity, but the others punished him, and that truth was passed down via myth. It's not like the Oricerans would be eager to confirm such past cruelty. Considering what we've already proven about Oriceran links to ancient Egypt, it's not impossible."

"I'd have to ask my mom. She's the expert in that kind of thing." Alison shrugged. "But interesting even symboli-cally. Humanity's strength is knowledge, a building and growing thing that can't be stopped or contained. It's weird when you think about it. All those thousands of years since the Great War, and in a lot of ways, the Oricerans ended up not advancing much. Earth went from stone tools to spaceships."

Scott nodded. "Indeed, Miss Brownstone. That's why I've thrown my life into advancing technomagic. I understand the restraint of the Oricerans, understand why they're leery given their history, but as a human, my soul calls out to remember the sacrifice of Prometheus, even symbolically. It's my greatest hope that before I die, the true potential of both planets will be brought out." He shook his head. "Perhaps Zeus was wise to punish Prometheus because what he feared came to pass. The gods thought mere lightning bolts were impressive, but humanity took to the stars, as you noted, and gained weapons to make the gods weep." He chuckled. "And we even managed not to destroy ourselves in the process." He stared at the painting for a few seconds before he shook his head. "But you didn't come here to discuss Greek myth or paintings, did you?"

Alison shook her head. She wasn't sure how much Scott already knew, but it wouldn't hurt to be careful.

"Derek Chesterton," she began. "He's up to much worse stuff than trying to assassinate you and destroy your company."

Scott's brow lifted. "Worse is a subjective judgment, I suppose, especially when it ends with my death. Would you care to clarify?"

"I've been looking into some things, some medical experiments." Alison furrowed her brow. "Dangerous medical experiments, maybe even biological weapons, and I think Chesterton's funding them."

Scott frowned. "Biological weapons? Derek's an arrogant fool, but I don't see how that can benefit him. His ruthlessness has always been more directed. Unless..."

"Unless?"

He shook his head. "I don't know. I thought I had a thorough understanding of the situation, but perhaps your presence here has unsettled him more than I realized."

Alison shrugged. "I'm pretty sure he was doing this kind of thing before I moved to Seattle. I only have some very basic circumstantial evidence right now, and I have my infomancer probing our best bet, a medical testing company that might have been doing contract work for Chesterton. He's making progress, but from what he's told me, these guys are locked down more than a spy agency, which makes me a little suspicious."

"Perhaps." Scott rubbed his chin. "Though magic has made corporate espionage harder to defend against, and those with the resources do expend them when they have secrets to protect. The government, as always, lags in understanding the nature of the world. I'm hesitant to admit this, but if what you're saying is true, I've underestimated how far my enemies are willing to go."

"He's not only your enemy."

"Indeed." Scott smiled at Alison. "You continue to impress me, Miss Brownstone. I presume you've come here to seek my aid in this matter. Perhaps you'd like my people to look at some of the information you've recovered?"

Alison shook her head. "No, we've got that covered, and I have some contacts in the government starting to move on this once I get them a little more direct proof as well. The thing is, everyone's afraid to move because of how powerful this guy is. I think I can get the evidence to put him down, but that still requires the cops, the feds, and the courts to do their job." She pointed at Scott. "Once I've got my evidence, I'll need your political clout and influence. I want you to help me take Chesterton down once and for all, and I don't want to hear any whining about stock prices or investors." She snorted. "When it's all done, I will have helped you take down your number one competitor, and I'll have done all the hard work. It's either that, or I solve this the Brownstone way, and I'm guessing that'll get messy for the entire city, if not the country, because it's not exactly like I sneak into places in the middle of the night and do quiet assassinations."

Scott sighed. "Indeed. I would have hoped to resolve this in a manner with minimum secondary impacts, but if your conspiracy charges are true, it's important to stop Derek before he does something foolish that not only harms a lot of innocent people but also makes them wary of technomagic and harms my business."

"Always the bottom dollar for you, huh?" Alison scoffed.

"Money is power, and you can't change anything in either world without power." Scott's watch buzzed, and he glanced at it. "I'm sorry, Miss Brownstone, but I have business to attend to. As for your request, I'm willing to commit my influence if and only if you can provide me direct evidence linking Derek to your conspiracy. If we go after him without that evidence, he'll be able to bury his involvement in this and become even more untouchable. Understood?"

Alison grinned. "Don't worry. I'll get what you need. I'll be making some noise. Keep an eye out."

Scott adjusted his tie. "Very well then, Miss Brownstone. Good luck."

"We need to review." Alison paced Tahir's small living room and Hana's gaze followed her as she walked back and forth in front of the couch. "Like I said, I've got Scott on board for the final kill, but Tahir's still gathering evidence."

The wizard nodded from his desk. "I'm making progress on breaking some of the other servers I've found, but the level of protection necessitates me being cautious."

"That's fine. We're moving forward on this, and that's good enough for now." Alison frowned, deep in thought. "But I wonder if there are more fronts where we can apply pressure."

Hana scrunched her face up as she considered the issue. "Other than simply going straight to him to kick his ass?"

Alison chuckled "This situation will probably end up there, but if I go after him now with force, Latherby might not be able to cover for me. Right now, we only have a lot of circumstantial evidence. Nothing concrete linking him to the experiments, and barely anything concrete linking him to the assassinations." Alison shook her head. "We need more evidence and quicker."

"I could charm him." Hana shrugged.

Tahir chuckled. "That would be fascinating to see."

Alison shook her head. "There's no way a guy like that doesn't have some sort of defense against that, either artifacts or a wizard on standby watching for mind control. But maybe you're on the right track. Maybe we should go straight to Chesterton and talk to him—press him a little, without revealing how much we know. Enough to make him nervous so he maybe lets something slip but not enough for him to come at us in a big way. With the PDA and Scott now watching his ass so carefully, we might even produce an opening for them."

"But what about what Scott said about going after him without firm evidence?" Hana replied.

"At the end of the day, Scott cares more about AMS share prices than he does anything else, and he doesn't even know the full extent of what's going on. There's no way Chesterton will bury this entire project simply because we're sniffing around." Alison stopped pacing. "Agent Latherby told me Chesterton's been quiet lately— real damned quiet—which means he's worried. But that means he'll be careful, and we need him to be a little less careful."

Tahir rubbed his chin. "If you worry him too much, he might lash out."

"This time, we'll be ready for him. We'll be expecting him." Alison nodded at Hana. "I'll want you to stick by me just in case. Probably no concerts for a while."

"Fine with me, girlfriend." Hana grinned. "It's a small price to pay to take down a billionaire scumbag."

"Then we'll move forward on this." Alison pulled out her phone and held it up. "Can you get me a number for his private line, Tahir?"

The infomancer scoffed. "Of course I can. It'll be difficult, but after what I've done lately, it'll feel trivial in comparison."

"Fine. Do it. I'll let the PDA know I'm going to rattle

Chesterton's cage so they can help keep an eye on things. Just in case..." Alison shrugged.

Tahir smirked. "Just in case he sends a battalion of men in power armor to kill you?"

"Something like that, yeah. But no risk without reward. You get me the number and continue probing those systems. We can't sit around for months or years and allow Chesterton to ready himself for a final strike." She frowned.

Hana laughed. "You're raring to kick ass."

Alison thought that over for a moment. Myna's news had inspired her more than she expected, but it didn't change the fundamentals of what needed to be done. Waiting favored the enemy, especially in a battle that would likely end with government agents arresting Derek Chesterton rather than Alison fighting through his guards.

A little angry revenge never hurt anyone, especially when it's justified.

Alison shrugged. "I'm tired of being a target. Sometimes, the best defense is a good offense."

Alison decided to wait until the next morning to call Chesterton. Something about threatening a billionaire involved in a bioweapons project seemed like a morning thing to her. Armed with a phone number Tahir uncovered with minimal effort, the next phase in her battle was about to begin.

She dialed and waited.

"How did you get this number?" Chesterton answered after the first ring.

Even though she'd seen television interviews, deep disappointment at his normal voice struck her. The man hired an entire assassin firm to go after her. The least he could do was have a cool accent or rant about his evil plans.

"Is it really that surprising, Chesterton?" Alison replied. "I might not be as rich as you, but I have my resources. You do know who is calling?"

"Alison Brownstone." Chesterton snorted. "The ill-mannered thug."

"I don't know about the ill-mannered part. I try to say please and thank you all the time." Alison chuckled. "And glass houses, Chesterton. I'm not the one who sent professional killers after someone, and you didn't even have the balls to do it directly but hid behind Two Worlds Security."

"You've no proof of anything," Chesterton replied, his voice cold. "If you did, you wouldn't be calling me. Let me guess. You and your thug father are so used to threatening people and having them give up that it probably didn't even occur to you that you're not the first enhanced criminal to come after me."

Alison rolled her eyes. "I'm not the criminal. You're the criminal, and you don't think I know you were up to more than simply messing around with Jacobsen Associates?"

"Let me make this abundantly clear, Miss Brownstone," Chesterton replied, his voice dripping with open contempt. "If you contact me again, I will bury you in so many lawyers King Oriceran will be dead and dust by the time you come up for air. This is already harassment as is, but in the spirit of mercy, I'll let it slide."

Alison snorted. "How magnanimous."

Chesterton chuckled. "And I'll provide an additional hypothetical of potential interest to even a lackwit thug like yourself."

"Hypotheticals are always interesting, even if they're from ruthless evil assholes."

"If there was a businessman who was only dedicated to advancing his company, and he was targeted by an arrogant assassin who believes herself beyond the law, then no one could blame them if they took proactive measures to protect themselves," Chesterton explained. "It'd be foolish if they didn't. We live in a dangerous world, after all."

Alison narrowed her eyes. "I'm not an assassin. I fought Jacobsen to defend a client, and then I took them down after that because they came after me. I'm the one defending herself, and I know all about your dirty little secrets."

Chesterton scoffed. "You know nothing. Seattle was an orderly place before. It no longer is, and I intend to survive that transition. Good day, Miss Brownstone. Don't call me again."

Chesterton ended the call.

Alison stared at her phone and shook her head. "Huh. I'm not sure if that went well."

CHAPTER TWENTY-TWO

Tahir had just finished pouring a cup of coffee when his left and right monitors filled with alert windows. Multiple alarms sounded from his computer. An intrusion alert even sounded from his phone.

"What the hell?" he muttered.

He dropped the mug and the coffee spilled over his kitchen counter before he rushed to his desk. Frantically, he clicked around to take in all the warnings and silence the alarms. Multiple traces and several active system intrusion attempts were in progress. There was no way this was a single attacker. A whole team was coming after him, probably both magical and non-magical.

A few quick uploads started the process of active defense, but Tahir accepted the obvious. It was already too late. The barbarians were already inside the castle. That many simultaneous attacks meant the enemy knew exactly where he was. The sheer volume of attacks was already overwhelming.

Tahir's gaze cut from window to window as he tried to

take in the scope of all the attacks. He hissed as he spotted a small window with a simple but terrifying message: **Intrusion in core building systems.**

The warning informed him that his enemy had already penetrated his apartment building. Cameras and door controls were theirs.

A shrill alarm sounded in the hallway. He'd almost forgotten. Fire alarms were also theirs.

Why are they sounding the fire alarms? What's the plan?

On a hunch, he checked the building diagnostics through an existing backdoor program he'd established, while the fire alarm continued to scream.

His eyes narrowed as he noticed one important line.

Emergency Lines (1, 2, 3) Outgoing Transmission Status: FAILURE! Reattempting transmission IN 10 Seconds. 9 Seconds...8 Seconds...7 Seconds...

The hacked fire alarms wouldn't bring any first responders.

Tahir checked the building door status quickly. All door locks had been released, which was consistent with the fire alarm protocols. The attackers apparently wanted everyone out of the building. But why?

No witnesses? Or are they trying to limit casualties to only me for plausible deniability later? One dead wizard, who cares? A building full of dead people, Homeland Security, and FBI will overwhelm Seattle.

A loud harsh buzz sounded from his computer. Tahir's stomach tightened. He turned his head to see if the expected warning had popped up.

Possible extended range aerial perimeter alert: most-likely estimates: aircraft (87%), unusually large bird

(50%), dragon (23%), flying humanoid (12%), normal-sized bird (6%).

Tahir took a deep breath and moved to click the alert. It was an algorithm. Even if he'd programmed it and supervised its training, it wasn't perfect. False positives were always a possibility.

An image of a distant dark shape appeared on the screen. He magnified the shape with a few clicks and frowned. No mistake. A low-flying dropship was heading directly toward his building. It skimmed the trees in a way that had to draw at least some attention.

What's the point of getting rid of everyone else if you're going to go and do that? Do you hope people will simply assume you're AET?

A few seconds later, the vehicle shimmered and disappeared. Considering the poor state of technological active camouflage, he assumed a wizard, or maybe more than one, provided the invisibility.

Tahir laughed. "At least they're going all out. I'm almost honored."

He rattled off a quick command to execute a script he never thought he'd need to run. It held the rather banal name of **lastresort.**

PLEASE CONFIRM lastresort Y/N.

Tahir pounded the Y key. He'd have to recover as much as he could from backups later, assuming they weren't compromised.

He flipped his keyboard over, and his hand hovered near the wand for a few seconds before he ripped it out. A yank opened a drawer, and he grabbed a small silver disc with a button from inside.

His fingers flew over his phone as he sent a text to Alison.

Under attack. Incoming dropship. Running. Sorry. Sloppy.

Once transmission of the text was confirmed, he dropped the phone to the floor, pressed a button on the silver disc and dropped it on the phone. Blue-white arcs shot from the disc and the phone died as smoke poured out of it.

Tahir threw his door open and ran toward the stairwell, his heart pounding. With his systems and primary phone dead, his transmitter to Alison would be useless. The magic was tied too closely to them.

She could be anywhere from minutes away to in another country. He'd need to depend on himself as he always had.

The wizard took the stairs two at a time and kept going until he hit the parking garage. A Camaro peeled out—someone who lived on the first floor. Its tires squealed as it raced toward the open door.

Tahir rushed over to his Toyota and flourished his wand with a quick incantation. The trunk popped open to reveal a briefcase and a backpack.

He opened the briefcase. A half-dozen microdrones, each the size of his hand, sat parked inside, along with a backup phone. He grabbed the phone and tapped out a few quick commands.

The drones whirred to life and rose from the trunk. After a few more commands, they cruised out of the garage and soared into the air, their video feeds now sent to his secondary phone.

Tahir shifted one of the drones to thermal and smiled as he spotted the yellow-red heat signature of the invisible dropship's engines.

Not thorough enough, fools.

He sent a few more commands, and four of the drones screamed toward the dropship. His phone screen updated with system information.

Explosive charges armed on Drones Alpha, Beta, Gamma, Delta. Closing on target. Estimated contact in five seconds.

Tahir sent one drone as a chase camera while he held the other hovering over his apartment building.

The drones weren't fast in and of themselves, but the rapidly closing dropship made it an easy approach. One pair of drones split off and charged one engine, and another pair charged the other. The impact detonated the explosives inside and produced a fireball that engulfed the back of the ship. It wasn't enough to obliterate the aircraft but more than enough to leave the engines sputtering and smoking.

The ship banked hard and it's vertical thrusters kicked in. Whatever strike team was aboard would survive, but they'd have to clear a lot of ground before they could come after him. Every minute he could stall increased the chance that the police or Alison would arrive.

I can call her on the backup phone.

Movement near the remaining apartment drones caught his attention as a large black van screeched to a halt outside. A couple of seconds later, Tahir's phone died, along with all the fire alarms. A massive EMP.

Tahir sighed and unzipped the backpack. An EMP-hardened laptop lay inside, along with similarly protected AR glasses and a haptic glove. He pulled on the haptic glove before he slid his wand into a groove until the glove clicked.

After pushing the AR glasses on, he rushed toward the exit, making a few quick motions and muttering some voice commands to activate a feed to a drone hidden on the roof. The EMP would have taken most of his backup drones, but this one was large enough to be hardened.

The video feed from the drone winked to life. Darkness lingered for several seconds until the drone flew into the sky, free of its container and with a clear view of the black van.

The van door slid open, and four men with rifles stepped out, frowns on their faces.

Running while one eye saw the world in front of him and the other saw a video feed strained Tahir's balance and concentration. He primed the few small rockets available on the drone and waited until he arrived at the exit to the garage to fire with the flick of his glove.

The rockets hurtled away from the drone. The men jerked their guns up and opened fire but they were too slow. The rockets exploded and launched their scorched bodies into the air.

Their bullets got their revenge, and Tahir's stomach lurched as he had a first-person view of the drone falling toward the ground.

His video feed died, an overlaid error message near the top.

Transmission feed from Drone Iota disrupted.

"Thanks for the update," Tahir muttered as he emerged

from the garage and deactivated the status display on his AR glasses.

He rushed toward the street as a crowd of people pointed toward the smoking van and dead men less than thirty yards away. He couldn't hear any sirens in the distance. Several people shook their phones and frowned.

They've fried your phones with the EMP. Don't you get it?

The average person fleeing the building probably assumed the automated system would summon the authorities. By the time they realized something worse was going on, even if only from his rocket attack on the van, it was too late to make a phone call.

When Tahir had moved into the apartment, he didn't care much that there was a tree-filled park across the street, but now, it offered him his best chance for survival.

The wizard rushed across the street and made a few more quick motions with his haptic glove as he all but shouted an anti-tracking spell.

I'll admit you're worthy foes, but right now, all you've done is inconvenience me and lose four men. Don't take me lightly.

CHAPTER TWENTY-THREE

S weat beaded down his face as Tahir ducked into a small copse of pines. He suddenly found he regretted not living in rural Maine. He'd read once about a man how a man disappeared into the woods there decades before and lived half his life without anyone ever knowing he was there, despite the fact he stole from nearby houses and campgrounds.

He'd let himself get sloppy. Security by obscurity wasn't security at all. If he survived, he'd have to be a little more careful, and he intended to survive.

A few minutes. That's all it'd take. He'd launched a rocket barrage and set off several explosive drones. Chaos had a way of getting noticed, even in Seattle, and when chaos happened, the police or Alison weren't far behind.

I'm beginning to see the wisdom of being stronger in direct battle magic.

Tahir never carried guns. They offended his personal sense of elegance. He'd always prided himself that his greatest weapon was his mind, but he wouldn't have minded an automatic rifle or rocket launcher about then.

If Alison had her building finished, would we have been safer there? She mentioned hiring security just in case. I suppose it's no stranger than military bases being covered with military police.

Tahir narrowed his eyes as whirring grew louder in the sky above. A dozen small drones circled the park, none with the markings or lights that suggested they belonged to news organizations, the city, or the police. Not all the floating sentinels might belong to the enemy, but that was too many for such a small area to ignore the potential.

With line-of-sight and his glove and wand, he could hack the drones, but that'd only signal his enemy that he was there. They might only be searching and have no clue if he was even in the park. The spiraling flight paths of the drones suggested they'd still not spotted him, but that wouldn't last, not with that many drones, even if their operators were lackwits. If he waited too long, they'd have his exact position.

Time for some calculated risk.

Tahir made a few precise movements with his gloved hand before whispering, "Upload invisibility 2.15."

An acknowledgment message appeared in the left side of his AR glasses, and his glove glowed. He held his breath for ten seconds, then crept deeper into the trees, hoping his spell would keep him off the feeds of the drones, even if he wasn't sure that the sky spies were close enough to be affected.

The spell wouldn't work on people, but he only hoped to buy himself more time. They weren't in the middle of some forsaken warzone. They were in Seattle. Civilization. Of sorts.

Tahir frowned as the trees thinned and opened to a paved jogging path. He looked at the sky. Drones continued to circle above, but none reacted to his emergence from the trees.

It worked. Interesting. I knew I could have pushed it more when I tested it.

He considered taking a moment to make a call to Alison via the internet, but that also risked giving his position away to the enemy, depending on what they monitored.

A slight grin snuck onto his face. It'd been a long time since he'd dealt with infomancers or hackers with enough skill to threaten him.

Complacency is a mistake and a character flaw. This only proves I need to continue to improve my skills. Still, how many wizards did they need to take me on? Whatever the number, next time, they'll need ten times as many.

Tahir ran down the jogging path, which took him farther from his apartment building. Distant sirens sounded, and he slowed.

Finally.

Should he head back to the apartment? If he could hear the sirens, the police would be there soon. Given the explosions, there was a good chance the AET or SWAT might be the first on scene. They would be able to take on the enemy.

Tahir furrowed his brow.

Or perhaps they couldn't. The massive, coordinated cyber attack along with the dropship and high-power EMP pointed to a well-trained and equipped group, someone closer to the level of Jacobsen Associates than the Eastern Union. AET would have a chance, but regular cops, even SWAT, would be slaughtered.

He pursed his lips. While he had no love for the authorities, he wouldn't hide behind human shields. His pride wouldn't allow it. Whether it was conscience or arrogance, he'd have to continue his solo escape.

Something crunched in the distance behind him like someone had stepped on a pinecone. He looked over his shoulder and narrowed his eyes.

At least I made them work for it.

Three men in black body armor with rifles emerged from the trees. After a moment of hesitation, they ran toward Tahir.

The wizard sprinted down the path and considered whether he should start working out with Alison and Hana. He exercised enough to keep in shape, but as his heart pounded and his legs began to burn, he wondered if a few more hours in the gym each week would have made the difference between his death or survival.

Knowing Hana, she probably wears some very nice outfits when she works out. That wouldn't be an awful thing to see.

Tahir managed a laugh despite more men joining the chase from a different direction. For all the pride he had in his intellect and skill, he was simply another man in the end, his mind colonized by thoughts of a beautiful woman interested in him.

He leapt to the side as he sensed magic and spotted something bright out of the corner of his eye. A blue bolt hurtled right through the space where he'd stood. His body hit the ground hard, and he gasped as the impact emptied his lungs.

The armored men closed on him, and a man in a light suit with a bright red wand in hand appeared from behind a tree.

Tahir shook his head and took a breath, desperate to fill his lungs with precious oxygen. He pushed himself to his feet and looked at the different groups pursuing him. A resigned sigh escaped his mouth, and he raised his hands. He would die with some dignity and take some small comfort in the fact that it'd taken an entire team, complete with a dropship and EMP, to take him down. That was almost an Alison-level expenditure of resources.

I'm sorry, Hana. I tried.

The enemy circled him and stopped, the guns and wand still pointed.

"If you're waiting for me to beg," Tahir shouted. "It won't happen." He smirked. "How are your friends in the dropship? Tell them their pain is because of Tahir Arain, the greatest infomancer who has ever lived."

One of the men with a rifle nodded to the wizard. "Do it already. I don't want to listen to this crap."

"Helping Chesterton," Tahir interrupted, "is working against yourself. Did anyone tell you what he's doing? You're a short-sighted fool."

The wizard sneered and pointed his wand. He shouted a quick incantation. A blue bolt shot from it and struck the infomancer.

Tahir only had the briefest of moments to realize he'd been stunned, not killed, before he collapsed to the ground unconscious.

Alison frowned at the street and parking lots in front of her Fiat. Fire trucks, police cars, vans, and officers filled them. Armored AET officers clustered near a van, inspecting their weapons. A huge crowd stood gathered near the police, with several officers pushing back a few reporters but not doing anything about the news drones swarming the area.

Please be all right, Tahir. Please.

Hana looked ahead, her face a mask of pain. "He's dead, isn't he?"

"We don't know that. Tahir might not be tough, but he's a smart guy." Alison shook her head. "There's no way he'd get taken out easily. Knowing him, he had all sorts of backup plans and traps or something."

"But you said your tracking spell wasn't working." Hana took a few deep breaths. "That means he's dead."

"No, it could mean a lot of things." Alison parked the Fiat along the street. "Whoever is after him could be blocking the spell. Even Tahir could be blocking the spell if he's worried about enemy wizards. I don't have anything of his with enough personal connection for a resonance spell." She killed the engine and looked at Hana. "I want you to stay here for now while I go figure things out. He'll be okay."

Hana gave a shallow nod. "And if he's not okay?"

Alison curled a hand into a fist. "Then we track down everyone involved with hurting him and make them pay."

"Good." Hana's eyes turned yellow, and she extended her claws.

Alison threw the door open and pushed her way through the crowd toward the police line. A smoking, half-burned van was parked down the street. CSIs and their small drones inspected the four bodies—mercenaries based off the weapons nearby, their outfits, and the tactical vests.

You took out a van full of mercs, Tahir? Good job. You're better than I thought.

A police officer held up his hand as Alison approached. "Ma'am, this is a crime scene, and there are possible explosives in the building. I don't care if you're a resident. You'll have to stay back."

"I'm not a resident." Alison pointed at the apartment building. "One of my people lives in that building, and he sent me a message saying he was under attack. I need to verify whether he's still alive."

The cop shook his head. "I told you this is an active crime scene, and there could be explosives. I won't tell you again."

Alison shook her head. "I'm Alison Brownstone."

His lips twitched. "I...still can't let you through. I'm sorry."

"Let her through," called a familiar voice. "I'll take full responsibility."

Alison looked to her side. A grim-faced Agent Latherby walked straight toward her, his mirror shades hiding his eyes.

Do they teach them to all wear those kinds of glasses in federal agent school?

The cop nodded and motioned Alison through.

She hurried toward Latherby. "I'm surprised PDA got here so quickly."

The PDA agent nodded toward the van. "A few dead mercs is one thing, but the reports of a temporarily disappearing dropship made us think magic was involved, and the scale of this...incident requires a coordinated multi-agency response."

Alison blinked. "Disappearing dropship?" She frowned. "Tahir sent me a message and mentioned a dropship."

"There was a temporarily invisible dropship until someone slammed some explosive drones into it," Agent Latherby explained. "Your man, I assume, was responsible for the drones. It was a semi-invisible smoking dropship until it crashed. The mercs inside managed to flee the scene and blew the whole thing up to cover their tracks, so now we've got half the Seattle PD over there, and the other half over here. At first, Homeland Security freaked out, thinking it was some sort of coordinated New Veil attack."

"It's not them. It's Chesterton." Alison snorted. "And now, Chesterton can attack random apartment buildings and get away with it."

"We have to investigate, Miss Brownstone, but I can assure you this incident is an escalation that no one finds acceptable, especially if Chesterton is the one behind it."

"Because someone else randomly decides to send those kinds of forces against one of my people?"

"You have to admit you have a lot of enemies." Agent Latherby pointed to the van and dead bodies. "Based on the equipment, they are your basic scum underground mercenaries, expensive but lacking some of the elegance of your Jacobsen Associates types. As they're all dead and their dropship buddies escaped, we can't exactly interrogate them. It'll take some time to piece things together."

"Then go kick in Chesterton's door and interrogate him!" Alison threw her hands up in the air. "It's obviously him." She gritted her teeth. "We pushed him a little, so he pushed back."

Agent Latherby shook his head. "I'm a federal agent, Miss Brownstone. Not a vigilante."

Alison narrowed her eyes. "Maybe I should go kick his door in, then."

"You could, but that might not be the best idea."

"I tried playing this slow and careful, and one my people might be dead," Alison scoffed. "It's time to apply the Brownstone Effect to Derek Chesterton. I won't let him get away with this."

"Listen to what you just said." Agent Latherby sighed and shook his head. "Your man *might* be dead."

"What are you getting at?"

He pointed toward the bodies. "Thus far, we have a building that from what preliminary evidence indicates, was hacked from the outside, with the emergency lines purposefully blocked. We've got a downed dropship and some dead mercs. But what we don't have is a dead body belonging to one Tahir Arain."

"He only sent one text. There have been no calls." Alison shrugged.

"Which might mean he's dead, or it might mean they have him, but he's still alive." Agent Latherby surveyed the crowd. "Think about your other recent issues. Your little performance with the Eastern Union, from what I could tell on the video, was predicated on concern over Miss Sugimoto."

Alison nodded, her brow furrowing. "Yeah. So? What's

that have to do with anything?"

"It means the Eastern Union had her but didn't kill her. Mr. Arain might be a similar situation." Agent Latherby removed his sunglasses. He stared at Alison, a stern look in his eyes. "And also, if you think going after him will help you find your man, you should keep in mind that Derek Chesterton wouldn't be so foolish as to keep a hostage near him. He's too smart for that. You do realize that, don't you?"

Alison pointed to the apartment building. "At least let me in there to check for clues."

"This is a government matter now, Miss Brownstone." Agent Latherby shook his head. "As much as I respect you, we can't have you tampering with evidence."

"You expect me to sit on my ass and do nothing? There's no way that's happening."

He gave her a tight smile. "I'll only note that in hostage situations, hostages often die during bungled and ill-planned rescues. That said, *if* Mr. Arain is located, and *if* someone decides to go after him, they should make sure that their first effort is their only effort. In addition, if someone were to track Mr. Arain down somehow and mount a successful rescue, perhaps because someone is unencumbered by the red tape of law enforcement, I'm sure that the criminals involved won't exactly come crying to the police over it. The police, FBI, and PDA have plenty of other concerns in Seattle other than worrying about dead kidnapper mercenaries."

Alison spun on her heel. She walked several feet before she stopped and looking over her shoulder. "*If* someone goes after Tahir and finds out he's dead, then someone will end this bullshit once and for all."

The PDA agent nodded. "All actions have consequences."

"And for every action, there is an equal and opposite reaction." Alison kept walking. "You can't fight physics, Agent Latherby."

CHAPTER TWENTY-FOUR

Silence smothered the inside of the Fiat as the women drove back to the condo. Alison worked through idea after idea in her mind in an effort to decide how to track Tahir down. In most circumstances, she'd rely on him to help track someone, and her spell wasn't good enough for the situation.

Maybe I should call Peyton and get him to help. Heather, maybe? But Peyton and Heather might not be much help against infomancers. Whoever got the drop on Tahir must have had an infomancer, if not more than one. Maybe Lily can have her info-mancer help me?

"He hasn't called or texted," Hana muttered, her head against the window. "That means he didn't escape, even if he took those guys out."

"Latherby is right. It doesn't mean he's dead. We simply need to figure out a way to track him. Maybe my mom has some sort of artifact that can beat anti-tracking spells. Worst-case scenario, we wait until things die down, sneak into his apartment, and find some hairs or important personal items and I use a resonance tracking spell."

Hana frowned. "That'll take too long. We should bust in there now. Screw the cops."

Alison sighed. "I want to find him as much as you do, Hana, but if we go in there now, we'll take on the PDA, the normal police, and the AET. I need to figure out a way to find him. I've got money and resources. I'll figure this out."

Hana sighed and slumped her head against her headrest. "He's a good kisser, you know." She chuckled nervously. "I know that's a weird thing to think of right now, but I can't help it. He's a really good kisser. It surprised me."

Alison glanced her way and her heart speeded up. "Wait. You kissed him already?"

"Already?" Hana sighed. "Girlfriend, I've wanted him for months now, and when he finally agreed to go out with me, I wanted a sneak preview. Is that so wrong?"

"And you said he was a good kisser. That means he was into it, right? The kiss, I mean."

Hana groaned, closed her eyes, and put a hand over her face. "I don't want to talk about this anymore. We should think about how to find and rescue Tahir, not about him being a great kisser."

Alison grinned. "That's just it. You kissed and there was passion involved. You have strong feelings for him, and he obviously has at least some feelings for you. I think I can set up a spell based off those emotional and physical connections. You'd be surprised what you can do with a little physical and emotional intimacy when they're combined."

Hana blinked. "Seriously? You can track him?"

"Yeah. If there wasn't anti-tracking magic involved, your mutual feelings might be enough, but I'll need the mix of the physical and emotional for this to work." Alison whipped over into the HOV lane to pass several cars. "This will be difficult and take a little longer to set up than usual, but it should work. After talking to Agent Latherby, I'm convinced Tahir is still alive. I suspect that Chesterton wants to use him as a hostage to keep me off his back. Big damned mistake. All it's done is piss me off."

Hana's smile returned. "We can save him."

"Damn right we can." Alison nodded. "We'll head back to the condo, arm up, set up the spell, and then go rescue Tahir. Any assholes who get in our way will die. Agreed?"

"Agreed." Hana's expression turned serious. "I put in too much work to lose him now."

———

The Fiat rumbled along the dirt road. Dense pine and fir trees flanked the car on either side. They were well south of Seattle outside Spanaway. Alison sped the entire way, figuring if any police came after her, she'd lead them directly to Tahir and the mercenaries.

I really, really need to get a helicopter for the company.

She focused her attention directly ahead. There could be a trap or enemy ambush at any moment. She'd sacrifice her car if it meant saving Tahir, but if they lost the vehicle too early, it might cause them to lose the wizard as well.

Hana stared at the water bottle in her lap. A needle floated near the top. "It's been jerking back and forth a little, but not as much since we hit this road. We're definitely on the right track."

"Some drones would have really helped us here." Alison chuckled. "Maybe Tahir has a sister or something we can hire for backup in the future."

She slowed as a gated fence came into view. She stopped the car about a hundred feet out. "Let's go. Bring the bottle."

Hana nodded. "We're coming, Tahir. We'll save you."

They hurried out of the car. Hana pulled the sword belt from the backseat and strapped it on. Both already wore tactical vests they'd picked up from the condo loaded with extra magazines. They had no idea how many enemies they might have to take down.

Hana held up her pendant and murmured the activation incantation. It immediately glowed.

Alison tapped her ring three times and a red glow spread over her skin. She layered a shimmering shield with her own magic on top of it. If the enemy had infomancers, they might have other wizards who could toss a deadly spell or two.

They jogged off to the side of the road before sprinting toward the fence to reduce visibility. As they closed, they noticed weeds choking the rusted fence that surrounded an abandoned airstrip with a long, cracked runway.

Is it even safe to take off from here?

A single small building sat at the end of the runway, its paint long since faded. A collapsed antenna tower lay beside it. This looked less like a secret facility and more like a desperate attempt to use something forgotten.

Several vans with darkened windows sat parked near a

medium-sized turboprop cargo plane, but no one stood outside.

Are they already on the plane or still in the vans?

Alison and Hana crouched low behind a patch of thick weeds, their glow too obvious otherwise. If the enemy had spotted them, they hadn't given any sign.

Hana held up the bottle and stared at the needle as she waited for the water and metal to settle. "It's not pointing at that plane." She narrowed her eyes and gestured to one of the vans. "It's pointing to one of the vans. The far one on the left."

Alison nodded. "You don't go to the trouble of killing someone and taking their body out in a private plane at an abandoned airstrip. This proves that Tahir's alive."

Relief spread over Hana's face.

A loud mechanical whir sounded, and the cargo door at the back of the plane descended. The vans crept forward.

"Great timing. Good thing I sped all the way here." Alison narrowed her eyes. "They're going to load directly onto the plane. If they get in the air and out of the country, it'll be too late. For all we know, they might fly him to North Korea or some other place the US government can't touch."

Hana nodded. "What's the plan, then?"

"Misdirection and noise." Alison stood. "I'll draw their attention, and once they're focused on me, you rescue Tahir. Once you have him, we finish the clean-up and send a message about taking one of our friends."

Hana's tails appeared, and her eyes turned vulpine. She extended her claws. "Do we need to keep anyone alive?" Uncharacteristic anger filled her voice.

Alison shook her head. "We'll grab their phones and some of their other things. Tahir will be able to hack them and find out how close to Chesterton these assholes are. Ready?"

Hana nodded. "Ready."

Alison leapt and vaulted over the fence. Without hesitation, she sprang up and sprinted directly toward the plane, her hands held in front of her to feed a growing blue-white orb. There was something she needed to take care of to ensure they didn't escape in the air. As long she kept them in the vans, they could save Tahir.

The cargo door clunked down against the asphalt, and the vans accelerated.

Haven't you seen me yet? I'm pretty damned noticeable, you assholes.

Alison gritted her teeth as she funneled more magic into her orb and thrust her arms forward. The magical projectile rocketed through the air, crackled with energy, and collided with the left engine of the plane. It exploded in a massive blue blast.

Sparks and flames erupted from the engine, and the propeller crashed to the ground. Smoke poured from the burning engine and wing. The aviation fuel hadn't ignited as yet but it was out of action.

Alison took a deep breath at a spike of pain through her body.

I hope you're hurrying up with that ritual, Myna.

She pushed the thought from her mind, satisfied that she'd grounded the plane. The rest she could handle.

The vans all stopped. Their doors slid open and riflemen poured out and shouted defiance. Alison sprinted as they opened fire. Most of their bullets missed, but a few bounced off her defenses to her surprise.

Huh. Conventional rounds? You should have run anti-magic bullets. You got cocky because you were only going after an info-mancer, huh?

Alison stopped running and turned toward the men. She laughed but didn't draw her gun or knife, nor bothered to summon a shadow blade. Instead, she ran toward the plane at an angle and waved her arms like a drunk fleeing the cops.

"Come on, you assholes. Can't you at least land a single shot?" she shouted. "I thought you were badass mercenaries. You can't take down one little girl?"

The mercenaries all rushed away from the vans and closed on her as they maintained their fire. Several more rushed down the cargo ramp and opened fire as well.

Alison didn't dare look Hana's way. She needed to keep the enemy's attention on her. There was always the chance they'd execute their hostage.

Drawing a knife, Alison offered her best theatrical cackle.

I would have made a good Wicked Witch of the West. Much better than a flying monkey.

More bullets bounced off her defenses. "Is that all you've got?" Alison yelled.

She released her shield and let the bullets strike her ring-hardened skin.

I'm glad I didn't wear an outfit I loved.

A few more mercenaries rushed out of the plane, this time with grenade launchers on the top of their rifles.

Quick clicks and hisses preceded grenades that exploded around her and knocked her off her feet.

Alison hopped up, shook her head, and sighed at her burned shirt, pants, and coat, all perforated in a dozen places. Shrapnel fragments lay all around her, but her glow had barely dimmed.

The ring's getting a good workout tonight.

Alison charged toward the nearest mercenaries and flung her arm out to launch a curved blast of shadow magic through the air. It sliced into one of the men on the ramp and he slumped before his body rolled down the ramp.

The mercenaries switched to burst fire and a torrent of bullets now struck her. She closed on the first group and slammed her knife into a man's head. Without pause, she yanked the blade free and threw it into the next man's heart.

With frowns on their faces but no fear, the men moved backward but still continued their barrage.

Brave, considering how outclassed you are.

Alison kicked a rifle up from the ground and into her hand. Her skin continued to dim under the sustained fire. She fired quick bursts into the mercenaries, downing several before she dropped the gun and shunted magic into a shadow blade.

Someone moved to her left, and she spun to meet the new threat. It wasn't an enemy. Instead, Hana rushed toward the mercenaries' flank, the *tachi* held high in her clawed hands.

Alison grinned and hurtled directly forward. Without anti-magic deflectors or bullets, the mercenaries didn't have a chance as the two women sliced and diced their way through the entire group to finish up on the cargo ramp in under thirty seconds.

Her breathing ragged, Hana sheathed her sword. "Tahir's in the van with my gun. Bruised, but not seriously hurt."

Alison frowned as her skin tingled, and an overwhelming magical pressure poured over her from the cargo bay. "Do you feel that—or, I guess, in your case, smell that?"

Hana wrinkled her nose. "Magic. Lots of it. Wow. That's more than I smell from you when you go all out."

A rainbow of jagged bolts shot through the cargo bay. A loud rumble shook the plane.

Alison layered both her light and shadow magic into shields and tackled Hana off the side of the ramp as the entire plane exploded and a green shockwave enveloped them. The force of the blast scorched the side of the closest van and knocked it over. The women tumbled through the air.

They crashed into the roof of the farthest van and dented it as their weapons clattered against the hard asphalt.

Alison groaned. Burns covered her body, her shields were depleted, and her skin was now its normal color. She rolled away from Hana who was scorched on her limbs but thankfully didn't resemble a rotisserie chicken.

"Damn, girlfriend," Hana moaned. "You just saved my life again."

"Are you two okay?" Tahir called from below.

Alison rolled onto her stomach and grimaced as the

cold, sharp metal of the van rubbed her burned flesh. Tahir stood a few yards away, Hana's Glock in hand and his brow furrowed in worry. He had a few bruises on his face, but Hanna was right, he was in far better shape than either of them.

She held up a hand and waved before she yanked a healing potion from her pocket and downed the contents. Hana retrieved one gingerly as well.

The burns healed slowly, and most of the pain faded. Some weakness and throbbing remained from overextending her magic, but not as much as she would have expected.

I guess getting blown up all at once strains me less than taking five hundred different shots. Good to know.

Alison took a deep breath and shook her hands out before she jumped down.

Hana leapt down and ran to pull Tahir into an embrace. "You're okay, right? I know I ran off earlier, but I needed to help Alison."

He smiled and patted her back. "They stunned me and then tied me up and blindfolded me. Nothing much changed before you found me. I wasn't even awake that long when you showed up."

"We got your revenge." Hana smiled and stepped back. "We killed everyone for you."

"I can see that." Tahir frowned. "What happened at the end? I was in the van with the gun when I sensed all that magic and then the explosion happened." His gaze cut to Alison. "While I'm extremely pleased that you saw to my recovery and took out the men who kidnapped me, don't you think that was a bit excessive?" He pointed toward the burning wreckage of the plane. "We could have used the evidence."

Alison snorted. "It wasn't me." She frowned. "But something doesn't add up. Who the hell blows up a plane with a magical bomb but doesn't bother to give their guys anti-magic bullets? That was barely a workout until the bomb."

Tahir rubbed his chin. "Someone, perhaps, who finds their men expendable and is more interested in finishing off a vexing and continuous powerful magical threat."

Hana walked over to grab the sword and Alison's knife from the ground. "You're saying the whole thing was a trap?"

"I doubt that it was an explicit trap. It was directed to stop me, and I think the bomb was a mere opportunity. The timing of their attack as it correlates to my progress in tracking down Ajit Patel is too much to ignore." Tahir threw the back of the van open and looked around. He blew out a breath as he spotted a backpack. He opened it and looked around inside. "Good. They didn't throw out my computer, glove, or wand. I won't be totally useless."

Alison nodded. "I think we pushed too hard. I shouldn't have called Chesterton until you'd made it farther in your investigation."

Tahir shook his head. "I find myself rather annoyed— not with you, Alison, but with him. This is also partially my fault. Obviously, I didn't cover my tracks enough. I believed I had, but he would have never been able to send mercenaries to my exact location if that were the case. I almost escaped. Next time, I'll be better prepared."

Alison surveyed the area. The blast had incinerated many of the mercenaries down to their skeletons, but several bodies remained mostly intact, if crispy. "Let's grab what might be useful off them and get the hell out of here before the police get here."

Hana nodded and threw open the driver-side door of the closest van and leaned inside to rifle through the glove box and console.

Alison walked toward one of the dead mercenaries.

"Alison," Tahir called.

She looked over her shoulder. "Yeah?"

"Thank you. I've never had someone go so far to help me before. It's an...odd feeling."

Alison knelt by the dead mercenary and checked pouches on his vest and his pockets. "You got caught up in this because you work for me, but more to the point, you're also my friend. I never leave my friends behind."

She found and pulled out a phone. "Good start. One phone."

"Got a tablet," Hana yelled from the van.

Alison stood. "Good. The more we know, the less defense we have to play, and I'm so damned tired of playing defense."

CHAPTER TWENTY-FIVE

A lison glanced around at the cars surrounding the Fiat. Her bright red sports car stood out in a Costco parking lot packed with trucks and family SUVs.

I wonder if I'll ever be able to walk into a Costco and buy a huge box of healing potions.

She checked her mirrors and the rearview camera for the tenth time in as many minutes, but there was no one suspicious in the parking lot—besides the three of them, anyway. If Chesterton's infomancers were searching the city, they'd eventually find her, but at this point, she'd prefer the bastards come straight at her.

Alison leaned back in her seat. Her parents had dealt with people wanting them dead, and both related the same basic strategy. Minimize collateral damage and keep on the move until they could finish off the person at the top. Her dad had even once grabbed a pile of barbecue to feed himself while he drove around half of Southern California eluding hitmen, not sure how long it'd take.

Sushi won't keep as well. Damn it. I need to end this crap sooner rather than later.

If I kick in Chesterton's door, he might not even be there. Tahir could probably find where the guy is hiding. Or I could wait until Chesterton's next public appearance and take him out then.

Tahir typed away on his laptop in the backseat, his gaze locked on his screen. Hana thumbed idly through news on her phone. There wasn't much else to do until they had a better handle on the situation.

Alison started the car. There was no reason to linger in a Costco parking lot. "I need to come up with a better plan than sitting in a parking lot."

"Maybe we should go back to the condo," Hana suggested.

Alison sighed. "What if they attack the condo? Myna's right. I need better defenses, and they're using magic, so that means we'll need to be more careful. I don't want my neighbors to get caught in the crossfire. I depended on my name to keep people from attacking me at home, but I'm not so sure that's enough anymore."

Tahir snorted from the back but didn't look up from his computer. "Your condo is fine, at least for you. Chesterton has too much to lose from a massacre. His actions already prove it. The attackers who came after me at my apartment went to the trouble of activating the fire alarms to clear the building, and they used invisibility on the dropship. If he has his hirelings openly attack an upscale building, AET and the PDA will descend on his home within hours, if not the National Guard. In addition, given that we just saw a powerful magical bomb, if simple assassination was the goal, they could have used that on my building or your building without bothering with trying to capture me." He shook his head. "I suspect I was meant to be simple leverage, nothing more. As much as you have your limitations, he has his as well. You've defeated all his hired killers, and he must realize that he can't simply solve this problem with brute force. You even survived his bomb."

"Asshole," Hana muttered. "I hate his fucking ass so much."

Alison backed out of the parking lot. "Then Hana's right. We should simply go back to the condo. I can't drive around to parking lots for days. The PDA might eventually find a clue, but they're still the government, and that means they're slow."

"You should go back to the condo, yes, and Hana should as well," Tahir replied. "But I'm unsure what sort of magic they performed on me, and their having access to me means I'll need to spend some time setting up proper countermeasures so they can't easily hack your systems. There are a lot of ways to weaken you that don't involve blowing up your building. We can't have them spying on you and knowing your plans. I'm not overly concerned, but I think now is a time for an excess of caution given everything that has happened. At least for a few days"

"Do you want me to take you back to your place?" Alison joined the flow of traffic on the street.

Tahir shook his head. "I'd think it wouldn't benefit either of us if I was forced to answer too many of the police's questions. I don't even think you should let the police know immediately that I've been recovered. Given how reluctant the authorities are to move against Chesterton, he undoubtedly has at least some police on his payroll —at least enough to leak important information to him."

"Good point. Damn it. It's always easier when it's underworld pieces of garbage rather than alleged captains of industry."

Hana snorted.

"Obviously, we'll have to eventually deal with the police," Tahir continued, "but until we resolve the immediate situation, it might be better if I hide in a hotel. It'll be easy for me to book a room under a false identity."

Alison frowned. "I don't like the idea we have to hide people. Maybe we should track Chesterton's ass down and deal with him."

Tahir sighed. "Although he's avoided innocent casualties thus far, if we back him too far into the corner, we do risk targeting people who have nothing to do with this." He frowned. "I should point out, for example, that your father's home was destroyed in the past by people who thought him too threatening. A mysterious explosion at your family's current home could be a way to get at you."

"Chesterton wouldn't dare," Alison scoffed. "That would get my parents after him, and if he thinks I'm bad, he should see my dad."

Tahir snorted. "Chesterton's a man paranoid enough to conduct anti-magical biological experiments. And you're right, one of the few people in the country more dangerous than you is your father. I'm merely saying we might want to be careful about pushing Chesterton into a corner to the point where he lashes out blindly. Consider this an overreaction to my recent experience, but I think if we truly want to bring Chesterton down, we should consider letting me finish my investigation into Prometheus and Ajit Patel. I was close, and I still have access to my backups. I'll be able to continue probing to seek the information we need, and the authorities can descend on him en masse."

"But don't they know about you? They sent mercenaries to kidnap you."

Tahir averted his eyes. "It's my fault. There was possible detection before, and I thought I'd handled it. Obviously, I hadn't fully, but now I know to be more careful. As I told Hana recently, all mistakes are learning opportunities. I have my pride, and I won't be beaten in my realm by Chesterton's lackeys."

Hana smiled over her shoulder at him. "I have confidence in you, Tahir, and I really want to see a perp walk for that arrogant billionaire bastard."

Alison pulled a hand off the wheel to hold up two fingers. "Two weeks. If you don't have more information we can turn over in two weeks, then I'll handle this Brownstone style and kick in some doors. I'll warn my family and they can be ready, and if Chesterton's a stupid enough dumbass to go after my family, he better find a way to fly to Pluto before my parents show up, let alone me."

"Noted." Tahir held up one of the recovered phones. "Incidentally, I've identified our mercenaries. They aren't Two Worlds Security and have no ties with Jacobsen. They are an underworld mercenary company of modest renown. A step down from Jacobsen. Based on the number of men I killed at the apartment and the number of men you killed at the airstrip, we've already depleted most of their strength. From what I can tell, they don't have any wizards, so they must have used contractors during the initial attack on me. It is curious that Chesterton would go from an elite group with access to anti-magic weapons to more straight-forward thugs."

Alison nodded. "He probably figured it'd be easy to grab one infomancer, and maybe he wanted someone more disposable for the bomb if and when it came to that. Angering a top-level outfit would put his life at risk." She narrowed her eyes. "The fact that it went off means he might have been watching through a feed. I know they had no ties to Jacobsen, but do the mercenaries have any known ties to Chesterton?"

Tahir shrugged. "None that I've found thus far, but I can't be sure. Doing my work on a laptop in the back of a car is hardly optimal conditions. It'll take time to fully explore the phones and the tablet."

"Forget about them, then." Alison shook her head. "Concentrate on Prometheus and the hidden servers. That's the key to everything. Ajit Patel must be a big deal if they're going out of their way to hide him so well. I don't care about what third-rate mercenary company Chesterton's used as sacrificial pawns. I care about him. The only reason I'm not driving over there right now to kick his ass is that you got in my head about innocent people and my family. Otherwise, I'd go after him like I went after the Eastern Union."

"Very well." Tahir tapped something into his laptop. "I was close before, very close, and now I understand better the kinds of attack they might use. I won't get caught this time, and I'll get that information. Once I fully access my backups, I'll have a list of additional servers. I suspect the ones I targeted have already been strengthened or destroyed."

Alison changed lanes and her gaze lingered for a few seconds on a police cruiser driving the opposite way. "And this is something you can still do with the equipment you have from a hotel room?"

"Yes, it'll be less efficient, but I take pride in my abilities, even in non-optimal circumstances." Tahir lifted his chin, a glint of arrogance in his eyes. "And, like with you, Derek Chesterton has made this a very personal affair and has presented a direct challenge to me."

Alison snorted. "Racking up friends. He's so lovable that way."

Hana cleared her throat. "There's something else we should consider."

"What?" Alison responded.

Hana sighed. "I think, we should…consider extra security for Tahir while he stays at the hotel."

Alison glanced over at her. "Like what?"

"He didn't even run off with a gun." Hana shrugged.

"I prefer to follow my core strengths," Tahir replied. "I'm terrible with weapons, so it's pointless for me to carry them."

Hana looked into the back and smiled. "I'm decent with a gun, and when I fox out, I'm faster and have claws. If I can fight my way half out of an Eastern Union building drugged, I can handle most mercenaries. Plus, I've got the pendant." She looked at Alison. "I think I should stay with Tahir until we're ready to move or the cops are." Her cheeks reddened. "If that's okay with him."

Tahir blinked a few times. "I'll concentrate on probing Prometheus and Ajit Patel, but I don't mind."

Is this a bad idea? They both need to keep their focus, but she's also right. If they caught him once, they might catch him again, and Tahir's also right about his presence and the condo.

Alison sighed. "Fine. Get yourself a room, Tahir, and I'll take you both to the hotel. After that, I'll try to push this whole thing along from a different angle. I'm tired of us doing all the hard work."

CHAPTER TWENTY-SIX

Alison stepped into the PDA office. The young receptionist looked as bored as ever as she typed, but she didn't bother to look up even as her mouth curled into a frown.

What do you even have against me? You've been rude from the first time we met. You know what? Who cares? Get in line. At least you're not trying to kill me.

Without waiting for an acknowledgement, Alison marched toward Agent Latherby's door.

"Excuse me, Miss Brownstone," the receptionist called out, but she still didn't look up. "You can't simply march in there without an appointment. Agent Latherby's a very busy man."

Alison stopped and stared at her. "I get that, and I'm about to insist he become a lot busier, so I'm sure he'll be annoyed. But here's the thing. Today, I've been shot at multiple times. Men launched grenades at me, one of my friends and employees got kidnapped, and someone tried to blow me up with a magical bomb. Oh, that magical bomb totaled a plane and bordered on strategic-level magic. But, who cares, right?" She shrugged. "It seems like something the PDA should care about, but if you want to stop me, sure, go ahead and try. Otherwise, I'll go talk to Latherby and he's going to listen to me, damn it."

The receptionist rolled her eyes and muttered something underneath her breath.

The door to Agent Latherby's office opened. "It's fine, Helen." He looked at Alison. "Come in and stop making a scene, Miss Brownstone. She's only doing her job."

Alison continued toward the office. "Latherby, this is simply me bitching. You don't want to see me making a scene. Trust me. It involves a lot more explosions."

The agent retreated to his desk as she closed the door behind her.

"We don't know the whereabouts of Mr. Arain," Agent Latherby reported. "I understand your frustration, but if you're here about that, I can only tell you that we're looking deeply into the incident. As he's a wizard, PDA has some jurisdiction and some tracking magic was attempted, but it's being blocked. We're considering other options, but we've no proof he was taken, which constrains us."

Alison crossed her arms and frowned. "Yeah, I know. That's the point. Don't worry. I recovered him myself. Like I told Helen, today has involved many explosions, including a magical bomb that destroyed a plane. A very powerful one. If I wasn't using an artifact and had my own shields up, it might have taken me out. Now imagine if something like that went off in the city."

The agent arched an eyebrow. "Now I understand. That clears up at least one immediate mystery. The process of investigating the explosion at that airstrip is still underway. It was detected via satellite and the information forwarded to local authorities for review. Your clarification on the matter is appreciated. I was worried, for a moment, that we had multiple unrelated incidents occurring in the city. With all the instability and baseline issues, it would strain resources if there was another threat."

Alison shrugged. "But since they're related, who cares, right? Derek Chesterton can set off magical bombs, kidnap people, hack buildings, send mercenaries with dropships into the heart of a major city, and we all simply shrug and say, 'Well, don't want the stock market to go down. Some rich assholes might not be able to afford an extra car this month.' Or people can go on and on about stability. Here's a little tidbit. A country where the wealthy can do what they want with impunity isn't a democracy. You'd think as a federal agent, you'd care about that."

"I understand your frustration, but I think you should keep in mind that your family is quite wealthy. You are personally quite wealthy. You certainly have far more money than I do. I wouldn't cast too many aspersions on the rich."

"You think I care about being called a hypocrite when a man who helped fund an anti-magic biological weapon is walking around freely?" Alison slammed her hand on his desk. "That bastard Chesterton had a bomb ready, which means he was ready to blow up his own people to clean up after himself. I don't get why he can't just be arrested already." She shrugged. "Put him under enough pressure, and he'll crack. The guy's already afraid. You said so yourself. If you don't want me to do something about it, then you should do something about it!"

Damn it. I'm starting to understand and appreciate certain things Dad did a lot more.

"I need evidence, Miss Brownstone. Concrete evidence." Agent Latherby narrowed his eyes. "As inconvenient as this might be, I think we can both agree the last thing that would be good for this country is for government agents to snatch people out of their homes without clear evidence of wrongdoing. If you claim to care about democracy, that should be considered."

"So what? Am I supposed to sit around while Chesterton does what he wants to who he wants?" Alison laughed. "I'll be brutally honest with you, Agent Latherby. Pretty much the only thing holding me back from going straight to Chesterton and killing him is the risk to my family. And I'll make it clear, if he goes after my family, I will kill him. If you want to send me off to an ultramax equipped with some of his nullifiers after that, I don't care."

They stared at each, neither daring to blink until finally, Agent Latherby sighed and shook his head.

"I'm not your enemy, Miss Brownstone, but unfortunately, Chesterton is not like the Eastern Union. His connections mean he has power, and so we must all tread carefully so that innocent people don't suffer when all is said and done." He folded his hands in front of him. "I've been in this job a while, Miss Brownstone. When I joined the PDA, the chaos of the opening of the portals hadn't fully abated. I've done my part to keep the peace and protect this country, and that's always what I will do, using every means available."

Alison looked away and some of her fire drained from her. "I'm not saying you're a bad guy or on the take. But there are only so many punches I can take from this asshole, and there are certain lines, like my family and friends, that once crossed, can't be forgiven."

"I presume he'd have issues going after your family for many reasons, not the least of which is the Scourge of Harriken himself, but your concern is duly noted." Agent Latherby held up his left hand.

"What?"

"See anything?"

Alison leaned closer and shook her head. "No, what am I supposed to see?"

"A ring, for example." Agent Latherby lowered his hand. "One of the reasons I've never married is because of the dangers associated with this job. Trust me, Miss Brownstone, I know what it's like to be hunted by the agents of chaos and corruption. I've been wounded in the line of duty, and I've been forced to make quick decisions to save my life and those of my fellow agents. I sympathize and empathize with you far more than you seem to realize." He shook his head. "I shouldn't share too many details with you, but I will let you know there has been an unusual flurry of activity involving Chesterton in the last few days. Several agencies are also close to connecting him directly to Jacobsen Associates even without the testimony of employees of Two Worlds Security." He leaned forward. "We're close. Very close. We will take him down. You merely have to be patient. Then, it won't be a security contractor and her friends. It'll be the full might of the federal government along with all the local authorities coming down on him. He's powerful, but he's not more powerful than that."

Alison stretched her neck to ease the tension. "Patient? It's hard to be patient when people are trying to kill you and kidnap your friends." She took a deep breath, closed her eyes, and released it slowly. "Fine. I'll tell you what I told my people. If this isn't over in two weeks, I'm ending it. If that involves the government coming after me, so be it. And remember, this bastard isn't only coming after me." She pointed at Latherby. "He's coming after all magicals and someone has to stand up to him, even if it involves risking themselves."

"I'm aware of that, Miss Brownstone." Agent Latherby folded his hands on the desk. "But there are some other considerations you should take into account. You're not in law enforcement, so you don't understand. Even when you did bounty work, you were involved in what amounts to the steps near the end."

"Yeah. So? What's your point?"

"Conspiracies rarely involve one bad man. The universe isn't so kind to those who care. Even if you kill Derek Chesterton, I doubt that will end this, at least the anti-magic biological weapon. We're moving slowly so we have enough to hold him and convince him to cooperate, to pressure him into giving up everyone else involved." He stood and adjusted his tie. "As you're so fond of pointing out to me, Miss Brownstone, you're not the only one at risk. We can't proceed like you're the only one at risk, no matter how emotionally unpalatable that is to your Brownstone sense of agency."

Alison sighed and took a deep breath, her fists clenched.

"I'm not telling you to not defend yourself," Agent Latherby continued, "but I am suggesting you give us time to do our jobs, not for your sake, but for every potential victim's sake and for the sake of the magical populations of both Earth and Oriceran."

"I am giving you time." Alison turned and opened the door. "I'm giving you two weeks unless he comes at me or my people again. Then, we'll have to reevaluate the schedule, but I understand what you're saying, and I'm glad—" She sighed.

"What?"

Alison managed a slight smile. "I didn't know what to think of you when we first met, but I'm glad you're one of the good guys."

"Good guy? Perhaps. It depends on one's perspective." Agent Latherby chuckled. "I'm a federal agent. Haven't you ever heard that joke about the government?"

"What joke?"

"What are the nine most frightening words in the English language?"

Alison shrugged. "No idea."

"I'm from the government, and I'm here to help."

Alison snickered. "You know what? You're all right, Latherby." She waved and stepped into the main office.

"Miss Brownstone," Agent Latherby called. "Don't do anything you'll end up regretting."

She threw up a dismissive hand. "You're about ten years too late to give me that advice."

CHAPTER TWENTY-SEVEN

Three days later, Alison knocked on the unassuming door of an equally unassuming motel room. The place wasn't trashy enough to attract too much police attention nor nice enough to attract the attention of thieves looking for an easy score.

I hope they've actually been doing work and not spending all their time tearing each other's clothes off. Hana made a good case for protection, but it's not like she's unbiased.

Magic radiated off the doorway and windows. Tahir's defensive spells, she assumed. She'd stayed away on Tahir's suggestion until he was ready to give her more information.

A dark eye peeked through the blinds, and a moment later, Hana opened the door.

"You never responded to my text. We didn't know if you were coming." Hana nodded to Tahir.

Alison stepped inside and looked around the hotel room. Glowing glyphs decorated several of the walls.

Tahir sat cross-legged on a bed, his laptop in front of

him and his glove connected to a port on the laptop and glowing. "The room's protected against eavesdropping, scrying, and tracking magic. Crude spells compared to the more subtle ones I had inside my walls at my old place, but fast to implement and easy to maintain."

"It's kind of obvious magic's in use, though," Alison replied.

Tahir shrugged. "Plenty of wizards use hotels. I'm not that worried about anyone sensing the magic."

"Hana's text said, and I quote, 'Come right away, girlfriend. Important.' And important was followed by twelve exclamation points." Alison moved to a chair in the corner. "I could use some good news. Please give me some."

Tahir typed for a few seconds before he shrugged. "Good news is relative. I have important news."

Hana sighed and sat on the edge of the bed next to him, her face lined in worry. "Brace yourself."

Alison frowned. "Now what?"

"I was able to locate some files related to Prometheus Testing Services. The information wasn't on any of the main servers, but on another server, I found an address when I was probing the hidden server that I thought referenced Ajit Patel." Tahir took a deep breath. "The files had additional details and mentioned resources related to the project, including more field tests with other code names. You came up a few times, Dark Princess." He cleared his throat. "It discusses the team lead. The reason we can't find the Ajit Patel on the other servers is because it's a codename." He snorted. "The guy's not even Indian. The actual team lead is a man named Lawrence Northwell. I've been able to locate some information on him, and he does seem to have an extensive background in molecular biology and virology."

Alison shrugged. "That's all a good thing, right? It's more information. We can hand this all over to the PDA, and they arrest this Northwell bastard and get him to roll on Chesterton."

Hana and Tahir exchanged glances.

"Okay." Alison frowned. "What is it that you're not telling me? I don't care if Chesterton's name isn't in the file. We have a trail to this Northwell. We can move from there."

Tahir furrowed his brow. "The problem is where I found the files. They weren't on a Prometheus System, nor were they on servers that were controlled by any entity associated with Derek Chesterton. It took me more effort because of my crude tools and less extensive background spells set up, but when I investigated the server with the file more thoroughly, I found, ultimately, that it was under the control of what proved to be a shell company, which was also owned by another shell. I'll spare you the nested details, but the trail ends at a familiar place—Advanced Magitek Systems."

Alison shot out of her chair. "That's impossible." She rubbed the back of her neck. "You're saying Scott's involved? But that doesn't make any sense." She paced as much as the small room would allow her. "It's a shell company, right? So someone in his organization is working for Chesterton, obviously."

Tahir shook his head. "And Chesterton's foolish enough to stick his files on an ultimately AMS-controlled server? Chesterton might be a businessman and ruthless, but he started as a technomagic engineer. He has a technical background."

"But all the other evidence points to Chesterton." Alison froze in place and her stomach churned.

Hana sighed and flopped back on the bed, defeat on her face.

"Does it?" Tahir raised an eyebrow. "Let's review the evidence. We know the virus was artificially created because of the original memo I found after following the trail from the Jacobsen systems. The memo was on a server I couldn't directly associate with Chesterton. Jacobsen was hired by Chesterton indirectly, but they obviously weren't involved in the creation of the virus."

"But what about Prometheus Testing Services and what the witch overheard?"

Tahir shrugged. "She heard an offhand reference to Chesterton, but Prometheus has been hired by every major technomagic company in the country, including AMS."

Alison groaned and scrubbed a hand over her face. "Chesterton hired men to kill me."

"Yes, he did, but assassins didn't come after you until you interfered with the attempt on Carlyle's life." Tahir frowned. "And as powerful as you are, if Carlyle was that worried, he could have doubled his guards. It's not like he'd anticipated being assaulted by a Drow princess. You weren't, strictly speaking, necessary."

Alison took a few deep breaths and slumped back into the chair. "Maybe he was simply doing it to get on my good side. Sure, a few more wizards might have helped him there, but what about next time, when someone worse comes?"

"I feel you, girlfriend," Hana murmured. "On one hand, I'm pissed, and the other hand, I've got to respect the level of con he pulled off. It's epic."

"I...can't... I won't believe it." Alison rubbed her temples. "It makes no sense."

Tahir took a deep breath. "Everything suspicious about this situation applies as well to Carlyle as it does Chesterton. He has the same resources and even more. The original memo mentioned observing the Dark Princess closer. Carlyle has had much more opportunity to do that than Chesterton." He sighed. "I think you were the ultimate test subject, a high-profile and powerful magical who is prone to getting into trouble. The second set of files I found even detail how they got the virus into you by having a cook contaminate food at a café you used to frequent nine months ago. It talks about how they needed to keep the employee away from direct contact with you in case you used your soul sight on them. They'd thoroughly researched you, even if there were obvious gaps in their knowledge." He shrugged.

Alison stared at her hands. "So, what? Chesterton's been innocent this whole time?"

Tahir shook his head. "No, he's exactly what Carlyle said he is, a ruthless competitor who isn't above murder, and all evidence still does point to Chesterton hiring people to kill you. I think Carlyle decided to test his virus and have you weaken his greatest competitor at the same time. Win-win."

Alison's face tightened as she remembered something Scott told her months ago.

Real business is win-win.

Hana shot up. "Wait a second. There's one big flaw in all of this, Tahir. I didn't think about it, but it proves Scott's not the guy."

Alison looked over at Hana, her heart kicking up in hope. "What?"

"Your soul sight." Hana smiled. "You still had it when you first met him. Just like you had it when you first met me, and you wouldn't work for someone who had a tainted soul."

Alison groaned. "That's just it. I did have it, but that stupid-ass magical tie of his…" She shook her head. "It was so bright that when I looked at him with my soul-sight, I couldn't see any of his soul colors." She closed her eyes and let her head roll back. "And when I first met him, he was with a dark wizard talking about buying a stolen artifact."

Hana rolled onto her side. "But he said he didn't know, and he killed the guy when he might have hurt you."

"At the time, that was enough to make me trust him." Alison shook her head. "But now that I look back on it, I have trouble believing that Scott would be so unthorough as to accidentally end up chatting with a dark wizard. That fucker has played me from the beginning. He wanted to see his Dark Princess test subject up close and personal. He probably killed McNamara, half to continue the tests and half to cover his ass in case I got suspicious."

Tahir nodded gravely.

Hana sat up. "What's the plan, then?"

Alison sighed. "The PDA and everyone else are all up Chesterton's ass, not Carlyle's, and he has even more influence with law enforcement than Chesterton does. If we go to them, it'll delay things more and he'll definitely find out. No, I've got one shot. I'll go to his face and confront him. I'll make him submit to a truth spell. If I'm wrong, then all I have to deal with is him being pissed. If I'm right, I'll beat him and drag him in myself." She stood. "Both of you stay here."

Hana hopped off the bed. "No way. If Tahir's right about this, you might be walking into your death."

"If that's true, then you might be walking into your death as well." Alison shook her head. "You and Tahir stay here. If I don't contact you in twelve hours, go to Latherby and tell him everything. If the PDA doesn't do crap, you should contact my mom."

"Why not your dad?" Hana suggested.

Alison shook her head. "There are…things you don't know about my dad. If he thinks I'm in real danger, it could be too risky. There might be…collateral damage and I don't want that on my conscience or his. Mom will know how to handle the situation and him as necessary."

Hana blinked and gave a shallow nod.

Tahir frowned. "You're being stubborn, Alison. We should simply go to the PDA right away. If you trust Latherby, he can help."

"No." Alison marched over toward the door. "Scott's manipulated me, the police, the PDA, and this entire city. We can't trust anyone in Seattle, even if they have good intentions, because they might all be Scott's puppets. Give me twelve hours. I won't bring my phone with me to Scott's in case he can hack it and trace my contacts with you. I'll pick up a burner, though." She looked at Hana. "In this situation, I want to protect my friends, and no, even if

Lily or my mom were here, I'd want them to stay behind, too."

"Martyr complex," Hana muttered.

Tahir snorted. "Are you sure you're going with the smart decision and not simply giving in to a desire for petty vengeance?"

Alison shrugged. "Why not both? This ends today, one way or another."

CHAPTER TWENTY-EIGHT

Alison was grateful the entire incident was unfolding in February instead of the summer. It gave her an excuse to wear a long overcoat, which let her conceal multiple magazines, knives, and grenades. Scott and his people had never checked her weapons upon entry, and that afternoon was no exception. His personal assistant ushered her not into a receiving room but into a sprawling garden in the back, complete with an extensive hedge maze with entrances on either side of the garden.

The colorful flowers and bushes were in full bloom, despite the cold temperature, and residual magic hung in the area.

I wonder why they have me outside? Is he just in a mood to show off?

"Beautiful, isn't it?" Scott called from behind her.

Her back still to him, Alison reached into her pocket to pull out the burner phone she'd purchased. She started recording and slipped it back into her coat. After a few deep breaths, she thought back to some of her school play performances before she turned and smiled.

"It is," Alison replied. "I don't know if that's a wasteful use of magic or a brilliant use of magic."

Scott advanced on her in a suit with his omnipresent glyph-covered tie.

"I hate to pressure you, Miss Brownstone," Scott began, "but you're the one who contacted me and said it was an emergency."

"Yeah, Chesterton tried to go after Tahir." Alison shrugged. "Because he was getting too close to the truth about the company he hired to help him test his biological weapon. Tahir got deep in their files and was getting all the information we need to get to the heart of the conspiracy. Tahir's safe, and I've got him stashed away, but Chesterton's declared open war on me and my friends. I came here for advice. I don't know the lay of the land in Seattle. You do, and I need to figure out how to move forward."

Scott rubbed his chin. "I think at this point he's left you little choice."

"Left me little choice?"

He nodded. "Yes. You need to kill him. I know he's in semi-hiding, but I can get you his location. Then you can do the rest."

Alison stared at him. "You want me to simply kill him? What about chaos, and stock prices, and all that crap you whined about before?"

"The market will settle as it always does." Scott shrugged. "Chesterton's become too dangerous. It's a matter of time before he does something foolish. If you kill him, I can use my influence. The authorities are already looking into him. I can guarantee you that they'll leave this alone as self-defense. I'll do what it takes. I'd rather have you handle this then let it spiral out of control and hurt the city."

"I'm no assassin," Alison replied. She folded her arms and frowned. "Last time we talked, you didn't even want to use your influence to help me without more evidence, and now you're telling me you'll cover for me if I kill him? Why the big change?"

Scott shrugged. "The situation on the ground has changed. I was aware of some of the chaos that occurred the other day, but what was behind it had escaped my understanding. Derek's obviously out of control. Your probing of Prometheus Testing has forced him into a corner. The fact he'd developed an anti-magic virus to begin with shows how out of control he is. We need to end this now before he further weaponizes it."

I guess we know who is the cornered person panicking now, don't we?

Alison turned and locked eyes with Scott. "How do you know all that?"

Scott frowned. "What are you talking about, Miss Brownstone? You're the one who has come and asked for help multiple times recently."

"Yeah, but I was very careful to keep certain details out. I never mentioned it was a virus. Never mentioned it being anti-magical." Alison shook her head. "I certainly never mentioned the company name. Now, that makes me wonder, how do you know all that?"

"I'm well-connected. I learn things. Many things." Scott sighed. "Don't let paranoia from recent events lead you down the wrong path. I know you find my financial focus unpleasant, but that doesn't change the fact that we both share a common enemy, one who is preparing a dangerous anti-magical biological weapon."

"The funny thing is, though. Tahir found files about the project on non-Prometheus servers, including one controlled by a company that is owned by you. Sure, there are lots of smoke and mirrors in the way, but that's the truth." Alison pointed at him. "Take the tie off."

Scott frowned. "Excuse me?"

"Take the tie off." Alison shrugged. "And I'll use a truth spell. If you're on my side, that's not too much to ask."

He snorted. "I'm not subjecting myself to your paranoid interrogations."

Alison gave him a hungry grin. "I'm not leaving until you take the tie off and submit to the spell. Yeah, your little virus works, but not as well as you hoped, does it? I mean you've seen what I can do even though I'm infected. You tricked me into pissing off your homicidal competitor so you can see the results first hand."

Scott's face darkened. "Be careful, Alison. You're beginning to worry me."

"Good. I'm tired of being your Dark Princess." Alison tapped her crystal ring three times and layered light and shadow magic into a deep shield. "It's over, Scott. All of this." She gestured around the garden. "I don't give a shit about shareholders or disrupting the status quo. You're a criminal and a terrorist as far as I'm concerned, and I'm here to stop you. I've come here not to listen to your excuses but to let you surrender before I go all Brownstone on you."

He scoffed. "Such arrogance. Whatever it is that you *think* you know, you have no proof. Some file? Pathetic. Just like Derek, and it's hardly like he's an innocent victim. He did send someone to kill me for purely petty business reasons, and he did send men after you because he thought you were a threat. I simply made sure the right people whispered in his ear to ensure he'd put more effort into it."

Waves of magic pulsed through the area, enough that Alison's body tingled.

She drew her gun and aimed it at him. "You're coming with me. I'm only not killing you because a certain someone told me that in situations like this, we need to squeeze all the conspiracy info out."

Scott stared down at his fingernails. "You really are used to always getting your way, aren't you?"

Alison shrugged. "I'm the one aiming a gun."

"Do you have anti-magic bullets in that gun?" Scott raised an eyebrow. "I doubt it, and this tie has a lot of useful functions. Come on, Miss Brownstone. A lot of magical people have tried to kill or threaten me. Do you think I haven't learned to take some precautions?" He motioned to the mansion. "It's already been cleared of all non-essential non-security staff. Oh, and I'm sure you like playing Junior Detective with your little recording, but I should inform you I'm jamming all transmissions. We'll have a nice, private conversation, and we'll come to an accord."

Alison glared at him. "Do you think I didn't feel the magic before? What do you think will happen when I tell all your witches and wizards about what you're doing?"

"What witches and wizards?" Scott shrugged. "You

forget, I run a technomagic company. There's not a single man or woman left on this property who is a natural-born magical. All are normal humans using artifacts or technomagic."

"Well, aren't we thorough?" Alison holstered her gun. If blatant intimidation wouldn't work, she'd have to adapt tactics. Maybe she could appeal to his sense of reason. "There's one thing that confuses me, though."

Scott chuckled. "Only one?"

"Yeah." Alison shrugged. "Why any of this? You obviously don't hate magic. You run a technomagic company, so why would you make an anti-magic virus? Is this some petty greed thing? Supply and demand?"

Scott scoffed. "I'm not a myopic fool like Chesterton." He nodded toward her. "People like you Brownstones are the problem. I don't know exactly what your father is, but I don't believe for a second that he's a normal human using a mere artifact, and you are the Dark Princess. Both of you are proof of the necessity of my efforts. Even weakened, your power is ridiculous, and you aren't even the most powerful magical on Earth, let alone Oriceran." He shook his head. "Technomagic can level the playing field, but it's not enough, not when more and more magicals flood the Earth." He sighed. "I know you think I'm a monster but think about it rationally and objectively. Think about the dark wizards you've hunted and all the dangerous men and women your father took down through the years. It's quaint but true, Miss Brownstone. Power corrupts."

"And what about your power? You're a billionaire. Money's power." Alison shrugged.

"Contingent power. Yes, I can hire people to kill others,

but I don't possess that power myself. I can't open a portal and teleport myself from place to place or heal my grievous wounds with ease." Scott's face twitched. "Prometheus Testing Services isn't the only company I could have used. Do you know why I used them?"

"A deep company commitment to a lack of ethics and morals?" Alison shrugged.

"Their name amused me. It's like the myth, Miss Brownstone. The Oricerans are gods. They have a king who will rule for a millennium. They have gnomes more ancient than our oldest human civilizations." Scott inhaled deeply. "And like Zeus, they held us back, and so-called human traitors aided them."

Alison shook her head. "You're the Zeus in this scenario, Scott. Not Prometheus."

"No, if magic had been allowed to flourish alongside technology, humanity would already rule the stars." Scott snorted. "I know what you're going to say. You're going to talk about the portals, the energy, but there was magic even before the portals opened. The kemanas were there. Proper scientific application could have found other ways, but no, the Oricerans wanted to hold us back because they were afraid we'd pass them, and we will. A static civilization filled with long-lived demi-gods too arrogant to truly advance. Don't you see? It's Mount Olympus. All of Earth is Prometheus, and now finally, Hercules has come to free us, and I won't let Zeus keep the chains on."

Silence stretched between the two. A light breeze blew the sweet scent of flowers into Alison's nose.

Scott smiled. "I'm not a monster, Miss Brownstone. Not a Rhazdon seeking to conquer. This virus isn't something that I intend to coat the Earth with. We can use it as a selective weapon against only the magicals who are out of control. Don't you see, Miss Brownstone? We're on the same side. We both want to protect people."

"Did you practice that speech in a mirror?" Alison folded her arms. "Give me a damned break. You're not a monster? You tested a biological weapon on unsuspecting people, and I'm sure you killed more than a few along the way. Once Tahir, let alone the government, starts digging into things, I'm sure they'll find all sorts of skeletons. Derek Chesterton might be a bastard who tried to have me killed, but I doubt he has any illusions his bullshit is justified by some high-minded crap about protecting humanity." She barked out a laugh. "You tested it on *me* and are worried about my dad, yet you act like I can trust you."

"Sacrifices are always necessary." Scott shook his head. "You, of all people, should appreciate that. Consider what Laena did years ago to your family when her will was challenged. Let's be honest. Idealism is the opiate of fools who refuse to see reality as it is. It's mere tradition that has kept the magicals in check, and even then, barely. I make no apologies for protecting the powerless."

Alison frowned. "Even if it means more sacrifices have to be made?"

"History is littered with sacrifice." Scott shrugged. "I read an interesting research paper the other day that suggested that the myth of the Minotaur and the sacrifices of the Athenians was based on actual sacrifices made to an Oriceran creature."

"Bullshit. There's no way they would have let some Oriceran over here to eat people."

"Perhaps. How do we know? Because they say so? They lied to us and helped manipulate our history for thousands of years. They can't be trusted." Scott clucked his tongue. "Your own mother lied to you, Alison, and that was after the truth of Oriceran came out."

Alison glowered at him. "Shut your mouth about my mother. She had her reasons."

"Everyone has their reasons. Besides, you should be reasonable. You can't win. I already had a good idea of why you were coming here." A sad expression slid over his face.

"Because you're the one who sent the men after Tahir because he was getting too close. You hoped I would fixate on Chesterton."

Scott gave her a patronizing smile. "Miss Brownstone… Alison, we can still work together."

Alison blinked. "Are you high on dust?"

"You won't be able to find a cure without my help. That's the next step. Infect and control. You can go and finish Derek off. I admit to manipulating him, but he still sent killers after you for his own reasons." Scott shrugged. "With him eliminated, it'll free up more of my resources to focus on expanding technomagic while assuring that dangerous magicals are kept in check. You could help with that, Alison. You could help make sure that Prometheus isn't chained to the rock again."

Alison sneered. "And be your Drow on a leash? Why would you need me if you have your precious virus?"

"Being a businessman has taught me that it's good to have options."

Alison lowered her arm and extended a shadow blade. "I have three words for you. Can you guess what they are?"

Scott's face contorted in irritation. "I find you're often unpredictable, so no."

"Aw. It's simple. Three words—go to hell."

He sighed and tapped at his watch. "Unfortunate. Such a waste."

Men in gray body armor covered in glyphs emerged from both sides of the hedge maze, all holding rifles and wearing anti-magic deflectors.

Alison scoffed. "Do these guards know that you're creating biological weapons?"

Scott nodded. "I'm good at filtering for loyalty. These men will fight and die for me."

Alison funneled energy toward her legs and glanced back and forth. "One last chance, Scott."

"That's what this was for you, Miss Brownstone. Your last chance." Scott adjusted his tie. "Kill her."

CHAPTER TWENTY-NINE

Alison jumped and released the energy in her legs. She soared toward one group of guards as bullets whistled past her and a few were deflected by her layered defenses. Undeterred, she slammed into one guard and knocked him into a few others.

In the midst of their confusion, Alison swung her shadow blade and sliced a rifle in half and quickly pivoted to cut another. If she couldn't kill them easily because of their anti-magic deflectors, disarming them was good enough. A lot of people didn't understand the limited range of the deflectors.

She leapt backward and yanked a grenade from her coat with her free hand. With a flick of her wrist, she tossed the primed grenade and launched herself backward with a pulse of magic. A stray bullet, slowed but not stopped by her shields, grazed her arm as the grenade went off, and the men screamed.

Definitely anti-magic bullets. Damn it.

Alison spun and flung a curved shadow blast toward

the other hedge maze opening and the men gathered there. The magical attack struck one of the men. He staggered back and the crystal of his deflector darkened.

Another bullet ripped into her side, and Alison gritted her teeth as she tossed a few grenades toward the men. She rolled into the other hedge maze with her wounds on fire and a faint throb throughout her entire body.

Alison took a few deep breaths. "Come on, Scott. That all you—"

A massive blast flung her high into the air and the pain in her body intensified. A dozen more men stood in the distance, closer to the mansion, their rifles held high and with full-coverage tactical battle helmets on. Her grenades wouldn't finish the new batch off so easily.

The guards opened fire, and several bullets struck her as she collapsed with a grunt. She hissed and rolled onto her back. Rounds ripped through the hedge maze and passed over her.

Alison grabbed a healing potion and downed it but stayed on her back as leaves, wood, and dust filled the air above from the heavy gunfire. She crawled a few feet and sat up, raised her hands in front of her, and forced energy into an explosive orb. The throbbing ache in her body intensified.

I only have to overwhelm the deflectors. It's too bad Myna couldn't have finished her ritual earlier.

Survive, Alison, a voice spoke in her mind. Even though there was no real sound, it *felt* old and female.

Alison blinked and almost accidentally released her attack at point-blank range.

What the hell? she thought. *Please don't tell me Dad slipped Whispy Doom's cousin on me somehow.*

I'm sorry, I wanted to take more time to do this properly, but the ritual has linked us, and your pain has helped to open a window to your mind.

Why does a healing ritual open a telepathic link?

Survive, Myna responded, *and I will give you back your power soon. Use it to crush your enemies.*

Another series of explosions flung Alison back. She grunted and released her own attack. The white-azure ball rocketed away and missed the armored men but slammed into the mansion wall behind them. The explosion knocked several of the men into the air and their deflectors turned black. A few shattered.

Dazed, Alison shook her head. The front of her hedge shelter had been reduced to a burning, charred mess from the guards' earlier attack, but the healing potion had taken care of her earlier wounds, even if it couldn't do anything about her AMDS pain. She threw an angled shadow line to her side and tried to move quickly and minimize magical strain. The line pulled her out of the way of another bullet storm.

If that's actually you, Myna, and not me hallucinating, hurry the hell up.

As you wish, my princess.

Too distracted by the enemy attacks to complain about the use of the title, Alison flung her last few grenades, more for cover than any hope of hurting the heavily armored men.

I should have brought the tachi, *but that might have been hard for him to ignore.*

Alison extended a shadow blade and wings and launched off the ground in time to avoid another explosion. Pain rippled through her body, even though the enemy hadn't landed a hit. Myna was working. Alison simply needed to stall long enough.

She released the wings, landed with a roll, and charged into a nearby guard. Her blade slashed at his rifle before she leapt up and pushed off him with her legs to cut through the next enemy's weapon. A bullet ripped through her shoulder. She hissed at the pain and did her best to ignore it as she pivoted to disarm the next man.

Overlapping dull roars from the sky sounded from behind her. She recognized the sounds. Dropships, but no sirens.

Alison let out a crazed laugh as she disarmed several more men. They stumbled back and rushed toward the hole in the mansion, clearly at a loss as to what to do without their rifles and anti-magic bullets. Her pain and wounds began to increase and the sound of the dropships grew louder and closer.

The rhythmic thump of a helicopter sounded in the distance.

More reinforcements. Fun. Between all the men and anti-magic deflectors, at least I'll make the bastard pay through the nose to kill me. I bet he's not had to spend so much to kill someone before.

Myna, how are you doing?

The ancient Drow didn't respond. Alison gritted her teeth, jumped, and kicked a rifle out of a man's hands. Maybe the woman's thoughts had been some sort of hallucination, a way to cope with the building pain.

Alison spun around in search of more enemies, but the remaining guards retreated into the mansion. There were no rifle cracks or explosions, only the approaching drop-ships and helicopter. She rushed back toward the half-scorched hedge maze to get a better view of the skies above the mansion.

The angular shapes of four dropships grew closer, and off to their side, she could make out a blob she assumed was the helicopter.

She took a few deep breaths as her vision swam. "If I go out, I might as well go out over the top. I have to make the bastard pay for each drop of blood."

Alison released her shadow blade and raised her arm to focus light energy into her hand. A bright lance appeared and its intensity and length grew with each passing second. The pain in her body increased as well.

"Where the hell is Scott?" She snickered. "You might have thought you were King of Seattle," she shouted. "But you couldn't stand up to this princess and had to hide behind your men in the end."

With a scream, Alison flung the energy lance into the sky. It soared toward one of the dropships. It banked, but the lance struck the craft and exploded. A massive fireball grew in the sky and debris rained down. One of the other ships dove low and several armored forms leapt out from the sides. Small jets in their legs and back pulsed to control their descent, and their long silver weapons gleamed.

Power armor and railguns. At least I took down a dropship.

Two of the others banked back and forth erratically as they continued their run.

What's the matter? Not full of guys with advanced power armor?

Alison collapsed to her knees. Darkness clawed at the edge of her vision and her body seemed on fire. She'd delayed the power armor reinforcements, but the other dropship still approached, along with the helicopter. Who knew how many men were inside?

She couldn't manage another lance.

Her summoned shields failed, and she looked at her hands. Only the dimmest of red light clung to her skin.

Myna, I'm at my limit here. Can you help a girl out?

No response.

Alison sighed and shook her head. She yanked out her 9mm and pointed at the two remaining dropships. The crafts' vertical thrusters kicked in, and their back doors lowered. Dozens of uniformed men poured out with rifles.

Huh. No deflectors? No armor? Even you have your limits, huh, Scott?

Each loud thump of the oncoming helicopter sent a spike of pain into Alison's head. She focused on it. She might as well take in the other tool of her doom.

The dark and long helicopter looked like it could fit a decent number of men in the back. The side door was open and a heavy machine gun pointed from the side with a pale form in dark clothing behind it, but Alison couldn't make out much more detail at a distance.

Scott's new arrivals paused, spun toward the helicopter, and raised their weapons.

What are they doing?

The side-mounted machine gun came to life and launched a river of bullets toward the men. The high-speed projectiles ripped through several before they ran for the cover of their dropships and returned fire.

"SWAT? AET?" Alison blinked through her bleary eyes and tried to make out details. No red and blue lights and she couldn't read the markings.

The heavy fire from the men below perforated the helicopter and smoke poured from several places as it began a rapid descent. Its machine gun still maintained heavy fire and raked the men and dropships.

One of Scott's men emerged from a dropship with an RPG and set it over his shoulder. A few seconds later, the round screamed away from the launcher, slammed into the tail of the helicopter, and exploded.

The aircraft wobbled and shook, descended fast, and headed toward the dropships. Something glowed in the cockpit and in the back. Two passengers and a pilot bailed and fell to the ground cloaked in light.

Scott's reinforcements scattered as the helicopter smashed into the ground and exploded. The flames of its burning carcass licked at one of the dropships, but it'd not managed a direct hit.

One of the passengers zoomed forward at an incredible speed. Alison's eyes widened. Even through her blurred vision and pain, she'd recognize those nine glowing tails anywhere.

Hana's fast and serpentine movement avoided the gunfire of the reinforcements as she closed on the first group, the *tachi* in hand. She leapt toward them with a chilling scream and decapitated the first man.

Alison's pained brain took a few seconds to register that Hana wasn't wearing her pendant, but she couldn't linger on the thought as another blur rushed into the reinforcements.

The blur refined into a man. His powerful kick slammed into a man's chest, the crunch of ribs audible. His victim catapulted and rolled several times before coming to a stop.

Alison stared at the man and thought her eyes might have tricked her.

"Mason?" she whispered.

If that wasn't enough, a loud crack in the distance sounded, and another guard's head exploded. A rifle glinted in the hands of a slender form with the familiar glow of a bronze pendant around her neck.

Alison rubbed her eyes and tried to concentrate. "No way."

Another rifle shot took down another Carlyle guard, and the sniper strolled ever closer.

Alison managed a pained laugh. "Of course Ava knows how to use a gun."

Hana continued to slash at men on every side. Mason punched, kicked, and fired his gun with his left hand. Despite the superior numbers, the enemy formation was breaking and panic began to show on their faces.

A harsh roar sounded nearby.

Those power armors are still out there.

Alison fell forward and gritted her teeth. Her friends might have saved her life, but they'd be shredded when the additional reinforcements showed up.

Myna! Help already!

Bright light blinded her, and a pleasant warmth suffused her body and wiped away the pain and weakness.

"I'm sorry it took so long, my princess," Myna replied. This time, her words were not a thought but a whisper right into Alison's ear. "I had to rush. I still wanted to make sure." A hacking cough followed. "But I grant this gift to you, Princess of the Shadow Forged. I grant you the gift of your power back."

CHAPTER THIRTY

Alison coughed again. Her vision cleared and something unpleasant was in her mouth. Earth and grass.

She jerked up. The pain and weakness in her limbs had vanished. She looked around. Hana and Mason were finishing off the last few guards while Ava reloaded her rifle.

Alison stood and shook her hands out. There was some mild fatigue, the kind she'd experienced whenever she used intense magic throughout the years. Even without AMDS, it wasn't an unlimited resource, but she felt no pain and no throbbing, not even a hint.

Hana let out a keening cry as she ran the last man through.

The fox, Mason, and Ava all ran toward Alison.

She layered new shields over herself and extended double shadow blades. No strain at all.

Mason slowed, a look of concern on his face. "You okay, A? I saw you collapse but I had to finish off those bastards."

Hana rested the flat of the blade on her shoulder. "Sorry it took so long."

Ava shouldered her rifle. "Incidentally, Miss Brownstone, you'll have to pay to replace the helicopter that was destroyed—perhaps extra considering some of the strings I had to pull."

Alison laughed. "Sure thing." She shook her head. "It's gone."

Ava nodded toward the helicopter. "Yes, it's a total loss."

"No, the AMDS. Myna cured it somehow. Just now. I can feel it. There's mild fatigue from heavy magic use but no pain." Alison blew out a breath. "It's like I'd forgotten how it could feel. But…why, what…I thought I said something about waiting twelve hours?"

Hana snorted. "As if. I called Ava right away and asked if she could find some way to get us here quickly since we didn't have a car. Then I called Mason and explained the entire situation after Ava said she could get us a helicopter but we needed a pilot."

Mason gave Alison a sheepish grin. "I feel terrible, A. That new job I was supposed to be working? It was for Scott Carlyle. Probably another way to get at you. I didn't know…all the shit you were dealing with, but I understand why you needed to keep it close to you." He nodded at Hana. "Don't be pissed at her for telling me."

Alison snorted. "You all saved my life. Why would be I pissed? Yeah, admitting I have a magic-sapping disease and my benefactor is part of a conspiracy to depower magicals does seem kind of like more of a six-months-together thing, but hey, now you know."

Mason chuckled. "At least I'll have some more time to spend with you while I look for a new job."

Hana grinned. "Anyway, Tahir's trying to get the police and PDA to show up, but everyone's confused because we're trying to get them to raid Carlyle and not Chesterton."

Alison grimaced. "Carlyle. That's right. The bastard ran." She frowned. "And I don't hear the power armors anymore."

Ava frowned and adjusted her glasses. "Power armors?"

"Yeah, four of them from before. I nailed their dropship." Alison frowned. "One second." She extended shadow wings and pooled some energy in her legs for a few seconds to launch into the sky. The four power armors were nowhere in sight. She dropped back to the ground and released her wings. "They must have gone inside to guard Carlyle."

Hana pointed the sword at the hole in the mansion. "Then let's go kick his ass."

"No." Alison shook her head. "This isn't me being stubborn. This is me pointing out that your defensive artifacts might not stand up to a railgun. Probably not. Thanks to Myna, my full power is back and it's time for me to end this." She pointed at one of the dropships. "Maybe wait in there while I find Scott."

Ava pursed her lips. "The authorities might be delayed, but they are still coming. Perhaps it's best to wait."

Alison snorted. "Screw that. I'm tired of waiting. I'll be back soon."

Mason and Hana exchanged looks before they both nodded.

Hana gave Alison a thumb's up. "You go, girlfriend. Kick his ass for all of us."

"I will."

Alison rushed through the hole and into the mansion. While the sprawling building had a seemingly endless supply of receiving rooms, she'd been in it enough to know the general layout. It wasn't exactly a maze. She sprinted down the hallways and toward the living room.

She skidded to a stop. Scott stood encased in the center of the living room in the middle of a massive exoskeleton that would have made a Kilomea look small. Yellow light shimmered around him, and numerous pulsating glyphs covered the exoskeleton. The frame held no obvious weapons, and his shirt was unbuttoned, and his tie gone.

The four power armors lay on the ground, unmoving.

Alison frowned and nodded toward the power armors. "What? Is this one of those, 'You've displeased me with your incompetence, now die!' type things?"

Scott chuckled. "No. A good leader lets his subordinates learn from their mistakes. I'd not expected to have to use my prototype so early. This is the future, Miss Brownstone, technology fused to magic to make every man a demi-god. The dream of Prometheus fulfilled. I sacrificed my tie, and it wasn't enough. Unfortunately, this prototype required some additional charging, and you'd be surprised how much power is contained in a life."

"Listen to yourself, Scott." Alison's face twisted in disgust. "Now you're not simply testing things on magicals, you're killing your own people. And look." She gestured to herself. "I'm still alive. You've lost."

He shook his head. "I'm impressed that you've done so

well considering how much pain you must be in, but you forget, Miss Brownstone, I've witnessed your limits first-hand. I imagine you've taken some healing potions and energy potions to help keep you on your feet." The massive arm of the exoskeleton lifted. "I've monitored you for a while. I know how good you are at intimidation and how much you rely on it. I understand your psychology better than you do. You squeezed out an admittedly impressive victory against my men, and now, you're trying to hold it together long enough for the police to arrive, even though you're in such agony you feel like you'll pass out at any second. You think that I'm desperate, so you can come in here and give me a big speech and I'll surrender." Scott scoffed. "But you're at your absolute limit, and I have this suit. I'm sorry we couldn't come to an agreement." He smiled. "But you'll die here. The police and PDA will come to believe you were consumed by paranoia over Chester-ton. Goodbye, Miss Brownstone." Scott lifted his arm. Yellow lines of energy crackled over it, and several of the glyphs grew brighter.

Alison layered more shields over herself and held her ground as much to prove something to herself more than to Scott Carlyle.

"The problem with men like you," Alison replied, "is that you always think you're one step ahead."

"What's the problem with understanding the truth?"

A yellow bolt blasted from the exoskeleton and slammed into her. She hissed and rocketed backward to slam into a wall.

Alison fell onto one knee and shook her head as she released her shadow blade. "That hurt." She stood and pointed her shadow blade at him. "Genuinely hurt. Not any AMDS crap. I think you got through the shields a little." She squeezed her thumb and index finger together. "Just a little. If you had that thing, along with those four power armors and your other guys, and maybe a few quality witches, this might be a fair fight." She clucked her tongue. "But now, it'll be a curb stomp."

Scott blinked. "Impossible. How are you still standing?"

Alison leapt toward the wall and shadows anchored her steps. Scott's exoskeleton came to life and spat smaller yellow bolts that exploded against the wall but narrowly missed her. She pushed off, now behind him, and summoned two shadow blades and sliced at him.

The blades bounced off, but the yellow field flashed. She hacked away, and the field flashed brighter.

Scott spun and flung a massive arm at her. Alison ducked beneath the blow and launched herself away to land on another wall and crouch perpendicular to the floor.

"You really thought you would win. It's almost cute." Alison winked. She burst away from the wall toward him.

This time, he caught her with a hit, and she grunted as she catapulted back and into another wall. she shook her head and pulled herself out of her indent with only a little pain in her back.

Alison released her shadow blades and flung two quick blasts at Scott. Both struck. His defensive field flashed again, and one of the glyphs stopped glowing.

She was already on the move when he fired another yellow bolt. As she alternated blasts of light and shadow magic, she bounded over tables and furniture. Each strike made Scott's field flash and more and more of his glyphs disappeared.

"Don't you get it, Scott?" Alison shouted. Dark wings appeared behind her back, and she leapt into the air. "You should have never taken on the Dark Princess."

Alison focused magic into her hands and let herself drop straight to the floor. He blasted away. His shots stung and one even broke through her shield and burned her.

She ignored the pain and slammed into the ground. A massive nova of dark energy erupted from the point of impact and sliced through the furniture present and even cut into the other rooms. The blast struck the armor, and the glyphs all died as the wave sliced through the bottom legs of the exoskeleton. Scott was only spared amputation by the unusually large size of his machine.

The structure tumbled backward and crashed into the ground with a resounding thud.

Alison stood, her breath ragged, and shook her hands. She marched to the downed exoskeleton and extended a shadow blade directly to Scott's throat. "You really, really deserve to die, you know."

He lifted his chin in defiance. "Everything I did, I did for humanity. I regret nothing."

"So has said every evil asshole throughout history." Alison rolled her eyes. "I think I prefer dealing with gang members."

Alison smiled and shrugged, enjoying the satisfaction that welled up in her too much. "Don't worry. Even though I really, really want to kill you, I won't let you be some sort of New Veil martyr." She grinned. "Besides, you're so used to being in control. I think you'll enjoy a few lifetimes in an ultramax. Sometimes, the best revenge is letting someone live." She smiled and released the shadow blade. "For now, though, I'll also settle for this."

She slammed her fist into his face. His eyes rolled up in his head, and he slumped to the side, unconscious.

"Money isn't everything, Carlyle."

CHAPTER THIRTY-ONE

Alison strolled toward the elevator in her condo when Ryan rushed over toward her, a huge smile on his face.

She stopped and returned his smile. "Hey, Ryan. Did you need something?"

"I only wanted to say thank you so much." Ryan closed his eyes and took a deep breath. "I got it today in the mail, a signed picture of the Granite Ghost himself. He even had a cool inscription on it, 'May you become a scourge to all your enemies and to those who are enemies of barbecue.'" He trembled with pleasure. "I'm going to frame it, put it in a vacuum-sealed box, and store it in my safety deposit box."

Alison chuckled. "Good for you."

"Thank you, thank you, thank you." He wiped a tear away. "It's the nicest thing anyone's ever done for me." He waved. "Now I'm sure you're still busy filling out reports or whatever is involved when a Brownstone takes down a major bad guy, so I'll leave you alone."

The man literally skipped away, joy on his face.

Alison blinked.

That was a good thing. I think?

Alison took a sip of coffee and yawned. She shifted in her seat at her dining table and watched the frowning PDA bald agent who sat across from her.

"I'm glad you guys showed up that day." She rolled her eyes. "Finally. Better late than never, but you've even come all the way to my place to chat. So what's up? Is the part where you bitch at me about the chaos in the business community or whatever?"

Agent Latherby shook his head. "Investors will recover their money eventually, and that's not my concern. I'm in the PDA, not the SEC. I just wanted to personally deliver this information. I pushed hard based on the evidence you provided me. I was worried that since your phone had been destroyed in the confrontation, it might not be enough."

Alison sighed. She'd not even noticed at first, but it made sense given how many explosions and bullets she dealt with.

"But the files you passed along were enough for a good start." Agent Latherby smiled. "He's going down for his crimes, Miss Brownstone, as is Chesterton. There are so many charges against them, they'll never see the light of day. While I wouldn't want to be a shareholder in either of their companies, I'm a proud American today. You should also know we've already raided Prometheus as well. The conspiracy is over. No more victims. I think you understand, Miss Brownstone, that this goes beyond helping magicals. If this weapon had spread, we might have risked war with Oriceran. You've caused a lot of trouble and chaos in the short-term and saved a lot of lives in the long-term."

Alison shrugged. "A lot of this was personal. I won't lie."

Agent Latherby chuckled. "I'm more concerned with results than reasons. Thank you, Miss Brownstone, for your service to Seattle, your country, and the two worlds."

Alison smiled. "You're welcome."

She rested her head on Mason's shoulder. "I think I forgot to tell you how cool it was to see you in action. The whole air cavalry to the rescue thing was pretty hot, too, but seeing you take those guys down, damn, you really are a badass. It might have been nicer to see you kicking their asses with your shirt off, but I'll take what I can get." She gave him a peck on the cheek.

Mason chuckled. "I live to serve, A. I am a bodyguard, and if I can't guard my own girlfriend, what good am I?"

"Have you looked around yet for a new job?" Alison pulled away and smiled at him. "I wasn't sure if helping take down a corrupt businessman engaged in anti-magical conspiracy was good or bad for your job prospects."

Mason shrugged. "I'm taking a few weeks off. The cops and feds still have questions for me."

Alison took a deep breath, and her heart rate kicked up. "I do know one company that could use a good ass-kicker. The boss is a real bitch, but she's pretty hot according to a certain life wizard." She winked. "I get that it might be weird to work for someone you're dating, but if you simply want to think of yourself as my personal bodyguard, that works, too."

Mason furrowed his brow. "That sounds like a good offer, but for maximum safety, I think I'll need a closer inspection of the body that I'm to guard."

Alison smirked. "For safety?"

"Yes. Safely."

She stood and tugged on his arm. "I think that can be arranged."

A few more days had passed when there was a light knock at the door. Alison rose and headed to answer it. She wasn't expecting anyone. No one had called, and Hana was out helping Tahir move into his new place.

Alison opened the door, surprised to see Myna.

The ancient Drow inclined her head. "I apologize for not contacting you ahead of my visit."

Alison motioned inside. "I'm more surprised you didn't portal in."

Myna entered and headed toward the couch, her movements slower and more cautious than the last time Alison had seen her. She settled on the couch and smoothed her skirt. "It's useful to preserve my magic for times of need."

Alison chuckled and found herself a chair. "You didn't seem to mind it before and I won't complain about you not portaling into my place, but it's good that you're here. I wanted to ask you about something."

"Please, go ahead," Myna responded. "Anything I can do to be of aid."

Alison leaned forward and threaded her fingers together. "So the government will be sorting out all this crap with Scott for a while, but they already have Lawrence Northwell in custody. The AMDS research is over, but it might take a long time to find an actual cure through regular means. I wondered if you could help with that. I get that you can't necessarily simply cure people back to back, but maybe we can do a ritual for a month or something and start to cure people."

Myna looked down with a slight frown on her face. "I wish I could comply with your request. I truly do, but that's not possible."

"Why not?" Alison frowned. "It couldn't be a one-of-a-kind thing." She sat up. "Oh, does it only work on you if you're Drow or partially Drow?"

Myna's face softened and she looked up. "Yes, that's a strong consideration. I apologize."

Alison sighed and nodded. "Well, it was worth a shot, but that doesn't change how grateful I am to you, Myna. I'm still adjusting to having my full power back."

"As you should be, but remember what I said. You still need training, and I wish to provide that in the time I have left." A hopeful look appeared in her eyes.

Alison smiled. "I'd be honored."

Hana sat on the couch, thumbing through news on her phone while Alison smiled as she juggled glowing balls of light in front of her.

"It feels good to be whole again." Alison let out a happy sigh.

Her friend looked up and smiled. "I'm glad for you. Oh, by the way, did you read the news today?"

Alison shook her head. "No. Why?"

"There's a big thing about your shifter buddy in Congress. He's pushing hard for more government investigation of the Carlyle scandal by the House. That guy Senator Johnston is pushing from the Senate."

"Johnston was always a decent guy for a politician." Alison's lights winked out of existence, and she moved to the couch to sit beside her friend. "I got another message from Latherby the other day. He was right. This went well beyond only Scott. They've nailed some other big corporate guys and several people in the government. The only people who are defending Scott are New Veil and the HDL."

Hana rolled her eyes. "Yeah, everyone loves the opinion of terrorists."

Alison grimaced. "You should have heard my parents when I told them. It's a good thing Scott's in protective government custody, or he'd be a bloody smear."

"Are you sure that's not better?"

"Yeah." Alison shrugged. "If I'd killed him, the government wouldn't have been able to track down his other partners."

Hana grinned and nudged Alison with her elbow. "But

let's not worry about the boring stuff. Let's worry about the important stuff."

"Important stuff? What's more important than a massive billionaire-funded anti-magical conspiracy?" Alison eyed her friend with confusion on her face.

Hana rolled her eyes. "Your love life. I've noticed you've spent more nights over at Mason's place. You don't have to do that, you know. You let me know if you want a little alone time, and I'll make myself scarce. If anything, I can go hang out with Tahir. It's not like he minds if I hang out there." She laughed. "I've never had such a relaxed boyfriend."

"I'll keep that in mind." Alison stood and walked toward her window to look over the bay. "I want you to remember that because we took Chesterton and Scott down doesn't mean we're safe. If anything, it'll raise our profile and our risk. That's what I learned from my dad's experiences."

Hana shrugged. "Who cares? You're the Dark Princess, and you have your full power back. They should be afraid of you."

Alison looked over her shoulder. "You're not worried? Even after everything that's happened lately? To both Tahir and you? Taking down those guys helped, but it's not like we're guaranteed any quiet. That's all I'm saying."

Hana snorted. "Who cares? Quiet is boring anyway."

Alison smiled.

Never change, Hana. Never change.

The End

The *Dark Princess* takes on a dangerous sect of dark wizards, worshippers of Michael Galbraith. Not someone you want to meet without the back-up of a certain Drow badass.

Her story is far from over. Alison's adventure continues in The Family Business

FREE BOOKS!

 WARNING:
The Troll is now in charge.

And he's giving away free books
if you sign-up!

Join the only newsletter hosted by a Troll!

Get sneak peeks, exclusive giveaways, behind the scenes
content, and more.
PLUS you'll be notified of special **one day only fan
pricing** on new releases.

CLICK HERE

or visit: https://marthacarr.com/read-free-stories/

THE FAMILY BUSINESS

The Dark Princess takes on a dangerous sect of dark wizards, worshippers of Michael Galbraith. Not someone you want to meet without the back-up of a certain Drow badass.Her story is far from over. Alison's adventure continues in THE FAMILY BUSINESS

<u>**AVAILABLE FOR PURCHASE HERE**</u>

AUTHOR NOTES - MARTHA CARR
JANUARY 14, 2019

I got a text from my brother this week that said, "Good news!" He had found more money my late mother had stashed away in a bank somewhere. It's been over five years since she's been gone, and we still don't know if we have found it all.

It turned out that my mother had been taking a little money from my father's paycheck every two weeks for over 50 years and investing it in different banks or mutual funds – everywhere – and never told a soul. She's the outlier that disproves the theory that eventually we all tell our secrets to someone.

After she died, we found a king's ransom all over the map and could only marvel at what she had accomplished. She's the poster child for the idea that anyone can build a safe retirement. Too bad she never spent a dime of it on herself.

I secretly hoped I had gotten this particular gene from her. Unfortunately, I did and in spades.

I was standing in front of the underwear sales rack in

Marshall's whispering, "Will keeping this dollar change my life?" It was 12 years ago, and I was struggling to spend even a few dollars on myself – for on-sale underwear. Here's the kicker... I was using gift cards I'd had in my possession for months.

A mentor told me I had 30 days to go spend them and I could only spend them on myself. I'd already spent a few dollars from one of them on the Offspring. That was easy. Taking care of someone else, especially Louie was no problem. That rule didn't translate to me.

Fortunately, I'm a good rule follower so I did as I was told and bought the underwear anyway, and then cried my heart out in the parking lot. I was so sure God was going to strike me down.

My self worth was riding on fumes.

But that same mentor also let me borrow the view she had of me – that I'm fine just as I am and what needed to change was how I saw myself - and kept giving me instructions to set out into the world and try a different way of doing things – all the time. It got me out of wishing and hoping and into action, even though I was scared and anxious. That was no longer a good enough excuse. Eventually, the doing taught me the world didn't fall apart when I put myself first. My view of myself and the world slowly changed.

I started to let in the good and make myself a part of life, instead of standing on the sidelines. It's the reason I'm writing this in my new dream house and could say yes to Michael Anderle when he asked if I'd like to collaborate on creating a new universe. I have something to offer the world (even two worlds) and there's a place for me at the table. No admission required.

In the end, my mother ended up helping her children in two ways. The first was with her savvy investments, but it also would have been okay if she'd spent that dollar and changed her own life, instead.

The second was even more valuable for me. It's the lesson to save some, invest some *and* spend some and enjoy this life every single day. Join in on all of it on equal footing and see what happens.

More adventures to follow.

AUTHOR NOTES - MICHAEL ANDERLE
JANUARY 15, 2018

THANK YOU for not only reading this story but these *Author Notes* as well.

(I think I've been good with always opening with "thank you." If not, I need to edit the other *Author Notes*!)

RANDOM (*sometimes*) THOUGHTS?

You can do it.

Ok, perhaps it will take a while to do it (it took me over thirty years), but the one thing I had was perseverance.

Actually, that's not true.

I didn't have perseverance so much as a streak of "Screw you, world" a mile wide and to the horizon long.

I would have ideas upon ideas of how to make money and kept plugging away at them (and kinda failing) for years… and years turned into decades.

I see perseverance as someone tells themselves, "I'm going to be successful, so I'll keep working it!"

My mind said, "Oh? Not going to let me win here? Well,

here is ANOTHER idea and I'll try to sneak into success around *this* corner."

My success came as a total shock, but what I *did* know to do was grab ahold, double down, and ride it hard and fast.

And I'm still doing that.

Do *you* ever think about writing a story? I can't promise you success, but I *can* promise you that NOW is the time to get that started if you care to try it. In five years, in this industry will be completely different.

I encourage you to take life by the horns and write those stories.

HOW TO MARKET FOR BOOKS YOU LOVE

We are able to support our efforts with you reading our books, and we appreciate you doing this!

If you enjoyed this or ANY book by any author, especially Indie-published, we always appreciate if you make the time to review a book, since it lets other readers who might be on the fence to take a chance on it as well.

AROUND THE WORLD IN 80 DAYS

One of the interesting (at least to me) aspects of my life is the ability to work from anywhere and at any time. In the future, I hope to re-read my own *Author Notes* and remember my life as a diary entry.

Bangkok, Thailand

I'll keep this short and sweet. I'm writing from a desk in a corner suite overlooking the river in Bangkok, Thailand.

How? I wrote a bunch of books that sold, and eventually, grew it into a business that paid for my research here in the interesting city.

See my comment above that now is the best time to get started writing. There are wonderful places to learn your craft (the art of writing) but possibly none better to start understanding the publishing side of indie writing than the Facebook group 20Booksto50k—a group I started three years ago.

The answers you seek (if you choose to go down this path) are there, grasshopper.

(Ok, *probably* there. Let's not push it too far ;-))

FAN PRICING

If you would like to find out what LMBPN is doing and the books we will be publishing, just sign up at http://lmbpn.com/email/. When you sign up, we notify you of books coming out for the week, any new posts of interest in the books and pop culture arena, and the fan pricing on Saturday.

Ad Aeternitatem,

Michael Anderle

CONNECT WITH THE AUTHORS

Martha Carr Social

Website: http://www.marthacarr.com

Facebook: https://www.facebook.com/
groups/MarthaCarrFans/

Michael Anderle Social

Michael Anderle Social
Website:
http://www.lmbpn.com

Email List:
http://lmbpn.com/email/

Facebook Here: https://www.
facebook.com/TheKurtherianGambitBooks/